"Do nothing rash. I wish to be the one who takes your worthless life."

She frowned at his laugh. Did he believe she was jesting?

Calloused fingers brushed along her cheek and lifted her chin. When he knelt next to her, Lyonesse was surprised to find him so near. Amazed that he'd removed his battle glove so quickly and so quietly.

His breath warmed the flesh beneath her ear as he spoke. "Little Lioness, my worthless life will be yours to take."

The loud, rapid beating of her heart drowned out the sounds of the coming battle. His lips touched hers lightly, as if seeking permission.

Her thoughts tumbled against each other in their rush to her head.

She hated him.

Yet his mere presence disarmed her soul. Embers glowing red with warmth filled her senses with a new, unfamiliar confusion.

Lyonesse pressed her lips against his....

FALCON'S DESIRE

Denise Lynn

First published in Great Britain 2006
Large Print edition 2007
Harlequin Mills & Boon Limited,
Eton House, 18-24 Paradise Road, Richmond, Surrey TW9 1SR

© Denise L. Koch 2003

ISBN-13: 978 0 263 19384 8
ISBN-10:   0 263 19384 5

Set in Times Roman 14¾ on 16½ pt.
42-0207-76756

Printed and bound in Great Britain
by Antony Rowe Ltd, Chippenham, Wiltshire

Denise Lynn has been an avid reader of romance novels for many years. Between the pages of books she travelled to lands and times filled with brave knights, courageous ladies and never-ending love. Now she can share with others her dream of telling tales of adventure and romance.

Denise lives with her real-life hero, Tom, and a slew of four-legged 'kids' in northwestern Ohio, USA. Their two-legged son, Ken, serves in the US Navy, and comes home on occasion to visit and fix the computers, VCRs or any other electronic device Mum can confuse in his absence. You can write to her at PO Box 17, Monclova, OH 43542, USA, or visit her website, www.denise-lynn.com

Falcon's Desire
is Denise Lynn's début novel in
Mills & Boon® Historical Romance™

Thank you—

Kim and Tracy, for taking the chance.

Lori and Tony for being the best
fairy Godparents ever.

Tom, my hero, my knight in armour,
for being the model I build heroes on,
the shoulder I lean on
and the foundation
I build dreams on.
I love you, yesterday, today and tomorrow.

Prologue

Scarborough—Yorkshire
England—1142

*M*urder.

The accusation rippled through the crowded hall. Carried from one courtier to the next, the word found its way back to the man accused of the foul deed.

Murder.

"Rhys, Lord of Faucon, for the murder of Guillaume du Pree your lands and properties are forfeit to the crown."

The black-robed holy man smiled with satanic glee as he finished his proclamation. "Your life will be forfeited to the devil you have served."

From his chair on the raised dais King Stephen leaned forward. "Rhys?" He waited but a heartbeat before continuing. "Faucon, have you nothing to say?"

Rhys wanted to say much, but he bit back his sarcastic retort. The hard, cold floor beneath his knees helped keep his tongue in check. Chained like a dog, he was in no position to test King Stephen's humor.

Instead, Rhys searched the crowded hall for one ally who would vouch for his honor. Those who would do so were oddly absent from this gathering.

He strained against the chains binding his arms behind him. His muscles burned with pain. Rhys glanced across the torch-lit hall, seeking the three men who'd roused him from his much-needed slumber. They glared back at him. Their odd array of blackening eyes, swollen lips and bloodied noses gave him a measure of satisfaction. He'd not made their task an easy one.

"Answer your king!" The cleric scurried toward Rhys. The man's robe flapped about his stout legs.

Rhys looked up at King Stephen, ignoring what seemed to him nothing more than a short, cawing crow. He weighed his words carefully. His life and the continued welfare of his family rested on his ability to control his tongue. "Sire, I have killed many men while serving under your standard. Who is to say whether those who perished during the heat of battle were friend or foe?"

"No one asked you about an honorable battle. We are speaking of a coward's ambush." The squawking man positioned himself in front of Rhys. With fisted hands resting on his ample hips, the holy man glowered at him.

Even though Rhys knelt on the floor, the cleric's hard stare was nearly at eye level. This man of God—if he truly was—had the power to take away all Rhys held dear. And it seemed at this moment a possibility.

The cleric shook his fist at Rhys. "You whoreson of the devil. What say you for killing the good master du Pree?"

Rhys burned the man's features into his mind. He would not forget, nor forgive, the man's actions this day.

He addressed the king. "Who accuses me of this foul deed?"

The cleric sputtered. "Who? What matter does that make? You are guilty and the Lord Almighty *will* see justice done."

The noise in the hall grew louder as those gathered voiced their opinion of du Pree's murder.

"Enough!" King Stephen's shout brought a semblance of order to the hall. He instructed the guards to release the bonds, then motioned to Rhys and ordered, "Follow me."

After struggling to his feet, Rhys waited impatiently as a guard freed him from the chains. While rubbing the circulation back into his burning arms, he followed the king. The hissing of disappointment shadowed his departure. Vultures behaved better than the scavengers gathered here.

Certain his executioner awaited him, Rhys paused in the doorway to the small chamber where King Stephen led him. He cautiously peered inside and almost cried aloud with relief. The room was empty save for the presence of William, the Earl of York.

His allies may have been absent from the hall, but here in this private chamber the only supporter Rhys needed raised a goblet to herald his arrival.

Once the three occupants were seated, Stephen addressed both men. His focus riveted on Rhys, the king began, ''Faucon, by permitting the tales about you to grow unchecked, you have brought this upon yourself.''

Stephen grew silent, giving Rhys time to realize the truth of his words. It was not a lie. He'd enjoyed the tales told of the evil Faucon—even if they were not true. His overblown reputation won more than half the battles he'd engaged in, saving him and his men from any defeat.

But defeat loomed before him now.

With a slight wave of his hand, the king motioned toward the door. ''While some of the barons call for your life, it seems not all believe this cry of murder. Just as they didn't believe the cry before. However, this time much more hangs in the balance. I can ill afford to lose any of the supporters I have over this accusation.''

Again, the king spoke the truth. This battle for the throne cost much. Every supporter who left Stephen's side to fight with the Empress Matilda took along their men and gold. Regardless of any friendship, Stephen could not permit this matter to come between him and his quest to keep the throne.

Rhys leaned forward and swore, "Sire, upon my honor as a loyal knight and subject, I have killed no man in such a cowardly fashion."

Stephen shook his head. "Your word held little weight when Alyce died, yet most looked the other way. We are not now speaking of a vile-tongued wench. Guillaume du Pree was well liked by some and mistrusted by others. I am afraid, Rhys, that outside of this chamber, your word means nothing."

Rhys flinched under the reminder of his faithless wife. Over five years had gone by. When would the mere mention of her name not cause his heart to constrict? He pushed the memory down into the recesses of his mind. "I can prove my innocence with nothing but my word."

"You need find another way—quickly. The men gathered here are bored, Rhys. A trial by combat would alleviate that condition."

Had the king cleaved him with a battle-ax, Rhys would not have been more shocked. His mouth went dry at the thought of proving his innocence in a fight where fairness and honor would be missing. Neither battle, nor death frightened him. However, his accusers would arrange this event, going to great lengths to ensure his death and the loss of his family's wealth and honor.

Rhys swallowed his uncertainty before admitting, "I can think of no other way." Against unimaginable odds, he would simply have to win.

"Let us not be hasty." William took a long draught of wine and then stared at Rhys over the rim of his goblet. "You are forgetting that someone *did* commit the murder."

"True. And this someone does need to be found." King Stephen agreed with William's statement of the obvious before adding, "Within the next four weeks."

Chapter One

Northern England—1142

A raspy grumble shattered the early morning quiet of the forest. "He is not coming."

"Shh!" If Edmund hadn't been her best archer, Lyonesse of Ryonne would have left the complainer at the keep.

She hoped the Lord of Faucon would pass this way before the sun fully rose. The lengthening rays already broke through the dense foliage, casting thick slivers of sparkling light on the dew-covered moss below. The full light of day would provide little concealment for the men hiding in the trees and bushes.

A rustling of branches preceded another grumble. "This is daft. By the time he arrives I will be too stiff to move."

"Cease. He will be here soon." If their prey didn't arrive shortly, she feared the men would desert their posts.

Nay, that was a senseless worry. These were Guillaume's men. They'd brought his body to her at Taniere and remained. Each swore their allegiance not to her father, the Lord of Ryonne, but to her, the rightful mistress of Taniere.

With her betrothal to Guillaume du Pree all was in place for her to retain her responsibilities as the Mistress of Taniere. Until Faucon had turned all her hopes and dreams to dust.

He would pay for all he took from her. Lyonesse scanned the men around her. They would help her exact revenge.

Their leader, John, had devised this plan to capture Faucon. By spreading word about Guillaume's death and telling all who would listen of Faucon's cowardice, John had been certain the murderer would seek him out. When the vile knave came looking for John, they would all be ready.

Lyonesse swallowed back the ever-threatening tears. While the act of capturing the Devil of Faucon would not lessen the tears, it would lighten her heart to know she'd avenged Guillaume.

If God smiled upon her quest for revenge, she'd have Faucon's lifeless body at her feet this day. By the time she finished with him, everyone would know he was not the great bird of prey they'd dubbed him. She would relish proving the tales false. All would know he was nothing more than a man. A man who could die like any other.

The abrupt rustling of bushes and tree limbs from farther up the path signaled the approach of riders.

Lyonesse peered through the branches and smiled. Their wait was almost at an end.

Rhys tugged lightly at the reins. The stallion suddenly became skittish. Steps that had been sure and steady a moment ago, now faltered. The horse weaved back and forth across the road, snorting and tossing his head.

"Easy, boy." He patted the thick, black neck in an attempt to calm the animal. The usually placid beast rolled his eyes to look up at the rider. Rhys agreed with the wild glance. He felt it, too—something was wrong. The hair on the back of his neck tingled with anticipation. A flash of cold passed down his spine.

He raised his hand, bringing the five men following him to a halt.

Rhys slowly continued ahead. He stared into the woods, but could see nothing that should upset the horse, or himself, in this manner. Yet the forest was too silent. He reached down and touched the wooden scabbard encasing his sword.

A shrill whistle split the air. Rhys gripped his knees tighter into the rearing horse's ribs. He grasped the hilt of his sword with one hand and yanked at the reins with his other.

His men charged forward. In the same instant another force dropped from the trees and sprang from behind bushes, effectively cutting Rhys off from his men.

Before he could pull his sword free, a thick fisherman's net dropped over him and his horse. He clawed and tore at the confining snare, cursing his inability to free himself.

"Nay. Hold." In the din of swords crossing and men cursing, his shout went unheeded.

Gloved hands reached out and jerked at his steed's bridle. When the animal was brought to an unwilling stop, Rhys felt the sharp tip of metal press into his side.

Unable to swing his sword, he kicked out and knocked the threatening blade away. Three more blades quickly replaced the one. After forcing his fingers to relax, he dropped his own sword and shouted for his men to hold their weapons.

They immediately followed his order and offered no resistance as the enemy escorted them back down the road.

One of the men holding a sword to Rhys's side asked, "Are you prepared to die, Faucon?"

Rhys gritted his teeth against the sharp pain of a blade twisting through the links of his chain mail and into his flesh.

A small figure dropped from a tree limb. "Nay! Hold your sword, Sir John. I want him taken alive. For now."

Rhys sucked in a quick breath when his assailant pushed and twisted the blade a little more before pulling the tip free. The jagged cut would not heal as quickly as a clean slice. He had an insane urge to bellow in rage when his blood ran hot down his side. He would rather die from a well-aimed blade than from an infection.

Aiming his attention down at the newcomer, Rhys sought to ignore the fire burning from his wound. Surely this wasn't their leader? Huge, green eyes stared out of a small, pale face. This was nothing more than a child.

Rhys lifted one eyebrow. A child playing knight in his grandsire's old, hardened-leather armor. How long was the lad going to just stand there and say nothing? Rhys had not the leisure to partake in any childish pranks.

A leather glove too large for the hand it covered quickly swiped through the air. Rhys growled as the men around his horse reached up and pulled him from the animal.

The confining net prevented him from landing on his feet. He gasped at the pain jolting through his side, yet Rhys rolled to his knees the instant he hit the ground.

He swung his tightly balled hand at the closest face. The pleasure he felt as his fist made contact with flesh was short-lived. He immediately quit struggling when the cold bite of a sword slipped easily between the links of his hauberk and coif to press briefly against his neck.

While three men kept their swords trained on his chest, two others tore away the net. Thoughts of escape flooded his mind, but the idea vanished as the man called John leveled the side of his blade against Rhys's neck. No one moved. Instead, they looked to the boy for guidance.

Rhys glared at the lad. His heart lurched to his throat at what he perceived.

Unblemished, pale flesh was broken by full, rose-hued lips. A courtesan would kill for lashes as long as the red-tinged ones framing the overlarge eyes. It would take more than ill-fitting armor to hide the female beneath men's clothing.

Certain the shimmering glare would lacerate him as surely as any uncut emerald, Rhys returned the glowering stare and asked, ''What do you want from me?''

''I want nothing from you, Faucon.'' She laughed at him. ''Nothing, except your worthless soul.''

He already knew the answer, still he asked, ''Why? Why do you seek my soul?''

''Why?'' She ripped off one of her metal-studded leather gloves and slapped his face.

A trickle of blood ran down his cheek. ''If I am to die, I would at the very least like to know the reason.''

She lifted her glove, as if to strike him again and

paused. With one hand raised in the air and one red-tinged eyebrow higher than the other, she stared at him for a moment. "No." She shook her head and lowered her hand. "No. You do not play with a simple girl, Faucon. You will not force me to forget my motives in a fit of rage."

"Then answer my question."

Calmly slipping the overlarge glove back onto her hand, she said nothing.

It mattered not. Rhys did not need to hear the words from her lips. Guillaume du Pree had no sisters, but he had been betrothed. The hatred written plainly on the face before him held the answer to his unasked question. Lyonesse of Ryonne had captured him.

The lady's well-planned actions would likely end in his death. King Stephen and The Earl of York had been wrong in their assumption that none from Ryonne or du Pree's holding would seek retribution for du Pree's murder until the month was up.

Her continued silence filled him with sudden rage. Rhys sought words to reason with her.

"I did not murder your betrothed."

"You lie, Faucon."

"Waste no more time talking." Sir John interrupted the debate. His menacing tone fit the evil scowl covering his face. "I will kill him now."

Rhys's attention shifted to John. Whatever held the knight in check thus far was quickly losing its tenuous hold. Every muscle in the man's body was poised for battle. The air around him was thick with the scent of bloodlust.

"Nay, be patient a few moments longer." Lyonesse placed a restraining hand on John's wrist. "I want to remember this moment for the rest of my life."

Thankfully, the man retained enough sense to listen. Rhys returned his focus to his captor. "I tell you for the last time, I did not kill du Pree."

"Silence, Faucon. Save your lies for your maker. I'm certain in hell they are worth something."

Fear was nothing new to any sane fighting man. Sometimes a healthy respect for fear could save your life. This would not be one of those times. Tendrils of both, fear and regret snaked through his veins.

Anger at the unjust accusation and rage at the coward's death he now faced, gave him the strength to fight off the creeping tendrils. Certain that his own death was imminent, he asked, "What about my men?"

"They will not be harmed. They have been taken to safety."

"Safety?"

"Aye, Lord Faucon, they are safe. However, it may take them a while to find their way free."

The men surrounding them laughed.

He ignored their oddly placed humor and took a

deep breath before asking, "And how do you plan to kill me?"

"You ran a sword through Guillaume's back." Sparks of fire shot from her eyes. "You will die the same way."

She removed her gloves and ordered, "Get him up."

John lifted his blade against Rhys's chin, forcing his head up. He had no option but to follow the upward motion of the weapon. He silently cursed as two soldiers began to secure his arms behind his back with leather straps.

He would rather die fighting than be slaughtered like a trussed boar. "No!"

Mindless of the weapons aimed at his body, he violently jerked around, shoved past John and sprinted toward the safety of the forest.

"Stop him!"

His escape was short-lived. Five men flew at him, knocking him from his feet. Fists pummeled him about the head and body. The gash on his side tore even more from the blows. They shoved his face into the dirt, quickly securing his arms and legs. Then they hauled him to his feet and led him back to Lyonesse.

His heart pounded loud in his ears. Rhys shook with a helplessness he'd never before felt. He riveted his attention on the woman before him and shouted, "Get this over with."

''In all due time, Faucon.''

Lyonesse savored the deliciously sweet taste of her victory. Certain the restraints would hold, she allowed her gaze to slowly roam up her captive's massive form.

The stories had not been completely accurate. This man was not simply big. Like the fabled warriors of old, he was a huge dangerous giant. Gaps in the laced seams of the chain mail protecting his legs gave evidence to tightly corded muscles bulging toward freedom.

She admired the richness of his plain, black surcoat. Even hanging in torn disarray, the fabric bespoke of quality. Lyonesse knew that while the material would be as strong as the muscles it covered, beneath her fingers it would feel as soft and silky as a kitten's fur.

Her attention trailed up the long, wooden scabbard hanging at his side. Soaring falcons were artfully carved into the sword's case. The wide belt at his waist served not only to anchor the scabbard; it also did much to accentuate the outward flare of his chest.

Muscles strained violently below flesh in his silent struggle to break the bonds holding him. Lyonesse could see the fierce expansion of his chest and arms with each effort.

She glanced up and shuddered. If his strength were as great as the determination etched on his face, he would soon gain his freedom. His full lips narrowed into a grim line. A rapid pulse beat against one cheek. His swarthy complexion was broken by the cuts her glove had made on one side of his face. On the other side a thin white scar trickled like a tear from the corner of one eye to his mouth.

He leaned forward. For a brief moment unruly hair hid his face. Sunlight glistened off the shoulder-length mane. When he straightened, one raven lock fell across his face. Lyonesse's fingers itched to smooth the wayward strands back into place.

She peered into his eyes and was horrified to find Faucon watching her perusal. Flecks of gold sparkled against his light brown orbs. The shimmering brightness flared and paled with a life of their own.

"Look your fill, milady," he taunted. "For I will be the one who haunts your nightmares. You will wish you'd never beheld me."

She quickly turned away to hide the rush of embarrassment that heated her face. Lyonesse gritted her teeth. *What evilness possessed her to so intently study this vile beast?* After collecting her wits, she turned back to him. "Those are bold words for one trussed like a gutted stag."

The black brows of the captive winged higher over his amazing eyes. It would be far too easy for a person to fall helpless under that striking glare.

To her amazement, he only laughed at her. The desperate tone of his laughter sent a ripple of guilt down her spine. She studied her captive and frowned. Behind the fierce anger that brightened his eyes lay something akin to…pain.

She'd seen that expression staring back at her from the polished surface of her mirror. Pain. Loss. They already haunted her nightmares.

What did Faucon know of pain? Or of loss? This man doled out death and destruction as a pastime. He gave no thought to the lives his actions touched, or ruined in the process. Nay, even though she could not name the emotion, she knew it was not pain flickering in his gaze.

Even if the demon did possess a tiny bit of remorse in his black-hearted soul, what did it matter to her? Nothing would change. Guillaume would still lie dead. How would she find a husband within the time left to her? For without a husband, King Stephen would take Taniere.

The sound of wooden wagon wheels clattering over the hard, rutted path interrupted her disturbing thoughts. A few more of the men arrived to dispose of Faucon's body, but John's loud curse unsettled her even more.

Suddenly losing control, Guillaume's man lunged toward her captive, intent on running his sword through the man.

''Nay! He is mine.'' No one else must finish the deed. Only her. As Lyonesse threw herself at John she knocked him off his feet and seized his sword.

She grasped the weapon with both hands and turned toward Faucon. Stiffening her spine, steeling herself for what she was about to do, Lyonesse walked toward him. She picked a spot on his chest as her target.

"Damn you, look at me." She did as he bid. "If you are bold enough to take my life have the courage to watch me die."

Honor and bravery—the ideals her father lived by, the qualities she strove for in herself, shimmered in his unflinching stare.

Horror stopped her. What was she about to do? This would not be revenge.

Her stomach rolled. This would be murder.

The sword wavered. His stare bore into her. He would accept death. Unlike a coward, he would not plead for his life. The sword wobbled and fell from her hand.

Lyonesse shook herself from her trance and stared at Faucon.

He returned her steady look. "You are making a grave mistake, milady."

She made her decision. "Get him in the wagon," she shouted at her men.

Faucon struggled uselessly against the men who nearly carried him to the waiting hay wagon. His threats and curses fell heavy on her ears.

Not wishing to listen to his tirade during the trip

back to Taniere, Lyonesse leaned over the side of the wagon and ordered, "Cease, Faucon."

"You will pay for this. All of you." Faucon glared at the men. "Do you take your orders from a mere slip of a girl? The king will hunt each and every one of you down."

His empty threats infuriated her. "Faucon, I warned you once. Cease. Else I will find a way to silence you."

He answered with a menacing snarl. "You puling little cub, do you realize what you are getting yourself into? The day will come when you regret this action."

"I know exactly what I am about. I'll not regret anything." Grabbing a dirty, rumpled cloth from the cart, she rolled it into a ball. "Maybe this will stop your threats."

The cloth stuffed in his mouth cut off Faucon's blistering curses. Lyonesse backed away from the hate and anger glowing from his eyes. No words were needed to understand his silent promise of sinister retribution for her act.

Had her need for revenge not been so strong, Lyonesse knew she would have disgraced herself. Had she loved Guillaume less, it would be easy to order Faucon's release and ride away. But the loss of her love hardened her heart.

Quickly mounting her horse, she left the others behind and headed toward home. Left to only her thoughts and the eerie cry of a soaring bird of prey, Lyonesse muttered aloud to the empty air. "Faucon must pay for his treachery. I have witnesses to provide proof of his guilt."

Guillaume's own men had brought the cold, disfigured body of their lord back to Taniere keep. They described the butcher who had ended du Pree's life.

Even more telling than their description of the murderer was the last detail Guillaume's men had told her. The eyes beneath the dark nasal helm glowed a riveting gold. Like the raptor he was named for, his eyes pierced their quarry just before the kill.

Aye, Faucon had mutilated the gentle Guillaume beyond recognition. Of that, there was no doubt. It mattered little if all of Faucon's forces arrived at her gates. Let them come. They would soon learn that their name alone would not always protect them from retribution for their sins.

The thick, gray walls of her keep were a welcome sight. Lyonesse cantered ahead, her hail of "Taniere!" brought instant reaction from the men in the twin gate towers. The drawbridge slowly lowered and the iron portcullis raised, giving entrance to the outer yard.

She rode past the inner gates and into the second bailey, then slid off the lathered horse. After handing the reins to a waiting stable lad, she paused only long enough to give the unneeded order, "See that he is well cared for, Simon.'' Lyonesse headed up the steep steps leading into the great hall.

She paused briefly to learn from her maid Helen that a missive from du Pree's holy man had arrived before reaching the welcoming silence of her private chamber. She hastily stripped the heavy armor from her sweat-soaked body. ''Sweet Mary, how can they wear this?'' A sigh escaped her lips as she peeled the thickly padded undershirt away from her hot flesh.

Relieved of the old, leather-hardened armor and protective underpadding, she snatched the rolled parchment from her bed before dropping down on the mattress.

Quickly sliding her fingernail beneath the wax seal, Lyonesse unrolled the missive and scanned its contents.

She couldn't hold back the laugh building in her chest. For the first time in months, she experienced a measure of relief and satisfaction. The Good Lord had heard her prayers.

Lyonesse stood just inside the tower cell. Even chained to a bed and sleeping, Faucon looked formidable. Was he indeed a spawn of Satan? Did he take pleasure from fighting and killing?

The many scars marking his body attested to his prowess. To have withstood so many injuries and survived gave credence to his strength and cunning.

Was he a champion to be lauded, or a devil to be feared? Bravery or sorcery?

Either way, he was still a murderer.

A living and breathing murderer.

Lyonesse frowned. She'd not expected this predicament. When she and John planned this revenge, there'd been no talk of what to do when Faucon was brought to Taniere. The only lengthy discussion was where to bury the body.

The body she'd not so carefully tended a short time ago. It had taken three men to hold Faucon while she poured Helen's sleeping draught down his throat. Gentleness had not been on her mind while she'd cleaned and stitched the gash in his side and seen to the bruises and cuts on his face and neck.

"Milady, do you require help?" Howard called out as he entered the small tower chamber that served as Faucon's cell.

"No, Howard, all is well."

The way her captain dogged her every step around Faucon was almost laughable. In less than one day, the keep's active grapevine had already begun to grow. Too many people already knew she was using this tower chamber as a cell—and they knew who she held prisoner.

Little more than a fortnight past, Lyonesse had left her father's keep at Ryonne in a hurry. She'd wanted to leave before he returned from the king's service and could stop her. Since she'd not had time to find her own work force at Taniere, many of his servants were in attendance. She'd not risk killing Faucon with so many of Ryonne's people about. Tongues would wag. Regardless of her reasoning, her father would not take kindly to her form of vengeance.

She could bide her time. After all, she'd captured the mighty Faucon, had she not?

Howard cleared his throat. ''Milady, do nothing rash.''

Lyonesse turned to face him. She opened her mouth and then quickly bit back the stinging reply so ready to fall from her lips. Howard's worried expression twisted her stomach with guilt. ''Howard, upon my honor, I will not kill this man today.''

He peered down and studied her face for a moment before warning, ''Keep an eye out for Sir John. I do not think he will give up quite as easily.''

Why Howard did not trust Guillaume's man was something Lyonesse would never understand.

Howard nodded toward the bed and asked, ''Will he die of his wounds?''

''Nay. His wounds were minor. 'Tis Helen's concoction that keeps him asleep.'' When concern etched even deeper lines in Howard's face, Lyonesse pushed him to the door. ''Go. Faucon will suffer nothing more severe than an aching head.''

She waited until the captain left before returning to the bedside to check on her rather shabby handiwork. Sadly, she was not always the most careful seamstress and wanted to make certain the stitches held.

Lyonesse knelt on the floor and pushed the covers from his side. Faucon shifted in his sleep, dragging the cover off his chest.

She paused, her hand in midair as she'd reached to check his wound. Her face flushed hot. A tingle ran down her neck and across her chest filling her breasts and intensifying the heat on her cheeks.

Lyonesse had tended many injuries for her father and his men. A man's body was no mystery to her. She'd lost her curiosity many years ago. Why did seeing just this man's chest cause such fluttering of her heart?

He was her enemy. He'd taken away her future. He'd killed her love. She'd prayed for his death many times over. She'd wished to see his broken body lying at her feet.

She bit her lip. Her heart did not cease its rapid pounding. The heat on her cheeks did not lessen.

She shook her head and steadied her trembling hand. She was tired, that was all. The excitement from capturing this man had been too much. She needed rest. Nothing more. Lyonesse pulled the salve-filled covering from his side.

His hand shot out like a snake and grabbed her wrist. ''What are you doing?''

The chain securing him to the wall gave little warning. If she'd not already been kneeling on the floor, she'd have fallen. How long had he been awake? She pried at his fingers. ''Release me.''

His grip tightened. ''What are you doing?''

Lyonesse smiled into his gold-flecked gaze. ''I thought I would take out these stitches and see how long it takes a devil to bleed to death.''

He returned her steady stare for a long moment before releasing her. ''By all means, proceed.''

His response surprised her. ''You would just lie there?''

Faucon raised an arm. The metal links permitted him limited movement. ''What could I do to stop you?''

She knew better. This was not a man who would simply accept death while lying flat on his back. ''How long have you been awake?''

His laugh was weak. ''Long enough.''

Her heart sank. She'd have no luck filling him with worry. He'd most likely heard her vow to Howard. Determined to complete her chore and quit the chamber, she asked, ''May I finish here?''

Faucon closed his eyes, tensed his jaw, and nodded.

Lyonesse studied him for a heartbeat. ''Does it hurt that much?''

''Only when you poke and prod at it.''

How long *had* he been awake? Suddenly, she didn't wish to know. Quickly, after checking the stitches, she smoothed on more salve. Her fingers shook at the contact with his flesh. The skin covering his frame was smooth to her touch. The muscles beneath were tight and well developed. Lyonesse bit her bottom lip, forcing her errant thoughts back to the task at hand. She not-so-gently slapped the covering back over the wound and pulled the blankets up over his body.

She rose and headed toward the door. ''I will send up a maid with something to drink.''

''Food, perhaps? Unless you want me to starve to death.''

She paused. '''Tis a thought.''

His laugh rumbled across her ears. ''That might please you, but your Howard would not be happy.''

Lyonesse sighed. He'd heard the vow to Howard. ''Faucon, you may be alive at this moment, but do not be so certain I will not yet gain my revenge.'' She smiled. ''I had you at the pointed end of a sword once. I can do it again if need be.''

''Maybe so, but I'll be ready for you and it will not be quite as easy.''

Lyonesse's blood rushed through her veins. She wanted to rip the smirk from his face. ''You think you are so invincible. You survive every battle. Do you think that will last forever? You are nothing but a man, Faucon. A man who can, and someday will, die.''

His smile widened. ''And you are but a woman. A woman like any other.'' His eyes seemed to glow from across the room. "Tell me, Lady Lyonesse, which scar did you admire the most? The one on my thigh, or one of those on my chest?"

Anger and embarrassment ripped a scream of rage from her throat. Not only had the swine heard her vow to Howard, he'd been awake the whole time.

Before charging out the door, she yelled, "Go to the devil, Faucon."

Rhys laughed. Lord Baldwin of Ryonne had chosen well by naming his daughter after his wife's father. This cunning she-cub was worthy of being called Lyonesse. Too bad she'd not inherited her father's even temper. For all her bravado and trickery, the Lady Lyonesse angered too easily. Her emotional displays would not serve her well. But it would provide him with some amusement while he was here.

Since she'd not killed him in the forest, he had a bad feeling that he might be here a long time. If that happened, he'd end up dying at King Stephen's orders without ever discovering the true murderer.

Rhys jerked his arm, grimacing at the bite of the iron manacle holding him to the bed.

Surely they didn't mean to keep him chained to this bed forever? They knew who he was, so they'd heard the stories about Lord Faucon.

His bitter sigh filled the chamber. How could anyone not have heard the tales? Rhys purposely let the rumors of his terrible disposition grow and spread.

Secretly he enjoyed the fear that sprang to men's eyes when they realized whom they faced. It suited him to build upon this dark image by dressing himself, his horse and his men in nothing but black.

Those who knew him well found the stories of his evilness amusing, even assisting Rhys in building the fables beyond the believable. He had to admit, it effectively kept the unwanted daughters of his peers from being dangled beneath his nose.

In truth, he'd not needed stories to keep women away. Word of Alyce's death had sufficed. That suited him well. He'd no wish to avail himself of another woman's lies and deceit.

Again, what he'd thought was a long-buried pain, stabbed at his heart. ''Blast it all.'' The curse echoed in his ears. He glanced out the arrow slit. The sun was already setting.

How much time would pass before his men found their way to his captain Melwyn? They'd broken the men up into two groups. Melwyn's group headed toward Faucon's keep, seeking aid from his brother Gareth. The other group rode with him, toward Richmond. The most logical area to begin his search had seemed the site where the rumors about the murder were circulating. Instead, they'd ridden into a trap.

A cleverly devised trap. Since du Pree's lands and Ryonne were to the south, he'd not expected to encounter vengeance on the north road.

Where was he? He knew what general area. His foolish captors had taken no pains to hide their direction. The cart had followed the north road before turning slightly east toward the coast. That would put him in either the Earl of York's, or the Earl of Richmond's territory. Since both men were considered friends, he was in a safe region.

Yet they were close to the Scottish border. All were aware that the Lord of Faucon was a staunch supporter of King Stephen in his battle against the Empress for the throne. No matter what had taken place during King Henry's reign, the Empress had no right to the crown.

Rhys refused to believe for an instant that Baldwin's daughter would be loyal to the enemy. So where had Lady Lyonesse taken him? He closed his eyes, recalling snippets of court gossip. Had he heard anything about Ryonne, Lyonesse or du Pree? Other than about the upcoming marriage ceremony, he didn't recall—*wait!* Rhys sat up. Yes, he did recall something…from last summer. *What?*

He smiled with relief. Taniere. How could he have forgotten the uproar when old Leon had handed his prized possession to his granddaughter?

His smile died. Knowing where he was did little to help him. His only hope was his men.

They were all to meet outside of Northampton next week. If his men could not find him, would either of his brothers be able to prevent the loss of all they held dear?

How did he let this happen? The ridiculousness of the situation wiped away his anger and worry. Unable to contain himself, he started to laugh.

Once started, his deep, throaty laugher was nearly impossible to stop. He did not care if the sound echoed out of the chamber and down to the hall.

"A female. The terrible Faucon has had his wings clipped by a female."

All his years of hard work to build a reputation wasted. Wiped out by the small hand of a grief-stricken female. He shook his head. "Not even a woman fully grown, but by an untried girl."

When he reached up to wipe the tears from his eyes, Rhys flinched at the bite of his chains. The flash of pain didn't stop the laughter from erupting again.

Lyonesse. Aye, she was well named. His shoulders trembled with mirth. In his mind a green-eyed kitten pounced on an unsuspecting falcon and shook the bird of prey between its small, white, sharp teeth.

Chapter Two

An early evening breeze brushed lightly across Lyonesse's cheek. The gentle current carried a fine, cool mist from the sea it just crossed, causing her to pull the woolen mantle more closely around her to ward off the chill. Her perch in the crenellation of the stone wall may have shielded her from a person's view, but it provided little shelter from the seeking wind.

She'd had two days to think. Two long days to figure out what to do with Faucon until his time ran out.

So far she'd come up with little else besides holding him in her tower. He'd only laughed at her with a deep, sinister laugh that sent shivers down her spine. He didn't realize that she knew about the king's command. Faucon had one short month to prove his innocence, or die. If she could hold him long enough, his death would not be on her hands.

Faucon would have to be content with being held captive—for a time. She'd ordered the chains securing him to the bed removed, making his lot slightly better. A thick, iron-studded door with a locking bar on the outside, secured him within his tower cell.

"The murdering scum be dead?"

Lyonesse jumped at the intrusion. "No." Intent on her thoughts, she gave Sir John little more than a glance.

He grasped her shoulder. "What do you mean, 'no'?"

She jerked away from his unwelcome touch, reluctantly climbing down from the wall. "No, Faucon is not dead."

"'Tis not what we planned." Anger tinged his words. "Milord du Pree will not wait forever for his revenge."

Lyonesse lifted an eyebrow at his impatience. "What does a day or two matter to one who is dead?"

Sir John loomed over her, his lips curled into a snarl. "Lord Guillaume trusted you. Like a besotted fool he was ready to give you everything." He spat on the wooden planks of the wallwalk. "You dishonor him with your hesitation."

"I dishonor no one." She swallowed her fear of the man and stared up at him. "Faucon will pay for what he did."

"When? You have had time aplenty to finish the deed."

Howard's dire warnings about trusting Sir John

rang in her mind. No. She would not tell him her plans.

"What would you like me to do, Sir John? Run a sword through him with Ryonne's captain at hand?"

Sir John's smile sent a tremor down her spine. "I can see to your captain easily enough."

"You will *not* endanger Howard."

The man stepped away. "If the deed is not done by this time tomorrow, I will see to it myself."

"Give me no ultimatums. I will deal with Faucon."

Lyonesse gasped when he grabbed her arm. "Unhand me."

He tightened his hold. "The time for games is over. I came to you to fulfill my lord's final wish and I will see it done. No one will stop me. I will kill any who get in my way. It will give me great pleasure when Sir Howard seeks to interfere." Releasing her, he started to turn away, stopping long enough to add, "Until this time tomorrow, Lady Lyonesse."

She watched his retreat and wondered why she had ever trusted him. 'Twas simple—because she'd been too distraught to think straight. Grief had made her more than eager to seek revenge on Guillaume's murderer.

And now she'd made Sir John an enemy. An enemy who threatened to kill Howard.

Sir John left her no choice. She would have to set aside her new plans of letting King Stephen deal with Faucon and fulfill the old ones.

She still thirsted for his blood, but would she be able to take his life? Is that what Guillaume would have wanted?

She turned back to the wall, watching the flurry of nighttime activities in the outer bailey. Fires for cooking and warmth glowed from the doorway of each cottage and hut. The smells of food being prepared set her stomach rolling.

The calls and laughter of those gathering their tools and closing their shops for the day made her smile wistfully. They were going home to wives, husbands and children. Their lives might be poor and humble compared to hers, but they had someone to go home to, someplace to call home.

While she had nothing and no one. Nay, her chance at having someplace to consider her own was lost. She closed her eyes tightly against the tears. Her chance at having a happy, fulfilling life had been taken from her.

Lyonesse turned and glared across Taniere's inner courtyard. Her heated stare swept across the muddy practice yard, past the stables and mews to fly up the earthen motte that supported the high walls of the keep. Aye, lost because the monster locked inside the tower knew not the meaning of honor.

He'd killed Guillaume as if the man had been

nothing but a mere foot soldier, instead of heir to a title and great wealth. It would have been of more benefit to take Guillaume for ransom, than killing him in such a cowardly fashion. No sane man would have mutilated Guillaume beyond recognition. Only someone of the devil's ilk could have committed such a deed. Someone like Faucon. What savagery lurked in the soul of the man she'd imprisoned? Perhaps he had no soul.

Perhaps killing him would *not* be a sin.

She crossed her arms tightly across her stomach. Every time she thought of Guillaume's death, bile rose to choke her. Pain, as sharp as that from a thrusted sword, pierced her temples.

She would never get used to not having Guillaume about. He had paged at Ryonne. Under her father's tutelage he had grown into manhood. Once he'd become an adult, he had a man's responsibilities. While many of his duties took him away from Ryonne for long periods, he'd never been away from her heart.

Anger thickened her blood. Renewed rage fired her resolve. Aye, she still desired revenge. From between clenched teeth, Lyonesse vowed, ''Misbegotten spawn of Satan, you will pay dearly for what you have done.''

A cool gust of wind made her shiver. Determined to end her growing nightmares this very night,

Lyonesse pulled her cloak closer about her and marched toward the keep.

The skin on the back of her neck prickled, making her stop in midstep. Someone or something was watching her. Watching her like a predator stalking its prey.

From the shelter of the forest he watched, biding his time. Faucon still lived. His minion's announcement hadn't been needed. He'd felt it in his heart. The gut-wrenching taunts rustled in the leaves—*he lives, he lives.*

Glaring across the open expanse of land separating Taniere's walls from the dense forest, he lifted his gaze to the keep. The beast had killed the most important person in the world, and her son. For that Faucon would pay.

For now Faucon drew breath—safely locked in one of the towers. But soon—very soon the devil's heart would cease beating and his breath would come no more.

When Faucon lost his life only one person would be held to blame. Lyonesse.

For five years he'd planned Faucon's death. The time had stretched like an eternity before him. An endless, lonely eternity. Lyonesse made a grave error by taking the murderer captive instead of dispatching him to his master. For that she would suffer the pangs of hell.

* * *

Rhys stared through the arrow slit and watched the sun sink from view. His heart fell in unison with the light of this remarkably strange day.

He cursed his forced inactivity. The idle solitude permitted unbidden images to form in his mind. Memories that he had not previously allowed to disturb, or interrupt his life, now threatened to overwhelm him.

The rushing thoughts were so vivid he could hear and see them. Shapeless thoughts from years past transformed into actions of now. Rhys groaned at the sound of a newborn baby's cry. His groans turned to a strangled gasp of horror when the screams of a dying infant and mother invaded his senses.

A sword cutting through his flesh would not be as painful as the piercing wails that rang relentlessly in his own mind. He could hear her accusations and her laughter.

She'd taken a naive, eager boy to husband and had effortlessly crushed his hopes and dreams with her vileness.

''By the Rood, cease.'' His growl bounced off the bare walls of the empty cell.

He jumped to his feet and paced the small confines of his tower jail. The act did little to comfort him. Nor did it provide the action his body desperately needed to quell the unwelcome memories.

The arrow slit silently beckoned to him. Drawn to

teasing thoughts of freedom, Rhys paused before the narrow opening and gazed down at the baileys and walls below.

He watched two lone figures on the closer wall. Unable to hear their words, he could only assess their moods by the posturing of their bodies. The quick motions of his captor expressed her agitation and impatience. While the tense, stiff movements of the man conveyed tightly leashed anger.

They took turns glancing up at this tower while continuing their animated discussion. Obviously, he was the topic of their argument. With a dismissive shrug, Rhys let his attention wander. He looked beyond the outer wall.

A large expanse of cleared land lay between the keep and the woods. No force of men would be able to approach the keep unseen. Not even his own.

The outer bailey of the keep drew his attention. Fires burned inside the thatched huts. It seemed like a lifetime since he'd enjoyed the contentment of hearth and home.

The lingering warmth and joy shared at his parents' hearth had once made him long for a wife and children of his own. A bitter marriage and too many deaths had driven that childish longing to an early grave.

He rested his forehead against the damp stone wall. What unholy saint drew those thoughts from the bowels of hell?

A key grated in the lock of the tower door, drawing him away from the arrow slit and away from his building gloom.

A young page carried a wooden tray laden with food and set the tray on the floor before turning to Rhys.

The boy looked up at him and asked, "You are the devil Faucon?"

Rhys smiled at the child's boldness. Only by keeping his voice low was he able to contain his laughter. "Aye, 'tis what some call me."

The lad squinted. "Why do you not look like a demon?"

Rhys crossed his arms against his chest, then looked down his nose at the imp. "What should a demon look like?"

An innocent knowledge of devils rushed from the child's mouth. "You should have horns and a tail. How do you wear boots over hoofed feet?" He paused to point down at the tray. "A true demon would not eat this food. It is already dead."

Rhys kicked his foot toward the tray, forced a growl to his voice and asked, "How do you know I will not eat you instead of this rubbish?" He took a step closer to the boy. "Should you not run for your life?"

The child drew his small shoulders back, held his ground and tilted his head up a little farther. He pointed at Rhys, insisting, "A true demon would not have been captured by—"

"Michael!"

The accusation was cut short by a shout from beyond the door. Michael instantly scampered out of the room.

Lyonesse stood in the doorway. "That child is innocent." She glowered at him and ordered, "You will leave him be."

Rhys's mouth twitched with sorely suppressed humor. He lifted one shoulder briefly. "A child is a delicacy that I have not tasted in many weeks."

Lyonesse paused. Not one muscle in her tense face moved. Then a look of uncertainty settled on her face.

Rhys provoked the confusion even further. He assumed an air of nonchalance, bargaining, "If you will turn a blind eye to my ungodly appetites I will promise to stifle the child's screams." He picked at an imaginary speck of dirt beneath a fingernail and waited for her.

"Have you not yet killed enough innocent people to satisfy your taste for flesh and blood?"

"By all the Saints' bones!" Had the woman no sense of humor? "I was but jesting."

She stepped into the chamber, the hem of her overlong mantle trailing across the floor behind her. "Your humor is ill-received here, Faucon. I found nothing humorous in committing Guillaume to his grave.''

''No, you probably did not.''

'''Tis all you have to say?'' She closed the door behind her, shutting out the guards. ''No apology for the havoc you have brought to my life? No regret for killing an innocent man?''

Every fiber of his being warned him of danger. ''I have never taken an innocent life.''

She smiled. ''You lie so well.''

The warning grew stronger. Rhys narrowed his eyes. ''What do you want?''

She unclasped the brooch of her hooded mantle, letting it fall to the floor. Rhys's mouth went dry. Her hair, worn loose, cascaded over her shoulders and down her bare arms. Pale, silken flesh mounded gently above the deep-cut neck of her sleeveless overgown. The bliaut hugged her body like a second skin. She wore no chainse beneath—nothing but flesh showed through the tightly laced openings on either side.

The soft, thin fabric of her gown clung to her legs as she approached. Long, shapely legs carried her almost silently across the floor.

He did his best to breathe. Rhys willed his riotous heart to cease its wild thudding inside his chest. The erratic rhythm made it nearly impossible to think.

''Why, Faucon.'' Her whispered words floated

like a spring breeze. ''I want the same thing that I have always wanted.''

The sweet scent of roses and spice acted like strong ale to his senses. He looked down at her. When had she moved so close? He resisted the strong urge to reach out and draw her against his chest. ''And what might that be?''

Lyonesse looked up at him. Light from the wall torches twinkled like stars in her eyes. She smiled and he felt his heart turn over itself.

He focused on her mouth. So near. So ready to be kissed. She trailed the tip of her tongue across her lips and he leaned forward, willing to do the task for her.

''All I want, Faucon, is you.'' The sharp, cold point of a dagger pressed against his chest accentuated her words.

Chapter Three

Lyonesse would always treasure the look of surprise and anger that crossed Faucon's face the moments before his death. It would sustain her in the long, lonely years ahead.

When he reached up to grab her wrist, she sank the blade through the top layer of his skin. He stopped instantly and lowered his arm.

"Faucon, how could you think I wanted anything but your life?"

His dark gaze bore into hers. "Considering what a base clod I have obviously become, I bid you hurry."

She was surprised by how calm his words sounded. Would he really accept death so easily? "It has taken me months to achieve this moment. Let me savor it a little longer."

"Oh, by all means, please do enjoy yourself."

"Always the sarcastic retort? Tell me, Faucon, do you take anything seriously?"

His eyes burned. Golden specks flickered into be-ing. "I take living and dying very seriously."

Suddenly her mouth went dry. "You may take your own living and dying seriously. What about others?"

"It depends."

His voice, deep and gravelly, whispered across her ears. She found it difficult to concentrate in the warm chamber. She needed to end this quickly. Now. Before losing her will to see it through.

No longer was waiting for his time to run out an option. She'd come this far—debased herself to catch him off guard. To her amazement and satis-faction it had worked.

Keeping her gaze locked on his, she took a deep breath and in the split second before completing her deed, she wondered if there would be much blood. With all the force she could muster, Lyonesse gripped the dagger, prepared to ram the lethal blade into his heart.

Like a hawk snatching its prey in midair, Faucon caught her wrist in a viselike grasp. "You have two choices, Lyonesse. Either end this now, or submit."

She stared at the hand gripping hers. The muscles and veins in his hands strained against confining flesh. Blood ran down the front of his tunic. She saw her entire life, her future ebb away as easily as his blood. Swallowing the bile caught in her throat, she looked back up at him. "You have to die. If I don't do it, Sir John will and he'll kill all who stand in his way.''

''Fine.'' His grip tightened over hers as he forced the point of the dagger deeper into his chest.

Dear Lord, she couldn't do this. She'd tried. Twice now. And failed. In a whisper, she pleaded, ''Guillaume, forgive me.''

Faucon whispered back. ''You will never *let* him forgive you.'' Pushing the lethal weapon another hair closer to his heart, he beckoned, ''Come, Lyonesse, this is what you want. I am helping you all I can.''

''Stop!'' She pushed frantically against his chest with her free hand. ''Oh, stop, please. I cannot.''

Entwining his fingers through her hair, he grabbed the back of her neck, stopping her attempt at escape. ''I thought this is what you wanted.''

''I do.''

''Look at my chest, Lyonesse. Can you not see my blood run? Does it not give you a taste for more? You are almost there. Why stop now when you are so close?''

She glanced past the blood and stared at him. ''I am not like you. I could never kill in cold blood.''

He laughed. ''You are more like me than you will ever know.''

''No.'' Lyonesse shook her head. ''I could never do the devil's work.''

''Then why do you come to this chamber dressed

like a temptress and close out the guards? Who gave you the idea of distracting me with your body, so that you could plant a dagger in my heart? If you think those thoughts came from God you need to think again, Lyonesse.''

She would burn in hell for her actions this day. ''You do not understand. If you do not die, Sir John has vowed to see it through. Howard will seek to stop him and when he does...'' She couldn't complete the horrifying truth.

''Do you place such little trust in your captain?''

Lyonesse shook her head. ''I would trust him with my life.''

''But not his own.''

She gasped. ''I could not bear him to die for my mistake.''

''Then correct your mistake now. Kill me. See it through.''

Her knees buckled. Faucon winced, but pulled her upright. ''Damn you, Lyonesse. Get it over with.''

Her breath caught on a choked cry. ''I cannot.''

''Then I will end this myself.''

Jerking the tip of the dagger out of his chest, he shook her wrist and the weapon clattered to the floor. Faucon pulled her to him. ''I gave you two choices, Lyonesse. The first was to kill me.''

His lips grazed hers. ''The second was to submit.''

The warmth of his blood seeped through her thin

gown. The heat of his lips tore through her veins. This was insane. Yet that knowledge did nothing to prevent her from leaning even closer against him.

Coaxing her lips to part, he swept his tongue across hers and the fire shot all the way to her toes. Heat and ice both rushed through her at the same time. It left her dizzy, breathless and wanting more.

Faucon released her wrist and wrapped his arm around her. ''You were a fool to come here alone.'' His hot breath grazed her ear. ''What made you think you would succeed?''

Before she could answer, his lips closed over hers. The half-formed response fled her mind.

He stroked her side, his fingertips barely brushing her flesh. Lyonesse shivered from the unexpected contact.

No man had ever touched her like this—igniting fires with a gentle stroke. Not even Guillaume had kissed her in this manner—turning her legs to water and causing her heart to beat so rapidly. Never had she imagined the feelings running through her now. Faucon was just a man and she'd been certain of his reaction upon seeing her indecent clothing. Yet she had not expected him to touch her—or to kiss her.

She'd not expected to become the prey.

He traced across her chin and up to her ear with his lips and tongue. She could no more stop the tremors rushing down her spine than she could stop the moon from rising at night.

Faucon cupped her breast and ran his thumb across her already swollen nipple. "Ah, Lyonesse." His whispered words against her ear drew a moan from her. His lips against her neck caused her to gasp for breath. He chuckled softly against her skin. "The next time you seek to kill me, do not get within my arm's reach."

Threading his fingers tighter in her hair, he pulled her head back.

Lyonesse stared into his eyes. The golden flecks shimmered with life. The fire in her veins cooled instantly. What had she done?

His brows rose and a smile lifted one side of his mouth. "Next time, Lyonesse, I will do much more than just kiss you. I will make you mine."

She bit her lip as the heat of embarrassment rushed up her face. Pushing against his chest, she swore, "Next time, Faucon, perhaps I will see you dead."

He laughed at her idle threat. "There won't be a next time, my love."

"Do not call me that!" Her gown stuck to the already drying blood on his chest as she pulled away.

Faucon looked down and pried at the cloth, freeing them from each other. "I would appreciate it, if you would summon Howard."

She backed away and turned to retrieve her mantle

from the floor, just as the door to the chamber banged against the wall.

''Again you could not honor Milord Guillaume's wishes.'' Sir John stood in the doorway. His sword already drawn, he started for Faucon. ''I told you I would see to it myself.''

Lyonesse grabbed at his arm, but he jerked away from her. ''Nay. Do not.''

Sir John paused and looked at her. ''Do not?'' Narrowing his eyes, he let his gaze travel slowly down her body. His rage, when he returned his stare to her face, was almost tangible. ''I see that even you have fallen under this blackguard's spell.''

Pulling her mantle around her, Lyonesse returned his stare. ''Nay. But I will not have him killed. We will let the king deal with Faucon.''

Rhys looked from one to the other. Who was his biggest enemy? Sir John with a heart of hate and a ready sword? Or Lyonesse with a heart of deceit and tongue filled with lies? He'd rather face the sword. At least with Sir John he knew when and where the attack would come. But his unexplained lust for Lyonesse would cloud her approach.

He studied the opponents as they confronted each other. No, his lust was not unexplained. Here was a woman who would fight for what she wanted. A woman who would follow her own form of honor— even if it was a bit misguided. A woman who could contain her fear.

This was a woman who could touch his soul. The thought excited him and terrified him at the same time.

Her last words registered in his mind. "You will permit the king to deal with me?"

Without shifting her gaze from Sir John, Lyonesse replied, "'Tis what I said."

And he'd just thought her honorable. "Are there any other games you wish to play with my life?"

"What is wrong, Faucon? Do you not like a taste of your own treatment?"

With a curse, Sir John shoved Lyonesse toward the door. Then he turned and brandished his sword toward Rhys's chest. "Sparring with words is not the way to deal with this murdering scum."

Quickly glancing about the cell, Rhys spied the dagger. Before he could get his hands on the weapon, Howard and five of Taniere's men rushed the chamber.

"Hold!" Howard's shout caught Sir John unaware. After disarming the man, Howard handed him over to the guards. "Sir John and his men will leave this keep tonight. From this moment forward they are to be considered enemies of Taniere and Ryonne."

He paused a moment and when Lyonesse offered no argument, he continued, "If you naysay me on this, milady, I will lock you in your chamber and summon your father from Ryonne."

Lyonesse bowed her head and sought to pull her mantle more tightly around her, but Howard saw the bloodstains on the front of her gown before she could hide them. Grasping her arm, the captain exclaimed, "You are injured. What has happened here?"

Pulling away, she reassured him, "I am fine."

Howard glanced at Rhys, back to Lyonesse and finally chose Rhys. "What have you done?"

Rhys shook his head. "Me? Nothing."

"Milady Lyonesse?"

"I said I am fine, Howard. Leave it be."

"Then how did you come to be covered with blood? If you are uninjured, then I assume it is Faucon's."

"An accident."

Rhys wanted to laugh at the pair. Where had Taniere's vicious kitten gone?

"Lady Lyonesse, I told you to stay away from this cell. Why did you come here alone? Who dismissed the guards?"

Straightening her spine, Lyonesse glared at the captain. "I dismissed the guards. They are, after all, my guards."

Much better. Rhys was pleased to see her return to normal. Since the two of them were obviously distracted, he took the opportunity to snatch the dagger from the floor.

Howard did not seem the least impressed with Lyonesse's demeanor. "Did Faucon's blood just suddenly run from his chest unaided?"

She lifted her chin a notch and lifted one tawny eyebrow. "Perhaps."

Rhys took a step forward. If he could get his hands on Lyonesse, maybe he could use her and the dagger to escape. "No, my blood was quite content in my body before she entered this cell."

She pointed at Rhys. "But he—"

"Cease!" Howard cut off her reply. "I have heard enough. I still insist that you do not have enough proof to know if Faucon murdered Guillaume or not. Call an end to this, Lyonesse. Send out a ransom note and be done with it."

Even though a ransom would be an accepted action, Rhys would not stand for that plan. It was unacceptable to him. "It would be better if you would just let her kill me now than wait for ransom."

Howard scratched his chin in confusion. "And why is that? It makes little sense."

Rhys pointed at Lyonesse. "Ask her."

She leaned against the rough-hewn door frame and smiled.

Howard rolled his eyes to the ceiling before focusing his attention on her. "What have you done now, milady?"

"Did you know that if Faucon cannot locate someone to take the blame for killing Guillaume that he will be forced to prove his innocence in a trial by combat?''

The captain looked to Rhys for confirmation. ''Yes, she is correct, but she left out one important detail.''

Her smile grew. ''Oh, silly me. Yes. He only had a month to accomplish his task.'' She paused and shrugged one shoulder. ''I will not release him in time.''

Gripping the dagger he still held behind his back, Rhys quelled his temper. ''I know you hate me. I seek not to change that. But what has my family done to make you hate them so?''

She frowned. ''Nothing.''

''If you follow through with this plan, you will be taking everything away from them.''

''I thought you did not fear death, Faucon? I thought none could beat you in battle? What trick do you now play?''

Rhys laughed bitterly and then looked at Howard. ''I play no trick. This trial by combat will be a farce. Guillaume du Pree's holy man will arrange the combat, ensuring that success will be his.''

''Surely you see the folly in this course of action?'' Howard pleaded with Lyonesse. ''Milady, please, you cannot permit this to happen.''

Rage contorted her face. She stepped away from the door. ''Permit it to happen? What do I care if his family loses everything? What about me? What about all I have lost already and stand to lose in a few short weeks myself? Where has your loyalty gone, Sir Howard?'' Her voice rose with each question. ''What do you care that we will be forced to leave Taniere? You will simply assume your duty under my father's command. I will be left with nothing and Taniere will no longer be in my family's possession.''

Racing by a stunned Howard, she yelled, ''I will not permit that to happen.''

Rhys was ready for the woman who literally flew at him. Catching her unaware, he wrapped his arms around her to stop her renewed assault on his already injured chest. When he did so, Howard saw the dagger and paled.

Rhys looked toward the door. Freedom beckoned. Tightening his grip on the dagger he drew his gaze back down to Lyonesse. He saw not the defeat of a vanquished foe, but the bitter agony of a young woman.

Rhys held Ryonne's daughter in his grasp. Ryonne was a trusted ally. Surely the man's daughter possessed a small measure of his honor. He'd already seen a glimmer of her loyalty and honor. Had grief caused her to become irrational? Could he take advantage of her and still live with himself?

So much had already been taken from her. Her betrothed. And soon her keep. No wonder she was at her wits' end. Rhys could not take her pride.

'Twas all she had left. He would find another way out of this predicament.

A sliver of light flashed across his face. The gleaming tip of Howard's sword pointed at his face with unwavering accuracy. Rhys relinquished the weapon he held to Howard's outstretched hand.

Ignoring her halfhearted attempts to free herself, Rhys drew Lyonesse closer and held her face against his chest. ''Hush.''

Whispering meaningless words of comfort, his thoughts raced to his sister's inconsolable grief at their parents' graves. Compassion flooded his heart. He was stunned by the urgent need to comfort the woman in his arms.

''Count Faucon. Nay, you must not. You cannot. 'Tis not seemly.''

Without looking at the man, Rhys shook his head at Howard's half-completed sentences. He also paid scant attention to the meager struggles of the woman he held against his chest.

''Aye, you are correct, Howard. *I* should not.'' His accusing gaze met the captain's look of concern and ill-concealed fear. ''But do you not think someone's lack of heart brought us all to this point? Why did nobody realize how du Pree's death distressed your lady?''

For an answer Howard stared at the floor.

''Good lord, man, is there no one here who cares for your lady?''

While the captain walked out the door and issued quiet orders to the guards, Rhys stroked Lyonesse's back.

Trembling fingers gripped his tunic. Her startling reaction surprised him. The warmth of tears seeped through the fabric of his clothing. Her choked sobs tore at his heart.

After lifting her in his arms, Rhys crossed the room and sat down on the floor. Resting his back against the wall, he settled her on his lap.

Gently, he pulled her tear-streaked face to his shoulder, coaxing, "'Tis all right, milady, I will not harm you."

He fought the warring of his head and heart. He needed to find du Pree's murderer. His own carelessness had allowed this woman to capture him. He was probably foolish to relinquish his chance at escape.

He should be angry. He should hate Lyonesse of Ryonne. But as illogical as it was, he didn't. Against his better judgment, against all the memories his mind conjured, he felt something for this she-devil that he'd never felt before. Something in her pain and rage called out to his own.

Her sobs lessened, but her tears still warmed his chest.

He could not leave Lyonesse to live with her mistaken notion about him. Why it mattered, he did not know. Nor did he care to delve into any of his irrational reasoning this day.

''Milady...Lyonesse, is there no one you can go to? Someone who will make you laugh? One who can bring a ray of sunshine back into your days?''

She pushed against his chest. ''No.''

Rhys lifted her chin with the crook of his finger and stared into her liquid gaze. It glittered with a brilliancy that rivaled a chest full of gems. Drawn unwillingly into the sparkling treasure trove he leaned closer.

The tantalizing scents of exotic spice and heady floral beckoned him still nearer. Their breath mingled, warm and moist between them. No more than a slight movement would bring their lips together once more. A space so close, yet more distant than the stars above.

A strangled cry left her lips. ''Unhand me.'' She pushed against his chest. He winced at the pain. This time Rhys did not stop her struggle for freedom.

Scrambling to her feet she pointed down at him. ''You have taken away everything I had.'' Her finger shook. ''You destroyed every ray of sunshine I could ever hope to enjoy.''

Rhys stood up and grasped her shoulders before she could flee. He didn't try to keep his frustration from his tone. ''Never have I denied taking another man's life. But I am tired of being accused of a murder I did not commit.'' He shook her lightly.

''Listen to me. I have been on the king's business for nigh on a full year.''

Blood drained from her face, leaving behind a ghostly mask of disbelief and fear. Had he not been holding her so tightly, Rhys was certain she would have fallen.

''No.'' Her hushed gasp sounded more like a plea to his ears.

''Yes.''

Barreling through the doorway, Howard crossed the room and grasped Rhys's forearm. '''Tis enough, Faucon. No more. Let her maid take her now.''

Eager to be rid of this bewitching siren, Rhys released his grip on Lyonesse's shoulders and allowed her maid to lead her away.

Rhys silently watched the two women and Howard leave the cell. When he heard the key turn in the lock, he stretched out on his straw-filled pallet and stared at the ceiling.

He crossed his arms over his chest and frowned. It was imperative to his family that he complete his mission. It was imperative to his own well-being that he remove himself from the presence of this woman.

And do it quickly before this emptiness he felt at her leaving became a regular occurrence.

Chapter Four

She was a clodpolled onion-eyed dullard. Lyonesse tossed another handful of weeds onto the growing pile.

A lackbrained nitwit. Perspiration trickled down her forehead and dripped off the end of her nose.

Since she'd confronted Faucon yesterday, she'd called herself every bawdy name she could think of—yet none seemed to be the proper fit.

Another clump of dead weeds hit the pile. Maybe she could bury herself in the brown, soggy plant life she was pulling out of what would someday be an herb garden.

What possessed her? She knew the answer. Grief over Guillaume's untimely death and fear of losing Taniere had stolen her sanity and common sense. Yet not even in her darkest moments of despair could she forget the lessons she'd dutifully learned—lessons that kept her from killing Faucon.

Right and wrong.

Good and evil.

Heaven and hell.

Brother Joseph had taught her by word, her father by example and deed. Her maid Helen had always seen to it that she never forgot the words, examples, nor the deeds.

For all their teaching and devotion, Lyonesse knew none of them could answer the questions that tormented her.

Did nothing fall between good and evil?

Could not something seem wrong and yet be right?

Lyonesse uncurled her legs from beneath her and sat on the damp, cold ground. Looking at the patch she'd cleared she wondered why she'd bothered. Less than a month from now King Stephen would take Taniere from her and all this work would be wasted.

Do not cry. She was done with tears. They gained her nothing more than an aching head and upset stomach.

Obviously, she needed to find a husband—quickly and she needed to release Faucon.

How and in which order was yet to be determined. Neither task would be easy.

Since she found killing Faucon an impossible feat, she needed to release him. The longer he remained at Taniere the more dangerous he became. His men would come and free him by force. Innocent lives would be lost.

Regardless of what her maid thought, Lyonesse doubted if finding a suitable spouse would be as simple as pointing at a man and bidding him ''come hither'' like some trained dog.

She wouldn't want that kind of man.

She wanted Guillaume. Instead, she'd dutifully marry any man her father picked.

Her father was a warrior. A knight. A Lord. He would choose a man like himself. A man like...

Breathless, Lyonesse tried to shake the fearful thoughts from her mind. But they ran in circles, one more horror-filled than the last. Until they came to rest on the one thought that would strike many a lady dead.

Her sire would choose a man like Faucon.

The type of man who had killed not only his wife, but his newborn child. 'Twas said he'd shown no remorse for his deed. Nor had he shed a single tear for his loss.

The type of man who had no regard for women or for those weaker than himself. A man who laughed at death and had no respect for life.

Seeking protection from evil, Lyonesse quickly prayed, ''Oh, Holy Mother, let my sire's love for me be true. Let him never seal my fate thusly.'' She pitied any woman who would become wife to that type of man.

The type of man she needed to remove from her keep. She was not lackwitted enough to believe that she could lead Faucon to the gate and bid him fare-well with no fear of retribution. There had to be a way to convince him that it would be within his best interest to forget anything that had happened. *How?*

She'd not seen him since their encounter in the tower. But she had ordered Howard to permit Faucon limited freedom. He could move about the keep and the inner yard as long as he was under constant supervision and chained about the ankles and wrists.

Howard assured her that he would guard the pris-oner himself. She'd made him swear to keep Faucon away from her.

"Milady! Lady Lyonesse! Come quick. Milady!"

"Blatherskite," Lyonesse cursed as the screaming page ran toward her.

"Milady, look, look—"

She quelled the urge to shake the stuttering boy. "Michael, cease your blithering. Tell me what is wrong."

Michael pointed frantically at the sky. "The king is coming! King Stephen, milady!"

Lyonesse bit back her sharp retort. Instead, she looked up.

Nay, the king had not sprouted wings and flown to Taniere. But Michael's cries were justified. Only a king could own so regal a huntress.

If her eyes did not deceive her, a golden eagle dipped and soared against the backdrop of a cloudless sky. A low, breathless whistle left her lips as the bird swooped lower. Lyonesse wanted a closer look. She sent Michael for Howard and then climbed the ladder to the walkway.

Her father had long ago told her about goldens. But never had she seen one. She now understood his fascination with the eagle. While Lord Ryonne's description enabled her to identify the raptor, his words of praise did little justice to its beauty.

Golden. They were well named. When the sun bounced off the many shades of brown, tan and white flecks, the bird truly did appear gold.

The eagle spiraled higher, almost out of sight, before falling into a dive that would carry a lesser bird crashing into the stone of the tower. Only the obvious strength and agility of this one pulled it out of its descent to circle round and round before beginning another ascent.

Bewitched, Lyonesse watched it perform the graceful dance over and over. Spiraling upward, diving down, screeching as it circled the tower. Again and again.

A strange notion entered her mind.

She pulled her attention from the eagle, shifting her gaze to the tower's arrow slit. Even though she could not see into the cell from where she stood, she knew without the slightest doubt that Faucon stood at the window opening.

Sweat beaded on her brow. Her breath stopped

when a shrill whistle answered the bird's loud screech. As if on command, the eagle soared up and out to become lost in the forest.

After gaining her breath, she looked down at the bailey. All activity had ceased while the guards and the others had watched the bird along with her.

''I have never seen an eagle hunt a man before.''

Howard's voice startled her. Lost in thought, she'd not heard him approach.

Lyonesse searched for a response that would placate not only those gathered below, but her own shaking nerves as well. Finally, she asked, ''Would it not act in such a confused manner if it were ill or somehow injured?''

She hoped that her question carried down into the bailey. It was enough that she tasted the icy chill of fear. It would do no good for Taniere's people to worry along with her.

Howard needed no coaching. He raised his voice, agreeing, ''Aye, milady, if it were diseased it would act strangely. Surely the beast must have escaped from the king's falconer.''

As the keep's people dispersed and returned to their work, Lyonesse leaned closer to Howard. ''Has there been any word of King Stephen's presence in the area?''

He shook his head, leaving her with little hope. ''Nay.''

Unwilling to speak her thoughts, yet unable to

contain them, Lyonesse said, "Then this bird was sent by someone from Faucon."

Howard looked out over the wall, then stiffened. "Aye, but 'tis worse than that, milady."

"What..." Her question trailed off when she followed his line of sight.

The clearing between the dense forest and Taniere's wall was an intentional manmade addition. Empty space provided an unobstructed view of any man or beast crossing the area.

At this moment Lyonesse was provided with a view of both. The man, dress in naught save black, mounted on an equally dark destrier, stared motionless across the distance.

Behind him, on what she could only assume was a falconer's contraption, perched the golden.

The manner of the man's dress and the eagle with him, gave her little doubt they were both from Faucon.

After swallowing hard, Lyonesse whispered, "Oh, Dear Lord, save us." Stiffening her spine, she marched to the tower gatehouse and waited for Faucon's harbinger of doom to approach her walls.

To her shock and dismay, the man turned his horse and rode back to the forest. While a confrontation may have frightened her, this action filled her with terror.

He would return for the man he knew resided within her walls.

The question now was when?
And with how many men?

If she lived through this day without taking a life,
Lyonesse vowed to increase the rations left outside
the gates for the poor. She rubbed a rose-scented oil
into her lye-chapped hands. Could anything else go
awry this day?

Helping with the washing had kept her from wor-
rying so much about the man she held hostage and
what would surely be an impending visit from his
men. It hadn't kept her from listening to Helen's
unending complaints.

Lyonesse patted a cool compress of elderflowers
to the bridge of her nose and across each sunburned
cheek. When her maid had finally stopped harping
about Faucon, Helen had brought that demented eagle back to her attention. Without missing a stride,
her maid groused about Faucon's man. When those
subjects had been thoroughly exhausted, Helen had
busied her tongue with dire warnings about young
girls who spent too much time in the sun.

Lyonesse sighed and left the chamber. If her only
concern were freckles, she would be content.

Men's loud laughter gave her pause halfway down
the steep, narrow stairs. The boisterous noise
bounced off the stone of the walls and echoed up
the stairwell. She'd not heard this infectious sound
since her father left last year to join the king. Her

heart missed many beats. Surely he would not have come to Taniere without notice?

A deep voice barked with laughter at a ribald joke told by one of the other men. Lyonesse tensed as the familiar tone rang clear in her ears. Worry gave way to anger. Anger quickly simmered into rage.

Rapidly descending the remaining stairs, she saw Faucon standing at Howard's side. The time the two men spent together discussing whatever they could discuss, was one matter. But to endure this man's presence in her hall was another matter entirely.

She yelled at the only person who could explain this unwelcome and unwanted presence in her hall. ''Howard!''

Lyonesse's shout immediately brought the men's merriment to a halt.

She pointed at the behemoth standing arrogantly in the center of the other men, and demanded, ''What is the meaning of this?''

Before Howard had a chance to answer, the object of the discussion interrupted. ''Milady, this means nothing more than a fine evening's meal in the company of a lovely lady.''

She ignored him and leveled her gaze on her maid. Lyonesse seethed inwardly, wishing she had the leisure to pale and flutter as Helen was doing now.

Chains clanged together as a large, warm hand closed over her fist and deftly pried her fingers open.

After kissing her palm, he stated, ''And nowhere have I seen a more beautiful creature than Taniere's lioness.''

Lyonesse tore her gaze away from Helen's wavering look, and stared down at her own hand. What sorcery had this Spawn of Satan used to bewitch her? Hot and cold tingles ran down to her toes when his lips briefly touched her skin. Was it the vile way he kissed her palm, instead of the back of her hand that caused the unsettling shivers? Or was it the devil's wicked treachery?

She glanced up at him. The toad smiled at her as if he were attending a festive celebration, instead of rotting in the tower where he belonged. Why did Faucon act this way?

In keeping with a chivalrous code of conduct, she'd permitted him limited freedom. But had she not gone out of her way to show him how much she despised him? Faucon knew full well his presence in her hall was unwelcome.

It wasn't for the lack of trying, but he'd not truly suffered any true physical or mental anguish under his confinement here. So why did he now play the simpleminded fool?

Her hopes for a peaceful end to this day fell to the hardened dirt floor and shattered like a fragile egg. Lyonesse willed her tongue to remain silent.

Never had a female impressed Faucon as much as the one standing before him now. It had to be difficult for Lyonesse to hold her outrage in check as well as she did. A less composed woman would have dissolved into hysteria by now. Or at the very least would have become too flustered to remain as visibly calm as Taniere's vicious kitten appeared to be.

Her appearance did not deceive him one bit. Some might have missed the bright glaze of anger that he'd so quickly grown accustomed to seeing. Or not have noticed that her jawbone was too well defined. The normally heart-shaped face was pulled nearly into a square by the tightness of her muscles.

His assessment of her features did not go unnoticed. The lady's eyes narrowed in apparent distaste before she tore her hand from his and wiped her palm across the folds of the vivid green gown she wore.

Rhys bowed his head slightly and reflected upon her name. Lyonesse. While it was true that her gold-red coloring was well suited for a feline, he wondered if she knew that her namesake had been a bastard in every sense of the word? Her grandsire had been blessed with a reputation that made Rhys's presumed evilness pale in comparison.

Certain that she could see no other emotion upon his face but pleasant interest, Rhys deepened his smile. How many times had he been told that his wicked grin could cause even a nun to succumb to his charms?

"Lyonesse? How did you come to be named for your grandsire?"

A faint blush tinged her delicate complexion, making her appear more of a child than the oversized armor had. "I am certain my father had his reasons. I have never found myself churlish enough to question the name."

Rhys ignored the jibe and offered his arm to lead the unwilling lady to the table. He held his snort of amusement as she rested her hand so lightly on his forearm that she barely touched his sleeve. Did she really believe that she could continue to assume such ladylike innocence? No lady would have dared to conceive his capture—let alone accomplished the feat.

By the saints, this was going to be an interesting evening. Even though he'd been free to walk about the keep, he'd been bored to his limits. He'd sought an opportunity to pay his captor back with a little of her own coin. Now that he was certain she'd regained her senses, Rhys looked forward to goading her. After seeing Jezebel this morning, he had an added boon. The knowledge that his men were nearby worked to his advantage with Howard. It'd been simple to convince the captain to permit him to attend the evening meal in the hall.

He placed his free hand on top of hers. The instant he wrapped his fingers around her wrist to effectively hold her near, Rhys wished he had not. The smooth, soft skin beneath his fingers reminded him of how long it'd been since he'd touched anything so warm and soft.

Even though he knew full well that he would drive himself to distraction, Rhys could not have stopped his thumb from stroking the silken flesh if he'd tried.

At first she flinched under his gentle touch, but made no move to pull free. He bent toward her, and groaned silently at the combined expressions of surprise and horror on her flushed face. She might have been betrothed to this du Pree, but his first impression had been perfectly correct; she was an untried girl.

He forced his thumb to stop its steady motion, and waved toward the table. "Shall we sit?"

She jerked away from him. "You should not be here. Be gone."

"'Tis my greatest wish to be gone from here." He looked at the door and snapped his fingers before looking back at her. "I willingly make you a deal. Have your guards release me and I will disappear from your life."

She glared up at him. "You know I will not do that."

After sighing loudly, Rhys shrugged. "Then I will be content to be your honored guest at this meal."

Lyonesse narrowed her eyes as she glanced at the chains binding his wrists and ankles. She kept her voice low while agreeing, "Very well, 'tis not as if you can do much mischief with the jewelry you now wear."

She signaled for Howard. "Count Faucon will be joining us for the meal."

Rhys noted that the captain had enough decency to look ashamed. "Milady, I—"

Lyonesse cut him off with a wave of her hand. "It matters little, Howard. He is here and will be my guest. I am certain his presence will cause little harm."

She looked back at Rhys and added, "Since I have already invited him, I doubt that he will decline my offer and return to his cell. However, should he think to try anything foolish, I would be delighted to have him become the main course."

Ah, yes, it was going to be a grand meal. Amused, Faucon followed her retreating form to the table on the raised platform at the head of the hall and took the only seat available—the one next to her on the bench.

He tried to ignore the large tapestry hanging behind the table. The stunning needlework depicted a lion and his lioness, staring out as if guarding those seated below. A brief chill raced up his back and lifted the hairs on his neck. For a moment, Rhys wondered if this is what prey felt like right before an attack.

Howard mumbled curses as he secured Rhys's leg

shackles to the bench before taking a position against the wall behind them. Rhys wanted to laugh at the absurdity. What would he do in a hall crowded with Lyonesse's men?

They were everywhere he looked; seated at the many trestle tables scattered about the great hall, standing in small groups alongside the whitewashed walls, leaning against arched support beams and lounging by the open fire off to one side. No, he would do nothing to incite those gathered for the meal.

He turned his attention back to his prey and touched the finely woven linen sleeve of her gown. ''Ah, but were I to leave, I would not be able to tell you how the color of this gown makes your eyes sparkle like gems.''

She leaned away from him. ''And I would not have to listen to your silly lies.''

He trailed his fingertip up the back of her arm to stroke a ribbon entwined in her loosely braided hair. ''Or that your hair would be a magnificent silken veil were it loosened from its confinement.''

Rhys leaned closer, ignoring her soft gasp of shock at his familiarity, and touched the jewel-encrusted gold torque around her neck. ''If it were not for me, you would never know that this collar and your hair should be your only adornment.''

He lowered his voice. ''Just envisioning the sight could make any warrior wish to take you somewhere private to see if your beauty did indeed match his dreams.''

Her flaming face, blazing eyes and sudden intake of breath should have prepared him for the slap that landed on the side of his face.

Chapter Five

At the sound of the loud, stinging smack, all talking in the hall ceased.

Howard stepped away from the wall. The scraping sound of metal swords being pulled from wooden scabbards caused Rhys's heart to miss a beat. At any other time, the noise would have been music to his ears. Now the reverberating sound reminded him of a hissing, deadly serpent intent on striking its helpless prey.

The smile froze on his lips as Rhys wordlessly watched the ire in her eyes recede. When fear quickly replaced her anger, he leaned away from her. After turning to look at the many tight faces watching them, Rhys lifted his goblet of wine. "To your lady. May she never again have to deal with another such as me."

A quick glance at the stiff figure beside him made him urge in a whisper, "I am chained and unarmed, but I will not go down without taking a few of your men with me. Smile, Lady Lyonesse, live up to your name and put them at ease.''

Her temples throbbed. As much as she would like to see this loathsome creature's blood, she did not wish it spilled at this moment.

''Milady.'' Howard moved closer. ''I can return him to his cell.''

She shook her head before taking the goblet from the vile miscreant. Lyonesse lifted it toward her people. ''Eat, drink. We should be thankful that Lord Faucon took no offense at my ungraciousness.''

When a few of the men did not waver from their ready stance, she added, ''Having never been to court, I knew not that he was jesting. Surely you can forgive my lack of humor?''

The apology tasted bitter on her tongue and she longed to take it back. She'd not been the one in the wrong. He deserved the slap.

She breathed a sigh of relief when all but Howard relaxed at her words. The captain sheathed his partially drawn sword and moved back to his position against the wall.

Faucon took the untouched goblet from her hand and raised it to his lips. ''Such a pretty speech, Lady Lyonesse. Your people will be grateful that you kept the peace so readily.''

It would be so much easier if he could simply choke on the wine he was drinking. ''What my people do or do not appreciate is none of your concern.''

She jumped when his hand closed over her own. ''I would say that as a captive in Taniere, there is much to concern me.''

Lyonesse was fascinated with the way he could make a soft-spoken whisper sound like a threat. Fascinated, but not afraid. She studied his face from beneath her eyelashes.

Not the slightest evidence of a frown marred his dusky complexion. In fact, the only visible creases were the laugh lines at the sides of his glittering eyes. She had an overwhelming urge to see that smug smile removed from his face.

She pulled her hand out from under his, straightened her back and asked, ''What can you find so amusing? Is the mighty Faucon so invincible that his confinement does not matter?''

Prompted by his silence, she continued. ''Do you not find yourself wondering if you will live or die? Or does death have no meaning to an offspring of Satan? Have you been given everlasting life in exchange for killing innocent humans?''

Lyonesse ignored Howard's groan. Instead, she watched Faucon's jaw tighten.

Still the smile did not leave his face.

After placing a hand on the bench for support, she leaned closer to him and lowered her voice. ''How many lifetimes were you given for the murders of your wife and infant son? Did you gain as many eternities for Guillaume's demise as you did for theirs?''

Now the smile was gone.

The dusky complexion was replaced by a paleness that did not seem natural for one so dark. His glittering gaze danced briefly to Howard before returning to pierce her with a look of anger and pain so intense that for an instant Lyonesse regretted her words.

Faucon's grasp on her wrist stopped just short of crushing the bones that connected her hand to her arm. His voice was still nothing more than a whisper. ''You may be able to coax or goad others with your quicksilver tongue. But, Lady Lyonesse, you are not dealing with one who is willing to play your games.''

''I am not—'' When he none too gently pulled her arm up, she forgot the rest of her sentence. ''What are you—''

He quickly cut off her response by slapping the handle of her eating knife in her hand and ordering, ''Eat.''

Who did he think he was? Lyonesse stared at their shared trencher. He was not the Lord of Taniere. This murderer had no right to speak to her in this manner. Faucon was a prisoner here. A prisoner who had no right to be in her hall, or at her table.

She trembled with rage. ''What gives you the

right…'' Suddenly she realized that she'd given permission for him to be here. If he'd pushed her good humor over the edge, she'd no one to blame but herself.

Lyonesse bit her tongue, stopping the rest of her words and viciously stabbed her knife into a piece of meat. It would have been much more satisfying if it had been Faucon's heart.

Rhys flinched. He could almost feel her knife rip through the flesh and muscles of his chest as the sharp point sought his heart.

The vengeance-seeking little wench succeeded where many grown men had failed—again. This inexperienced woman used words to goad him into losing his temper as if he was nothing more than a callow youth.

He'd crushed the life from men more than twice her size. His words could cut her show of bravado into ribbons. Rhys glanced down at her. A tinge of pink still colored her cheeks.

Nay, striking out at the spirit of so regal a cub would not sit well on his conscience. It'd be child's play and he did not intend to amuse the child in either of them.

She goaded him beyond reason and struck where no others dared. In the short time he'd known her, Lyonesse had made him feel emotions that he'd thought well buried. Hatred and anger blended with pain as raw as it had been years ago.

Yet beneath those mixed emotions lay something far more dangerous. And far more enticing than any great wealth. Passion and desire threatened to awaken from their long lonely slumber.

Rhys stood, seeking to escape to safety. He motioned for Howard. ''I would return to my cell now. The company there will be much more soothing for the digestion of my meal.''

While Howard unlocked his fetters from the bench, Rhys smiled down at Lyonesse. He'd not let her see the warring that took place in his mind and soul. Gently lifting her wrist, he placed a chaste kiss on the back of her hand. He felt the furious beating of her pulse against his fingers. Briefly, he wondered which upset her more, his lingering touch, their nearness, or his smile?

He leaned close, so no one else could hear him answer her last, half-spoken question. ''A devil needs none to give him the right to do anything he desires.'' Watching the blush fade from her cheeks, he added, ''Beware of what you cause to begin, little lioness, you may not be able to control the outcome.''

''Why, you—''

Her response was abruptly cut short by a loud commotion coming from the entrance doors to the hall.

Clearly unable to decide what to attend to first,

Howard looked from Lyonesse, to Rhys, then to the door.

Rhys spread his arms as far apart as the chains would allow and nearly barked, ''Good Lord, man, I am going nowhere. Escort your lady and I will follow.''

Quickly springing to action, Howard assisted Lyonesse from the bench and led them to the entrance.

Over the yells of the men, Rhys heard a loud cry that drew him through the open door and out onto the wallwalk. Ignoring Lyonesse's shouted order to halt, he breathed in the crisp air and gazed up at the sky. The familiar cry of an eagle broke through the gasps of those gathered outside.

Rhys turned and glanced at Howard, hoping the man would lend his assistance. He then crossed his left arm over his stomach, giving him enough length on the chain to hold his right arm up at about chest level. ''Cover my arm.''

Howard looked at him as if he'd gone mad.

To Rhys's surprise, Lyonesse grabbed a cloak off a passing guard and wrapped the thick wool around Rhys's forearm. ''I want to see her.''

He pursed his lips and gave two short whistles. Instantly, he was rewarded by another cry. His heart raced as he moved closer to the wall.

Within a heartbeat Jezebel circled those gathered

on the wall and reached out with talons that could crush a man's bone with one hard grip.

Lyonesse gasped as the eagle settled on his arm. Rhys rested his arm on the stone wall, crooning, ''Ah, my beauty, would that you could carry me away with you.'' He smiled at the eagle's gurgling response.

A commotion at his side startled him and the bird. Jezebel danced from one clawed foot to the other on his arm. He gritted his teeth and nearly begged, ''Please, stop.''

He stiffened when the point of a sword pressed against his back. Surely Lyonesse wasn't going to kill him now with his men so near.

''Release the chains about his wrists.'' When Howard hesitated to do her bidding, Lyonesse reasoned, ''The eagle carries a missive tied in her jesses. Howard, his legs are still shackled. I have a sword in his back. Release the chains.''

Before the chains hit the wooden floor of the walkway, Rhys plucked the scroll from Jezebel and handed it over his shoulder to Lyonesse. While stroking the chest of the nervous eagle, he urged, ''If you can read, milady?''

Howard's weapon replaced Lyonesse's while she stepped out of the keep's lengthening shadow and back into the light spilling from the entrance of the hall to unroll the parchment.

He continued to stroke Jezebel while waiting for

his captor to read the missive from his captain. Had there not been so many people gathered so near, Rhys would have laughed out loud at the absurdity of this event.

Lyonesse's sharp cry frightened Jezebel into flight. Instantly Rhys gave the bird the whistled command to return to Melwyn.

When he was certain of Jezebel's safety, Rhys turned around. Howard held the sword across Rhys's chest. "Do nothing brainless."

Rhys stared down at Howard. "Some day, Howard, I will feed you that sword. Take me to your lady."

After reaching Lyonesse's side, he hastily snatched the note from her trembling fingers and read aloud, "My Lord Faucon, an armed force approaches."

Howard broke the deafening silence first. "Does this army come for you?"

Rhys laughed. "Would my captain go to such great lengths to warn me of my own rescue? Would he seek to tell me if a friend of Taniere approached? Had Melwyn thought to rescue me, he would have approached Taniere on his own."

Lyonesse paled. Her maid raised a hand to cover her mouth and scurried back inside the hall. Howard cleared his throat and scuffed one foot across the timber of the walkway.

What was the reason for this? Rhys frowned.

They acted guilty. He pinned Lyonesse with a questioning gaze. ''You do not seem surprised to find my men so near.''

She looked out over the wall for a few heartbeats before replying. ''Would not that be expected?''

Her tone of voice was too uncertain. As if she searched for an answer. Rhys turned to Howard. ''Would it be expected?''

Howard glanced at his lady. ''Lady Lyonesse, please.''

''Howard!'' Quickly facing Rhys, she admitted, ''Yes, Faucon, your men are near.''

''For how long?''

She shrugged. ''How would I know? We did not speak.''

''Speak? To who?''

''Your man.'' Howard then explained about the man retrieving the eagle.

Lyonesse glared at her captain as if she'd like to rip his tongue from his mouth. ''Thank you.''

Rhys held back his laugh. ''Tell me, Lyonesse, how much longer did you think to hold me?''

''For as long as it requires.''

''I am certain my men would have ridden away from the area and just left me here.''

After glancing down at the bailey and back to her keep, Lyonesse muttered, ''Keep your sarcasm to yourself, Faucon. I have other things with which to deal.''

Howard sprang to action with a curse. He shouted for the troop to assemble in the bailey. Then he turned to Lyonesse. ''Milady, I will do what I must to ensure your safety.''

Before she could reply, Rhys interrupted. ''With God's blessing my men could easily defeat a force of fifty. The one approaching your gates now is too large to confront alone. Else, Melwyn would not have alerted me to the danger.'' He glanced at the men assembled in the inner yard, counting thirty. ''Do you think there are enough there to hold the enemy at bay?''

Lyonesse nodded and stiffened her spine. Rhys admired her bravado in front of her people, but it did not change the facts.

''How many battles have these lads fought, Lyonesse? I have watched Howard training these young and woefully inexperienced men to become a fighting force to be reckoned with. Are they ready, milady? For the reckoning is at hand.''

Lyonesse shrugged one shoulder. ''They have no choice. I cannot conjure more men at will.''

''I can.''

The lady took a small step back. ''What are you saying?''

Rhys thought that was obvious. ''Allow Melwyn and my men entrance to Taniere. With the added numbers your victory is assured.''

She glanced at Howard, then out over the wall at

the forest beyond. ''Perchance they wish not to fight. We have no proof of their reasons for approaching Taniere's gates.''

''Melwyn has no reason to lie.''

Lyonesse's gaze darted back to him. ''He has every reason to do so. Would this not be an easy trick to spirit you out of Taniere? And to spread havoc upon innocent people?''

Rhys could not contain his snort of astonishment. ''Innocent?''

She stepped closer. The scent of roses filled his senses with a desire to be alone with this rather amazing woman. Rhys forced his awareness back to her words. She pointed at those in the bailey and spoke in a hushed, raspy whisper, ''They are innocent. None captured you but I. Leave Taniere's people out of this.''

''Agreed.'' He nodded to confirm his words before turning to Howard. ''If you allow my men to assist you in this coming foray, I vow not to escape. But it is imperative that I answer my man.''

Lyonesse stepped between the two men. ''This is *my* keep, Faucon. You discuss this with me, not my man.''

Howard came to attention behind her. ''Milady.''

He fell silent when she raised her hand. ''I will not permit your men into Taniere, Faucon. You have given me no proof that we will be attacked.''

Rhys stepped back. ''As you wish. But I tell you

this, Lady Lyonesse. Every young man that dies here this night will haunt you. Every life that perishes will feed your guilt for the rest of your life.''

''Milady, please.'' Howard coaxed Lyonesse to join him a short distance away.

Rhys could not hear their words, but he marveled at Howard's patience. Even now, when Lyonesse knew the skirmish was lost, she refused to give in gracefully. Her clenched jaw and expressive hand motions conveyed more than words. Previous encounters told him that as soon as her spine stiffened she'd conceded to Howard's request.

Rhys could understand her anger and her reluctance to do his, or Howard's bidding. Had the positions been reversed he'd not have permitted a strange force into his keep.

While Howard removed Rhys's fetters, Lyonesse said, ''I will allow your men into Taniere, Lord Faucon. But I do not for a heartbeat believe you will not seek freedom.'' She bent, lifted the hem of her gown and pulled a dagger from the garter of her stocking. ''So, I will be like a flea at your side.''

Rhys wanted to laugh at the image forming in his mind.

Then he remembered the first time she'd held a dagger to him and immediately wanted to wrest the weapon from her hand.

He glanced down and suddenly wanted instead to run his fingers over the curve of her still-exposed calf. Would her skin feel like a kitten's fur beneath his fingers?

Howard cleared his throat.

Rhys jerked himself back to the task at hand. He rubbed the back of his neck and looked out over the wall. After whistling three sharp notes into the air he turned back to Lyonesse. "A flea, milady? So small a pest would be easily dismissed." He glanced back at her legs. "You are neither a pest, nor easily dismissed."

Following his gaze, Lyonesse tugged at her gown. The folds fell back into place. She leveled a lethal glare on him. "If you are going to summon your men, Count Faucon, do so."

He casually checked the darkening sky. "'Tis done." Taniere would be safe till darkness overtook them. He estimated how long it would take Melwyn and his men to arrive.

Lyonesse joined him by the wall. "What do you mean, 'tis done?"

He spared little thought for the woman at his side, instead turning his attention to the coming foray. He questioned Howard. "Someone will greet my men at the postern gate?"

The captain beckoned a guard forward. He explained the situation and sent the astonished man on his way.

Indecision wrinkled Howard's brow as his gaze darted between Lady Lyonesse and Rhys. "Milady,

I..." Howard paused, shrugged and faced Rhys. "Count Faucon, what can I show you of Taniere?"

"Howard!" Lyonesse's voice rose in chastisement.

While her attention was on her captain, Rhys snatched the dagger from her fingers. He placed an index finger beneath her chin, gently closing her mouth. "Flea, I do not want your keep." He handed the weapon to Howard. "However, I think your family may."

Howard agreed. "Milady, while I am well versed in defending Ryonne, I have never had to protect Taniere against an enemy. I would welcome any offer of assistance Lord Faucon wishes to provide."

Lyonesse started toward the ladder. "Then by all means, let us be off." She stopped to stare at both men. "Let us further make certain that Count Faucon is aware of each entrance and exit. Let us not miss one avenue of escape."

Rhys shook his head. "The vow I gave you was not given lightly."

The heat of her brief glare seared him. Rhys watched her descend the ladder and followed. He wondered, *does she distrust all men, or only me?*

The three of them had barely crossed the bailey when the cry of an eagle pierced the noisy yard. Rhys nodded at the look of wonder on Lyonesse's face. "I told you my men had been summoned."

Chapter Six

Lyonesse rested her head against the damp stone behind her. She was tired of waiting, of wondering, of the repeated knotting and unknotting of her stomach.

This time between evening and morning seemed endless. What were the men hiding in the woods waiting for? Nightfall? The sun had already set, let them be done with it. Lyonesse stood to peer over the wall.

A mail-covered hand grasped her shoulder. "If you wish to remain a flea at my side, sit down."

The order was naught but a brusque whisper, but she'd heard it often enough this night to recognize the lack of patience behind the words.

Surrounded by his men, Lyonesse was unwilling to anger Faucon further. Easing down to her hard, cold seat she leaned her head back and gazed up at the star-filled sky.

She asked, "Will not the moon give away their approach?"

The long, low huff of a sigh reached her ears. Faucon sat down beside her. "I know you must be tired and cold, Lady Lyonesse. Perhaps the hall—"

"Nay." She quickly cut off his suggestion. He wasn't going to be rid of her that easily.

"Your father will not be pleased if any harm befalls you."

Lyonesse laughed lightly at his weak attempt to reason with her. "Neither will I."

Sounds wafted across the open field. They were all easy to identify; the steady plodding of horse's hooves, the dull thudding of shields bouncing against armor, spurs clinking against stirrups and the scraping, hissing noise of forged metal being pulled from wooden scabbards.

Her heart faltered at the unmistakable sounds of an armed force approaching. Faucon rose and looked out over the wall. While dragging a breath of air into her lungs Lyonesse closed her eyes. The time had come. Now she would discover whether Faucon's words were truths, or lies.

She looked down at the bailey. Men cloaked in naught save black mixed freely amongst her guard. Which force would Taniere's men need to fight? The one approaching? The one already inside? Or both?

She drew her bottom lip between her teeth and bit down. Pain flared through the tender flesh. The self-inflicted agony did nothing to pull her mind away from her worries.

Would he honor his word? She held back a snort of disgust. Faucon had no honor. Yet his men had entered her bailey quietly and so far followed Howard's orders without fault.

She could only hope that just this once Count Rhys of Faucon would allow a portion of chivalry to shine forth.

A new worry flitted into her mind. Lyonesse allowed her gaze to drift up the man still standing beside her. ''Faucon?''

''What?'' His voice seemed to come from so far away.

''Do nothing rash. I wish to be the one who takes your worthless life.''

She frowned at his laugh. Did he believe she was jesting?

Callused fingers brushed along her cheek and lifted her chin. When he knelt next to her, Lyonesse was surprised to find him so near. Amazed that he'd removed his battle glove so quickly and so quietly.

His breath warmed the flesh beneath her ear as he spoke. ''Little Lioness, my worthless life will be yours to take.''

The loud, rapid beating of her heart drowned out the sounds of the coming battle. His lips touched hers lightly as if seeking permission.

Her thoughts tumbled against each other in their rush to her head.

She hated him.

He'd killed Guillaume.
He'd ordered her about in her own keep.
He'd laughed in her face.
He'd disarmed her of weapons twice.

Yet his mere presence disarmed her soul. A simple touch sent her pulse racing. The fingers gently stroking her cheek sent her worries and fears fleeing for another harbor. In their stead, embers glowing red with warmth filled her senses with a new, unfamiliar confusion. A wild, whirling confusion that softly beckoned her forward.

Lyonesse pressed her lips against his.

Faucon's mouth curved into a small, brief smile before he lightly traced her lips with the tip of his tongue.

She gasped at the intimate touch. No longer content to glow warmly, the flames jumped and crackled in her veins. She returned his caress, unwilling to escape the heat engulfing her.

She followed his coaxing lead and marveled at the sensations coursing through her. Fire, hot and compelling, surged into her blood. While ice sent shivers of welcome pleasure down her spine.

A longing she did not recognize urged her on. Lyonesse threaded her fingers into the hair at the nape of his neck and leaned against his chest.

Faucon's soft, broken laugh doused the flames instantly. After pulling away slightly, he placed his hands on her shoulders. "Lyonesse." Her name

again left his lips in a breathless whisper, ''Lyonesse.''

Thankful for the near darkness shadowing her
face, Lyonesse prayed he could not see the flush of
embarrassment that heated her cheeks. She knew not
what came over her, but she did not want him to
think she gave her favors away freely. She leaned
away and nodded toward the wall. ''The coming battle has set my mind to wander. I am...I am sorry,
my lord.''

Faucon lightly rested his damp forehead against
hers. He asked, ''For what? You did nothing that
requires forgiveness.''

''I am not a common strumpet, Faucon. I did not
mean to give you—''

A finger over her lips silenced her words. ''Lyonesse.'' He paused and began again, ''Lyonesse, this
is my error, not yours. I wished only to offer comfort, no more.'' He brushed his thumb across her
swollen bottom lip. ''I thought that a woman who
would bruise her own mouth needed to feel safe, not
afraid.''

She jerked her head away from his disconcerting
touch, and stared up at him. ''I am not afraid.''

His crooked smile looked out of place. Something
so boyish, so pleading did not belong on a man such
as Faucon. Lyonesse frowned at her thought.

''If you were not afraid, what worried you so?''

She blinked at his concern and shrugged her shoulders. "Nothing. You were mistaken."

Faucon remained silent for a moment before he rose and looked out over the wall. A sharp, venomous curse left his lips. The heart-wrenching smile was no longer upon his face when he turned to look back down at her.

Now his features were drawn into a familiar mask. His mouth was pulled into a hard line. The dark eyes glittered like black ice on a pond in the winter.

Lyonesse shivered. He needed no words to tell her that their vigil was at an end—it was written plainly on his face. She grasped his outstretched hand, allowing him to pull her to her feet.

Unable to find the courage to look out upon her enemy, Lyonesse stared at the mail-clad chest before her. She breathed deeply, seeking strength for what was to come.

The fingers still entwined with her own tightened briefly. "Taniere will not fall."

Faucon's words did little to reassure her. She peered up at him and asked, "How can you be so certain?" Lyonesse despised the tremor she heard in her voice, but could do nothing to still it.

His frown deepened. He pulled her a little closer. "'Tis simple." Faucon nodded toward the wall. "The force gathered outside will be defeated by naught save sheer surprise."

Before she could ask his meaning, Howard and Melwyn joined them.

"Lord Faucon?"

"Milord?"

Lyonesse heard the confused questioning tone in both men's voices. Curiosity overpowered her fear. "Who is out there?"

Faucon released her hand and pulled the hood of her mantle up over her head. "Say nothing that will give you away."

After steeling herself for what would surely be pure horror, Lyonesse took a step closer to the squared cutout in the wall.

Her heart crashed against her ribs. Its thudding roared in her ears. She was afraid the beasts lurking outside would hear the loud, wild beating.

She gazed down at the men encroaching on her land. They were just outside Taniere's walls. As if wishing to be identified, the enemy held their torches high.

Lyonesse forgot to exhale. The blood froze in her veins.

Impossible.

Her madly pounding heart tripped to a stop. She darted a quick glance to Faucon and back down at the men gathered before Taniere.

It cannot be.

Her breath left her body in a loud rush of air.

Before Lyonesse could voice her disbelief, Faucon clamped a hand over her mouth, pulled her away from the opening and held her against his chest.

Her heart resumed its rapid pounding. Fear clouded her mind, leaving her incapable of thought. The keep and her people were in immense danger. This night they would face the threat of death. A fate she alone had brought to these innocent people.

Yet Lyonesse could do little as Faucon issued orders to both captains. Orders that would ensure Taniere's destruction.

Desperate to stop her tears, Lyonesse closed her eyes tightly.

What had she done?

A tear trickled down her cheek, searing her soul with guilt.

Why had she not released Faucon when she'd had the chance?

Lyonesse tried to choke back the remaining tears.

"Milady. Lady Lyonesse?"

Howard's voice forced her to open her eyes. *Did he not know the terrors that awaited them? What lies had Faucon, or his own captain, spewed to Howard?*

Lyonesse knew her fear and anxiety had touched her captain. His concern etched frown lines across his forehead. He shifted his weight from one foot to the other and twisted a leather glove in his hands.

Faucon removed his hand from her mouth and

turned her around to face him. He reached out and lifted her chin with a finger.

With her captain standing beside them and her men on the walls, Lyonesse expected the count to play the simpleton. She expected him to ask why she cried. Or to again lie and tell her Taniere would not fall.

Instead, he lifted one eyebrow and nodded toward the force outside the walls. "Their guise works well, does it not? You believe those are my men."

Since he didn't ask a question that needed an answer, Lyonesse held her tongue.

Faucon leaned closer. "Who killed your betrothed?" He grasped her arm and led her back to the cut out in the wall. "Are you certain it was me? Have you proof it was *my* men?"

Lyonesse heard his questions. She also heard the tightly controlled fury behind them. Doubt overshadowed her fear.

Faucon's hands rested lightly on her shoulders. He urged her even closer to the wall. "Who told you I killed du Pree?"

She stared at the marauders. Their standard fluttered in the breeze. With the torchlight shining on it, all could see a hawk with golden eyes.

Lyonesse fought to ignore the worry threatening to choke the life from her. She jerked away from Faucon's touch and asked, "How do I know those are not your men? Your captain could have brought only a few into Taniere and left the rest outside.''

Faucon laughed. ''I should be blessed with so many men.''

Howard stepped closer. ''Think, milady. Don't be ruled only by what you see. How many men serve your father?''

What her captain said made sense. But Lyonesse still found it hard to discount what she saw with her own eyes. Was Faucon telling the truth, or had he devised a lie worthy of the devil?

She glanced from the men gathered outside the walls to those within. If his words were false could she find a way to outwit him before any harm befell Taniere? She had to try. If she wanted her people to escape his treachery unscathed there was no other choice.

Lyonesse gathered her courage about her. ''If you seek to destroy this keep with deceit, I promise you, Faucon, your head will adorn what remains of these walls.''

Flecks of gold burned brightly in his eyes. His already rigid jaw tightened even more. He clenched his hands into fists. The metal links encasing his chest and arms strained to hold the muscles flexing beneath.

''When I seek my revenge on you, Lady Lyonesse, I will not come like a thief in the night.''

He spoke not with the roar she'd have expected.

Instead, he used a tone lower and softer than she'd ever heard from any man.

Its sinister promise chilled her to the bone.

He took a step forward and backed her against the wall. "No army will be required to fulfill my mission." He did not touch her, yet she could feel the heat from his anger. His breath was hot on her face. "You will know, with all certainty, that I have come for my just due."

Here was the fierce murderer, as remorseless and unyielding as Satan himself. Lyonesse fought the urge to close her eyes. She knew that a beast would attack if it sensed fear.

"Taniere's enemy is outside the walls, not within. Do you hear me?"

Lyonesse nodded.

"I have already vowed to not condemn innocent people to harm or death."

Lyonesse held her tongue. Faucon relaxed his stance, spun around to both captains and issued orders for the keep's defense.

"Howard, ensure your men are the ones visible on the walls." He turned to his own man. "Have our men remove their tunics, strike all standards and keep out of sight." He paused for a moment before adding, "For now."

"Howard!" Lyonesse's tone was sharper than she'd intended.

However, it made little difference. Whatever

she'd been about to say was stayed by the motion of one mail-covered hand.

Faucon did nothing more than point at the men. Lyonesse watched in amazement as both scurried away to do his bidding.

Speechless, she turned around to survey the enemy. Faucon grasped her arm. ''We are not finished.''

''I see nothing left to discuss.''

He pulled her against him. ''Aye. You are correct. There is nothing left to *discuss.*''

Her back tingled where it rested against his chest.

''But there are things *you* should understand.''

Lyonesse gritted her teeth at his tone. He was not speaking to a lackwit. ''You are still my prisoner, Faucon. I will take no orders from you.''

With the ease of a child playing with a toy, Faucon shifted his hold and turned her around in his arms. ''If I ordered your captain to lock you inside your own tower, he would not disobey me.''

She was suddenly afraid he was correct. *Would he? Would Faucon lock her away in Taniere's tower?*

Lyonesse stared at the angry visage above her and knew he would not hesitate to make her a prisoner in her own keep.

This was a battle she could not win. The men would follow Faucon's orders. After all, she herself had requested their compliance with his commands.

Not long ago she had boldly stood in the bailey and explained the situation to Taniere's men. She could not belay her own orders now.

Lyonesse pulled her lower lip between her teeth. How, and where, would she find the trust necessary to see her through this night?

Her vision misted with tears of frustration. She studied the hands gripping her arms. Could she trust them to hold the safety of her people as firmly as they held her?

"Do not think to sway me with tears." Faucon's broken growl stopped her silent questions.

She thought to disabuse him of so silly a notion. "I see nothing to cry about. All you have stated is true. My men will follow your orders." She shrugged one shoulder and asked, "Did I not tell them to do so?"

He released her and stepped back. "Aye, milady, you did."

She turned and looked down into the bailey and across to the other walkway and watched her guard prepare for whatever was to come.

Faucon took her hand in his own. Then, hidden from the enemy by the shielding wall, above all those in the bailey, before all who lined the ramparts, he dropped to one knee.

Lyonesse looked down at him. *What was he doing now?* All activity in the bailey stopped as everyone, to a man, turned to stare up at the two of them.

Silence whirled about them like the fog rising to cover the fields.

''Lady Lyonesse, upon my oath as a knight of this realm, I will defend you and Taniere with my life.'' He did not need to raise his voice. His words were passed from one man on the wall to the next and down to the men in the bailey, until all present knew what he said.

''As long as there is breath in my body I will not forsake this vow to you.'' Again, the men spread his words.

''You may entrust your safety and that of every man, woman and child within your walls to me. I will guard them as well as your sire would if he were here.''

Shock held her speechless. Many men had sworn their loyalty to her father and Ryonne. But never before had any man knelt and sworn an oath to her. She knew not what to think of either—the oath-giving, nor the man.

She took a deep breath and closed her eyes. There was no time to mull his actions over in her mind. An enemy lurked outside her walls. And inside a warrior had vowed to protect all she held dear. She could rely on nothing and no one save her own instincts.

The whispers began deep inside her belly. They swirled and drifted to her heart. *Trust.* Even her mind gave into the gentle urging. *Trust this man to honor his vow.*

Lyonesse opened her eyes. She looked out at the men waiting for her response. Above all else, she could not forsake the brave souls ready to defend her keep from danger.

"Count Faucon—" she bit back a smile at the sudden absurdity of this situation "—gladly do I accept your vow of assistance."

Faucon stood and kissed her cheek. For her ears alone, he whispered, "Even a devil has honor, my little lioness."

A silent cheer of approval met them as they turned to the crowd. Both forces, Taniere's and Faucon's lifted their swords in deference to the vow given and accepted.

The goodwill was short-lived. A loud hail of "Taniere!" from the enemy drew everyone's attention to the force outside the walls.

Without releasing her hand, Rhys approached the gatehouse. She felt the fear slither back to chill her bones.

Howard spared her a quick smile as he hurriedly climbed the ladder and joined them. Melwyn skidded to a halt on the wall. Both captains waited for Faucon's nod before moving into action.

Lyonesse watched as the seemingly well-oiled plan unfolded before her. *When had they devised these plans?* Her defenses rose. *And why did she not know of them?*

"Who hails Taniere in the dark of night? For what reason?"

Howard's shouted questions drew her attention away from her own bruised ego.

A bitter twisted laugh floated up and over the walls. The sudden loss of Faucon's strong hand wrapped around her own made the laugh seem even more evil.

Lyonesse shivered with the fear coiling in her belly. She swallowed against the bile rising to her throat.

Finally, the laugh ceased. From within the ranks of the enemy outside her gates a man shouted the answer to Howard's question. "I, Captain to Count Rhys of Faucon, have come to take my lord and master back."

Melwyn glanced over the wall and silently snarled. 'Twas obvious to Lyonesse that Faucon's true captain cared not for this impostor.

She looked long and hard at the man standing next to her. All the stories she'd heard about Faucon flitted through her mind.

He was a warrior who had fought many bloody battles. He'd killed men in the name of honor, God and King. He was a man people feared with just cause.

Yet she'd accepted his vow to protect her keep

from the enemy beyond her walls—an enemy claiming to be from Faucon.

Her gasp of dismay broke the silence engulfing Taniere, prompting Howard to answer the challenge.

"'Tis a sad show of bargaining you make for your lord.''

"Nay, I come not to bargain. I come to take this keep.''

One man broke through the ranks. Everything about him—from the way he moved forward without pause, to the arrogant tilt of his head—spoke of confidence. But the mask covering his features reduced his show of bravado to mere mimicry.

Lyonesse looked from the impostor to Faucon. A man who hid behind a mask could be nothing but a liar and a coward. Faucon may be the devil's helper, but he was no coward.

The impostor pointed his sword at Howard. ''Old man, your lord is not present and you have not enough men to stop me.''

How did they know her sire was not present at Taniere? Who were these men?

Nonplussed, Howard responded, ''It will take only one man to kill you.''

The man shrugged. ''Many have tried, but none have lived to tell about it. Faucon taught me well the ways of death.''

Lyonesse had heard enough. When she sought to refute his false boasts, Faucon clamped a hand over her mouth. "Hush. Do nothing to give us away. I wish to know who this whoreson is."

When she nodded, he removed his hand. She took a step closer to the wall and demanded, "Why would Faucon's men attack with no bargaining?"

"Ah, the fair maiden bids us welcome."

"Welcome? I welcome only your death."

The man shook his head. "No. I think not, milady." He turned to his men and shouted, "Whoever captures the Lady Lyonesse alive, will share her bed this night."

Had it not been for Faucon slightly tightening his grasp on her shoulder, Lyonesse would have screamed her fear. She took a strange comfort from his touch and laughed at the cocksure impostor. "The only thing you will share with anyone this night is a grave."

Howard lifted his sword as a signal to the men along Taniere's wallwalk. In unison they rose and aimed already notched arrows at the fools below.

Lyonesse pointedly looked from the men on her walls to those below, then smiled in triumph. "Now, do you leave in peace or do you fill that grave?"

Obviously surprised by the force protecting Taniere, the man froze. She could not hear what he said to his men, but Lyonesse drew a breath of relief when they turned to retreat.

Her relief was short-lived. The impostor took a shield from one of his men and threw it toward the base of the wall. He then tossed a sword atop it. ''These gifts are for you. Neither I, nor my master have ever found a use for either of them.'' He laughed before joining his men in a hasty retreat.

When the enemy was a safe distance away, Howard motioned a squire to retrieve the items.

The young man quickly completed his task and climbed the steps leading up to the walkway.

Torchlight bounced off the painted shield. Lyonesse moaned. ''Oh, Lord, no.'' She could not tear her gaze from the crude picture adorning the shield.

She offered no resistance, when Faucon to led her into the hall. Some unseen hand snatched her breath from her chest. She nearly fell onto the seat Faucon placed before her. Wordlessly, she took the goblet he placed in her shaking hands and closed her eyes as the honeyed wine warmed her throat.

She thought she'd begun to conquer the pain of losing Guillaume. It was over. There was nothing she could do. Regardless of who had murdered her betrothed, God in his mercy would see justice done.

But as her chest constricted with the tears she'd recently tried not to shed, she knew the pain had not yet been conquered, it had only hidden for a time. Only waited for the right moment to rear up and strike anew.

Lyonesse wasn't certain she could withstand another onslaught.

"Milady?" Howard's low voice broke into her thoughts.

She heard a sword clank softly against a shield and knew what he'd brought into the hall. To fortify her fading strength she took a deep breath, then opened her eyes and stared at the familiar items of war.

Again, the crude picture adorning the shield seemed to reach out and hold her gaze. A picture that she herself had painted the last time she'd seen her brother, Leonard.

With her own hands, she'd drawn and painted a lion on his shield. She'd thought it only proper that the future Lord of Taniere display the symbol of his future title to the world.

Leonard had laughed at her, mussing her hair and telling her how silly it was to think that he'd ever be the Lord of Taniere. He'd insisted their grandsire would outlive them all.

He'd only been half-right. Leonard had not returned to Ryonne or Taniere alive. He'd left to take part in his first battle. A small skirmish with the Empress Matilda. That's what her father had called it when he'd sought to convince her that Leonard would not be harmed. An event that would give him a taste of battle without putting him at much risk.

They'd brought his body home across the back of a horse.

More to herself than anyone else, Lyonesse asked,

"Why do men fight? What do they gain from dying?"

Faucon grasped her shoulder. She let it remain only because she had not the strength to shake the touch from her. "We fight so our children and wives may live."

"Alone?" She looked up at him. "So your wives may carry on without their husbands? So your children may grow up without their fathers? So that parents can lose their sons? What sense is that?"

"Not all men perish in battle."

"Oh, yes, that is so true." She sighed and reached out to briefly touch the shield. "Sometimes men die by treachery."

He knelt beside her chair and stroked her cheek with one finger. "Lyonesse, it is simply the way of the world."

She averted her gaze from Faucon and glanced toward the sword Howard still held. "The way of the world? Maybe it is just the way of men."

Her breath caught in her throat. Lyonesse rose and took the sword. The hilt was wrapped in worn leather cords. An uncut emerald topped the pommel. Her grandsire's sword. A weapon she had given to Guillaume.

She turned the length of metal over in her hands. Her grandmother's name was engraved on the blade. The room began to spin around her. Her hands went numb. The sword clattered to the floor. "Guillaume!"

Cursing, Faucon kicked the shield and the sword out of the way. He then guided Lyonesse back down into the chair and keeling beside her forced her to drink from the goblet.

The pain she had thought unbearable before, became deadly now. She sought to free herself from the nightmare threatening to overtake her. A nightmare of death and loss.

She turned to Faucon, needing to lash out with her pain and fear. "How does this impostor come to have these items? How does he come to impersonate your man?" She leaned closer to him. "Why did you not seem surprised, Faucon? Did you plan this between you?" Unable to swallow the building panic, she let it free. "Did you kill my betrothed and my brother, too?"

Certain the force tearing through her chest would rip her heart to shreds, Lyonesse covered her face with her hands and let the waves of agony and horror wash over her.

She tried to pull away from the strong arms that closed about her shoulders, but the hold was relentless and like bands of iron they would not budge. "Let me go."

"No." His lips were against her hair. "Lyonesse, regardless of what you may think you know, or what you may believe, I am no murderer. I did not kill your brother. And I did not kill your betrothed.''

''But they said—''

''Yes. They blamed Faucon. 'Tis easy to blame another when your face is hidden. How did this impostor know your sire was not here in the first place?''

He stroked her back and ran his hands through her hair. His gentle touch chased all reason from her mind. She could not think with him so close. ''I do not know.'' Lyonesse pushed against his chest. ''Let me go, I cannot breathe.''

Faucon relaxed his hold, but he did not release her. A faint smile touched his mouth when he wiped the tears from her face. ''I am sorry for your losses, Lyonesse. I can only imagine your pain. But I must find this knave before he makes anyone else suffer in my name.''

He brushed his thumb across her lips before rising. ''I have already sent most of my men to follow this cur.'' A frown marred his face. ''It is imperative that I join them on this hunt. But I cannot—I dare not leave you here alone.''

A tide of loneliness swept over her, catching her unaware with its swiftness. Lyonesse looked up at him. Her heart missed a beat and she knew she'd miss this devil's helper. She could already hear the quietness of her days and realized how hating him so intensely had somehow brought her back to life.

She waved him away. "Go. You are no longer a prisoner in my tower. You are free to leave."

The smile that again flitted across his face was brief. "Milady Lyonesse, while it would be a lie to thank you for your hospitality, I will admit your company has been anything but dull." Faucon took a step away. "There is little choice. You cannot remain at Taniere, yet you cannot travel to Ryonne without escort."

He paused. A look that only a true devil could possibly possess lit his features. Lyonesse held her breath—what was he planning?

"I will take you to your father at Ryonne."

Lyonesse's breath rushed out with a gasp. Finally gaining the ability to speak, she shook her head. "You are demented."

"My mental condition is not in question at this moment. 'Tis your safety that concerns me."

Nearly jumping from her seat, Lyonesse fought to keep from shouting. "My safety is not your concern, Faucon."

"And I say it is."

"I will not stand here and argue back and forth with you like a child."

Rhys nodded. "Good." He motioned for Howard and Melwyn before adding, "We leave for Ryonne at first light."

* * *

How had this happened? How did Taniere's walls come to be lined with so many men?

Lord Baldwin was still with King Stephen, so the men hadn't come from Ryonne.

It should have been an easy task to gain entrance to Taniere, remove Faucon and dispatch with Lyonesse in the process.

"Damn!" The dark forest swallowed his curse. Angrily, he threw his nasal helm. The helm bounced off a tree trunk. He yanked the suffocating black mask from his head and threw it away. The concealing fabric hung from a tree limb.

Eager to be gone from here, he stomped to the clearing and shouted at the men to take down the camp and prepare to ride. He could not afford anyone from Taniere discovering him, or his men.

Everything had been thought out so carefully. He'd spent years perfecting each detail and surveying them again for chinks. All had been in place. Yet nothing had gone as planned.

King Stephen had not outright declared Faucon a murderer. Lyonesse had balked at the last moment and not run a sword through the blackguard's back.

What would it take to gain vengeance for Alyce's death? How much more would be required before he found peace for the loss of his love and his soul? Had he not been forced to rely on others for fulfillment of his plans, the deeds would have been completed by now.

Where was Sir John? Why had the man not informed him of the sudden increase of Taniere's
force? Why had he not appeared on the wall with
the other men? It had been John's responsibility to
ensure Taniere's men would permit Faucon's *rescue*
and to see to it that Lyonesse was alone long enough
to meet with an unfortunate accident. They'd discussed this part of the plan thoroughly less than a
few nights ago. He'd not seen Sir John since. Surely
the man couldn't have forgotten.

'Twas bad enough that the imbecile had failed in
the simple task of convincing Lyonesse to kill
Faucon to begin with. But this, this was inexcusable.

Sir John had failed twice now. He would not be
permitted to fail again.

Chapter Seven

The sun crossed the midday sky before they'd finally departed Taniere.

Rhys studied the silent woman riding alongside of him. She was a vision of autumn against the bright greens of the forest.

Leather boots, probably pilfered from a squire, peeked out beneath the heavy, serviceable skirt of her saffron-colored gown. A full-length, hooded mantle the same deep chestnut as her horse covered her gown and protected her well from the damp, forest-cooled air.

He would compliment her on her appearance, but she'd not respond. Lyonesse had spoken not one word to him, nor to anyone else all day. She'd surprised him by joining the traveling party with no further outburst.

What was she plotting?

Her compliance was naught but a ruse. Not for one breath did he believe she'd changed her mind about leaving Taniere.

This three-day journey would last an eternity if he had to watch his back night and day. His spine tingled. Reminded of his last sojourn through the forest, he peered into the canopy of trees above them.

''Looking for something, Faucon?''

Rhys flinched. His horse skittered sideways. After bringing the beast and his own anticipation under control, he silently cursed his edginess before responding, ''Could any blame me?''

The sound of her laughter trilled across his ears before winging its way through the dense woodlands. ''Nay, I suppose not.'' She glanced at him before quickly averting her gaze back to the well-traveled path before them. ''Take heart. I have no men hiding in the trees.''

''Tis good to hear. Since over half of them were ordered to guard the gates at Taniere, it means they did so.''

''Of course they follow orders. They are good men.''

''I have seen firsthand how well they obey you.''

The look on her face, when she turned toward him, made Rhys pause. Did more than lack of sleep cause the darkening circles beneath her eyes? Was her silent plotting responsible for the tightness around her mouth?

''Tell me, Faucon. How will I explain this to my father?''

He reached across the distance separating them

and touched a silk encased braid. "Is worry the cause for your silence?"

She jerked away from his touch and increased the space between them. "A man who is neither in my father's employ, nor a relative escorts me to Ryonne. 'Tis cause enough for worry."

"I thought your father was with King Stephen."

"I know little of his whereabouts." Lyonesse shrugged. "Since Stephen claimed the throne, I do not see my sire for months at a time."

"Then I see no reason to be overly concerned."

"'Tis not your reputation on the brink of ruin."

"You might have considered that earlier." Rhys shook his head. Was this her usual course of action? "Milady, do you always act rashly and then worry about it later?"

"Until this incident I have never acted rash."

He kept his snort of disbelief to himself. "You are the Lion...Lioness of Taniere. Do you not think your reputation can withstand a little tarnish?"

"You would not understand."

"Why is that?"

Lyonesse rolled her gaze to the sky. "Dear Lord, deliver me from idiots." After sighing heavily, she looked at him. "You are a man."

"So I have noticed."

"Tell me, Faucon, is your reputation intact?"

"Which one?"

Lyonesse tipped her head and smiled at him.

"The one about The Mighty Falcon never being bested. Is that still intact?"

"And why—"

She cut off his reply with a laugh. "What will your peers think of your reputation when they learn a mere woman captured The Invincible Falcon?"

Rhys moved his horse closer to hers. "Tell me, little lioness, who will spread that rumor?" He grabbed her horse's bridle, preventing her escape. "And who do you think people will believe? You? Or me?"

Lyonesse had a sinking feeling in the pit of her stomach that he was right. But she'd already given in enough today. She glowered at him. "They will believe the truth."

"The truth?" His laughter echoed in the darkening forest. He leaned even closer. "They will believe what I tell them." His warm breath rushed across her cheek. "None would dare question me." His eyes sparkled like gold in the flicker of candlelight. "And those who do…"

She was well able to supply the ending of his unfinished sentence. Faucon smiled. Lyonesse forgot what she was going to say. She fumbled with her reins and lowered her gaze. *How did he do that?*

This spell he cast on her drove her mad. He spoke in those deep, low tones and her mouth went dry. He looked at her with his eyes half closed, her heart raced. When he leaned close enough that she could smell him, she forgot to breathe. *By the Saints, the man smells like sweat and horses.* Not exactly an aroma she wished in her bed.

Her face flamed with the errant thought. *Where had that come from?*

Her stomach tightened at Faucon's gentle laugh. "Where has your mind trailed off to, Lyonesse?" He stroked her cheek and her heart nearly leaped from her chest.

"Cease." She jerked on her reins, pulling her horse from Faucon's hold. "Do not touch me."

"Milady?"

Lyonesse turned to find Howard behind her. "What?" Instantly regretting her sharp tone, she repeated less heatedly, "Howard. Yes?" She tried to ignore Faucon's chuckle as he moved away.

"Milady, is anything amiss?"

"No. All is fine. Please—" she waved her captain forward "—continue on." To her surprise Howard did little more than glance at Faucon before riding ahead.

"You should have requested he stay to protect you."

She looked around before asking, "Why is that? I see none to bring me harm."

Faucon shook his head. "First you bemoan the ruination of your reputation. Now you act as though it is of little consequence."

"Riding beside you cannot possibly cause any more harm than permitting you to escort me to Ryonne."

"Tongues will wag."

"About what?"

"About the undivided attention we have paid to each other on this journey."

"Undivided attention? Milord Faucon, I was content to ignore you until you rode alongside me. But I thank you for the warning. From now on, I will pretend you do not exist."

Again he flashed her that crooked smile. "You may ignore me, but I will be watching you every moment."

"Why is that?" She forced herself to remain calm. "Do you think we'll be attacked?"

"Gallant try, but you fool me not." He brought his horse right next to hers. His leg brushed against her gown, sending a torrent of heat through the heavy fabric. "You are plotting something and if I must, I will chain the two of us together until we reach Ryonne's gates."

With a flick of his reins he rode ahead, then stopped and turned around. "I warn you only this once. Do nothing rash."

The moment she was certain that he was far enough away, Lyonesse let a string of curses fly.

His mocking laugh raced back to her.

* * *

Lyonesse moved closer to the fire. The night air had turned chilly and she missed the comforts and warmth of Taniere.

While the rabbit the men had caught filled the empty spot in her stomach, the cook knew nothing of herbs or spices.

And while the woolen blanket Faucon had draped around her shoulders kept the breeze from her, it was nothing like the fur coverlets that warmed her at night.

She ducked her face into the folds of the blanket and smiled to herself. In truth, she was spoiled. To be honest, she preferred it that way. Not that she wanted to be waited on hand and foot, but she did enjoy the benefits of her home.

She'd be miserable without the comforts Taniere provided. The many fireplaces and braziers that kept the damp and chill at bay. The cooks who could turn spoiled meat into a feast. Forests and streams filled with ready game kept her larder full. Rich fields and orchards provided vegetables, grain and fruit.

She'd never been without creature comforts—food, clothing or shelter. She'd never been denied anything she truly desired—until recently. She watched Faucon across the clearing. It didn't surprise her to discover his gaze on her.

He'd been partially correct. She was plotting. She plotted her future and the continued good of Taniere.

But if he thought he was going to stop her, he had a surprise coming.

Nobody—not Howard, not Helen, not her sire and certainly not Faucon would stop her from securing what was best for Taniere. She would not arrive at Ryonne with an escort. Aye, she'd return to her father's keep—she needed his help and his goodwill. But not under Faucon's protection. Doing so would not gain her a husband. If her name and Faucon's were mentioned in the same sentence, any prospects would be scared away.

Rhys watched her watching him. He wanted to laugh. The minx was calculating her next move. Her furrowed brows and intent, unseeing stare made that obvious. Even a lackwit would realize she was up to something.

Thieves and murderers plagued the forests, not to mention the band who had attacked Taniere. How could she for one breath consider doing anything rash?

Simple. It was Lyonesse.

As he'd threatened, chaining her to him would be safer. It would be easier to keep an eye on her. But the mere thought of having her body pressed against his on a horse, or on a pallet at night was more than he could bear. Some might call him inhuman, but when it came to desire he was human enough.

He cursed softly as Lyonesse headed toward the stream not far from the clearing. The woman seemed intent on getting herself killed. He grabbed a torch and followed.

Rhys lengthened his stride when the fire's light no longer outlined her retreating form. It would be too easy for her to lose herself in the cover of the dark forest.

In his haste, he tripped over a root. "Damn you, Lyonesse, where are you?"

She stepped out from behind a tree. "Right here, Faucon."

He wanted to wipe the smirk off her face—with his lips. Instead, he leaned against the tree and glared down at her. "Where were you going?"

She tilted her head and looked up at him with wide, innocent eyes. "Here."

Rhys scanned the area. "There is nothing here. What did you seek?"

"An answer to a question."

He frowned in confusion. "Did you find it?"

Lyonesse laughed. "Oh, yes, indeed I did."

Two breaths later he realized that she'd tested him. "I warned you what I'd do if you acted rashly."

"Milord, I came out here for a walk. I am not your prisoner. You are not my father, nor my guardian." She turned to leave, adding, "Do not seek to give me orders, or threaten me. Neither will work."

Rhys wrapped his hand in the blanket draped around her shoulders and pulled her against his chest. "Enough." Even to him it sounded more like a growl than a word. "This is not a game I play with you, Lyonesse. I will give you any orders I see fit and you will obey them."

He jammed the torch into a knothole in the tree. He ran a hand down his face, seeking a moment to find patience and a way to make her see reason.

Lyonesse pushed against his chest. "Let me go." She broke free, ending his search for patience.

Before she could take another step, Rhys caught both of her arms, swung her around and pushed her up against the tree. The torchlight flickered across her face. Her eyes blazed. Her cheeks burned. When she opened her mouth, he quickly ordered, "Do not scream."

She narrowed her eyes. Rhys lifted his brows. "I said, do not."

He was ready for her and caught her scream with his lips. He could not believe that anyone, let alone a woman, would seek to rile him at every turn. But she did. And knowing Lyonesse, she did it just to see if she could.

She'd succeeded—again.

What was it about the little hellion that set him so easily aflame? Aye, she was pleasing to look at, but so were many other women. Even Alyce, at five years his senior, was pleasing to look upon.

Lyonesse was headstrong, not exactly a desirable trait for a woman. She spoke what was on her mind, a habit that could get her into trouble. But speaking her mind was preferable to a lying, conniving woman who would seduce him with one hand and rip out his heart with the other.

Even though Lyonesse would go to her marriage with much wealth, Rhys pitied the man who took her to wife.

The thought of spending every night in bed with her drained the blood from his head, and sent it rushing to his groin. The nights would be pure delight. Lyonesse pushed against his chest. The days would be pure hell. But there'd be one difference—he *would* be her guardian. Would the hellcat listen to him then? He doubted it.

Quickly releasing his grasp on the blanket, Rhys slipped his arms around her and drew her tightly against his chest. When she sagged against him, he knew the action for what it was—a ploy to gain freedom. He deepened his kiss. Only when Lyonesse returned his hungry embrace, did he relax his hold.

After breaking their kiss, he leaned his forehead against hers. ''I thought you were worried about your reputation?''

''I am.'' Her response was but a brief, gasping reply.

Rhys trailed kisses along her cheek and down the side of her neck. Every time his tongue found a new morsel of untasted flesh, his desire for more flared. He paused just below her ear, whispering, ''You need worry about it no longer, Lyonesse.''

The blanket she still held around her fell to the

ground with a soft whoosh. Lyonesse threaded her fingers through his hair. "Why is that, Faucon?"

"Rhys, my name is Rhys."

"Rhys." She whispered his name like a warm caress. "Why do I no longer need worry?"

He hesitated. If he answered her, he would be committing the rest of his life to a challenge he was not yet certain he wanted. Instead, he claimed her lips for one more kiss.

At this moment, Lyonesse cared about only one thing and it wasn't her reputation. She had either been bewitched, or lost all reason, but nothing anyone thought or said about her mattered in the least. The devil's work, or insanity were the only explanations for the way she felt when Faucon—Rhys— touched her. Like a handful of butterflies had been set loose in her stomach.

Their wild fluttering made her dizzy and the only anchor she could find in the odd storm was the man holding her. Yet he could provide no stability against the firestorm assaulting her. He could give her only more turmoil.

But when their breath mingled and their lips touched, she knew nothing. And when their tongues caressed and their hearts beat together, she knew only a longing for more.

When he broke the kiss and stepped away, she felt a sharp, cold loss and the rapid return of her senses. The heat of shame fired her cheeks.

Faucon reached out a hand and then abruptly pulled back. ''We have been gone too long. You must return to the camp.''

He was right. She no longer needed to worry about her reputation. All gathered around the campfire had seen her leave and him follow.

She needed to get away from him, quickly. He was too dangerous for her to be around. She so easily forgot all the morals she'd been taught. Becoming a wanton whore for Faucon would not help her snare a husband.

She grabbed her blanket from the ground, pulled it around her shoulders and forced herself not to break into a run as she headed back to the camp.

Rhys watched her leave. It was going to be another long night. But this night he wouldn't be guarding Taniere. He'd be protecting and fortifying the walls he'd so carefully built around his heart.

He desired this woman. Something unidentifiable in each of them, called out to the other. Yet every kiss, every touch weakened another part of his wall.

Their passion would know no boundaries. But passion and desire had blinded him before. He'd mistakenly thought a woman's total abandonment signified the depth of her love and he'd willingly given all. Not only his passion, but his trust, his loyalty, his future and his heart.

He'd been foolish once. It would not happen again—no matter how much he desired her. He refused to permit another woman's hand to crush the life from him.

Dear Lord, what was he doing? He had a mission to complete and here he stood dallying with Ryonne's daughter. Somewhere he'd lost his mind. If Baldwin, the Earl of Ryonne, found out, Rhys wouldn't have to worry about Lyonesse crushing his heart—Baldwin would do it for her. The earl would take great pleasure in accomplishing the act while Rhys was alive to watch.

Lyonesse crawled to the tent flap. She looked over her shoulder and breathed a sigh of relief. While she'd dressed and packed a small bag, Helen had not wakened. The older woman had tossed a little, but her snoring never ceased.

She peered out, noting the nearly burned-out fires. Whoever was in charge of keeping them lit must have fallen asleep.

Her plan was set and she saw no room for failure. She'd slip out of camp and head to a small farm they'd passed not too far back on the trail. Every farmer needed gold and Lyonesse had enough tied in the overlong hem of the man's shirt she wore beneath the woolen tunic she'd stolen from one of the squires. She'd pay the farmer's family well for any horse they had. If she rode hard, she'd reach Ryonne a full day ahead of Faucon.

She slipped out of the tent, issuing a silent prayer

for success. Unnoticed, Lyonesse crept behind her tent and then sprinted for the woods.

Her heart pounded so hard, she wondered if it would burst. If Faucon caught her, she'd regret not having killed him.

When she reached the edge of the clearing, Lyonesse dared a quick look behind her. In the light of the moon, she saw that no one followed. Earlier, while warming herself before the fire, she'd noted which area being patrolled had the largest gap. She'd selected the right one. She paused to catch her breath before continuing on with her escape, and to thank God for His help this far.

"Milady."

Her heart ceased to beat. She recognized Sir John's voice.

"Milady Lyonesse."

What did he want? Why was he here? Lyonesse's breath caught in her throat. Was he here to complete his threat of killing Faucon? She took a step deeper into the forest then stopped. Should she leave, or should she warn Rhys?

Before she could make up her mind, Sir John grasped her arm. "Milady, we must talk. Guillaume—"

His words ended abruptly on a choked gurgle. Lyonesse jerked her arm from his hold. As she did so, he toppled forward, knocking her to the ground and pinning her beneath his weight. His head came to rest alongside hers. Something sharp tore through her clothing and into her shoulder.

Thrown into the underbrush, unable to see or to push Sir John off her, Lyonesse fought the overwhelming fear gripping her mind. She'd wanted to escape Faucon's escort, to return to Ryonne by herself. She'd not wanted to die in the attempt.

Through the fog of terror, she realized Sir John was not moving. He lay atop her like a dead weight. She pushed against his head, struggling to free herself. The object poking into her shoulder dug deeper and tore across her flesh.

Lyonesse reached up with her free hand and found an arrow protruding from the back of Sir John's neck. An arrow that morbidly connected the two of them together.

Over the frantic pounding of her heart, she heard a twig snap to her left. Faucon's men would come from the other direction. Whoever had killed Sir John was near. Unable to contain her fear any longer, she screamed.

Chapter Eight

"Lyonesse!"

Faucon's shout cut through her fear. Feet pounded on the forest floor as the men rushed to her. Vile oaths falling from their lips heralded their arrival.

Faucon tore the arrow free and rolled Sir John off of her. He pulled her from the ground into the safety of his arms.

While shaking her, he cursed, "Damn you, Lyonesse."

Everything was now ruined. Her worst fears would be fulfilled. She bit her lip, refusing to cry. She would not beg, nor would she grovel before him. Instead, she took a long, shuddering breath and stared at him.

His eyes glittered in the torchlight. His lips were pulled into a tight line as he tore her mantle from her, untied the laces at the throat of her shirt and tunic and slid the garments over her shoulder.

Obviously satisfied that the wound was nothing more than a scratch, Rhys pulled her clothing back over her shoulder and asked, ''Where the hell were you going?''

He didn't release her, but he no longer shook her. He'd no need. Lyonesse trembled with fear at what had almost happened and anger that she'd been foiled. Not caring who heard, she shouted back at him, ''To Ryonne. Where else would I go?''

Faucon's eyes grew large with disbelief. ''Are you addled? I am already taking you to Ryonne.''

He wanted to know if *she* was addled? Had he no idea what his grand gesture of protection would do to her? This was Faucon—man of the king, peer of the realm. Of course he knew. So the question now became, did he care?

Lyonesse stared at the rage so evident on his face and knew the answer. He cared not at all what became of her. Ire stiffened her spine and her shaking knees. Determination not to fail in her quest to save Taniere, and herself, fired her blood. ''Damn *you,* Faucon, how many times must I tell you? I will do what I must to save Taniere.''

''I care not about Taniere.''

''I do! 'Tis all I have.''

''You little fool, you almost lost your life. Who would have saved your precious keep had you been killed?''

Lyonesse shivered.

''Damn Taniere and damn you, Lyonesse.''

She said nothing to his repeated curse. His low,

menacing tone left her with the realization that she'd not win. There was no doubt in her mind that she would be damned. She would return to Ryonne in disgrace.

One of Faucon's men interrupted them to confirm what Lyonesse already knew. Sir John was dead.

Without taking his hard stare from her, Rhys ordered, ''Bury the body and scour the area.''

When his man left to do his bidding, Faucon shook her again. ''Did you think I jested?'' His tight voice broke and then rose. ''What would I tell your sire if anything happened to you?''

''Nothing happened. So there is no need for worry.''

''Worry?'' He turned her around and pushed her toward the camp. ''Worry?''

His voice sounded odd. Choked. She looked over her shoulder and asked, ''What is wrong with you?''

He pushed at her back. ''Close your mouth and keep moving.''

When he forced her to walk past her own tent, Lyonesse tried to swallow the dread building in her chest and throat. ''Where are you taking me?''

In an attempt to halt their progress, she sidestepped and was caught off guard when Faucon swept her into his arms and marched wordlessly to his tent.

''No!'' She struggled to get away, but he tightened his hold, brushed the flap out of his way with his shoulder and dumped her none too gently onto his pallet.

She scrambled backward for the opening, kicking at him when he tried to grab her ankle. ''No. Leave me alone.''

Faucon's mirthless laugh sent shivers down her spine. He caught her leg and dragged her toward him. ''Leave you alone?'' He reached down alongside the pallet, pulled up a shackle and slapped it around her ankle. Bile rose to her throat at the sound of the lock clicking into place. ''I will leave you alone as soon as I can hand you over to your father. Alive and well.''

She tugged at the cold metal circling her leg. ''Faucon, you cannot do this.''

With a smile only a demon could possess, he held up the long length of chain and dangled it before her. Torchlight from one corner of the tent glimmered off the thick links.

Dread snaked up her spine. ''What are you going to do?''

Faucon slapped that end of the shackle around his own ankle—effectively chaining the two of them together. Before Lyonesse could put voice to the curses racing to her tongue, he hauled her to her feet.

He forced her to meet his cold glare by grabbing her chin with one hand. ''I warned you. But would you listen? This—'' he jerked his foot, making the metal links binding them together rattle ''—is what you asked for.''

Lyonesse swallowed. There had to be something she could say.

He shook her head. ''No. Say nothing. Anything that comes out of your mouth will only make it worse.''

Who did he think he was? This was more than enough. She stamped her foot, narrowed her eyes and demanded, ''You will take this thing off. Now.''

Faucon smiled before laughing at her. He released her chin before bending to pick up the length of chain. Just when she thought he'd do as she ordered, he yanked the chain and she fell backward onto his pallet.

Before she could scramble off her back, he dropped over her. He pinned her legs firmly between his knees and stared at her for a moment before asking, ''Lyonesse, do you have any idea exactly what your position is right now?''

Her fear and anger fled in the face of warmth uncoiling low in her belly. She fully understood her precarious position. ''Let me up.'' She slapped at his chest. ''Get off of me.''

He grabbed her wrists and with one hand pinned them over her head.

She froze. Suddenly the sour taste of fear bit her tongue, chasing away all the warmth. ''Please, Faucon, I am sorry.''

He doubted that, but the tear trickling down her face amazed him. He'd intended to frighten her, but this was a bit much, even for him. He rolled onto his side, pulling her against his chest. He wiped the tear from her cheek. "Hush, you will come to no harm, but I cannot let you go, Lyonesse."

"Why—" Her voice caught. "Why not?"

He held her close, encircling her with his arm. "Do you think that arrow found the back of Sir John's neck of its own accord? They got too close this time. There will not be another chance."

Her shoulders shook and he knew she was crying. "Lyonesse. Do not." She would rip the heart from his chest with her tears.

"I cannot help it. All is lost."

"How can you say that? You are alive. All is not lost."

She sucked in a raspy breath. "You do not understand."

That was untrue. Rhys did understand. She feared losing her keep—a fear he well knew. Was he not in the same position? Whether he could save his own holdings remained to be seen. In the meantime he could assist Lyonesse.

The thought startled him. Why would he sacrifice his well-protected unmarried state for a woman who had thwarted his mission by capturing him and seeking to kill him?

Marriage would provide him the perfect opportunity to get even with the scheming wench. It would serve her right to find herself truly shackled to the man she'd thought to kill.

While he'd long ago given up his belief in love, he'd known that someday he would wed—if only to carry on his blood. Why not Lyonesse? Theirs would never be a boring marriage.

Her obvious scheming, so different from Alyce's secretive conniving, would keep him ever on alert. The flames of passion Lyonesse buried beneath her quick temper would make arguing with her worthwhile. He was wise enough now to not let passion carry away his heart. Of that he was certain.

Rhys closed his eyes and waited to see if God or Satan would laugh at him. When no sound of wild mirth reached his ears, he took a deep breath and pulled Lyonesse more firmly against him.

"Taniere will remain in your holding. Your husband will see to it."

He loosened his hold when she turned over in his arms. "My husband?"

Rhys winced at her hesitant tone. "Yes."

"And who might that be?"

He paused no more than a breath away from her lips. "Me."

Before he could silence her with a kiss, she gasped, "My God, you have lost your mind."

He ran his tongue across her lips and agreed. "Yes, I have, haven't I?"

Lyonesse was in shock. No woman in control of her senses would marry Faucon. Merciful heaven, he had killed his last wife and their newborn child.

While he had helped her defend Taniere and probably did not murder Guillaume, that didn't change the facts. He was still Satan's servant.

She couldn't breathe. This time his kiss did not fill her with heat, or desire. Instead, it froze her blood. She pushed at his shoulders and shook her head, breaking the unwanted kiss.

"Stop." She backed away from him. "I cannot marry you."

He rolled onto his side, propped his head up with one hand and rested the other on her hip. "I see no other choice."

His touch was warm. Yet it did not chase away the chill. "There are always choices."

"Everyone saw me carry you in here." He caressed her hip before sliding his hand up to her waist. "You will be here all night."

The chill began to fade. She grasped his hand and placed it on the pallet between them. "Do not think to force a marriage by seducing me."

He pulled her closer, ignoring her attempts to stop him. "Would that be such a terrible thing?"

Her heart leaped to her throat with the realization that he could very easily seduce her. "It would be a terrible thing. Faucon, I cannot—I will not marry you."

"And why is that?" He stroked her back.

She tried to ignore the tiny flames licking her flesh beneath his touch. She hated him. She feared him. But the harder she tried to convince herself of those facts, the harder it became to ignore what his touch did to her.

"Why?" His warm breath blew across her neck with his words.

He found the soft spot between her neck and shoulder with his lips. Lyonesse thought she'd faint. "Oh, please. I cannot think."

His soft laugh vibrated against her skin. "That is the idea." For a moment, he relented and looked down at her. "Is this better?"

Not much, but at least she could form a coherent thought. She needed to find a way to turn down his ludicrous offer without garnering his anger. "You do not need a wife, Faucon."

"Every man requires a wife."

"Not all. Not you."

His eyebrows disappeared beneath the dark hair that fell over his forehead. "Why am I different?"

Slowly choosing her words, Lyonesse stared at his chest. "You are King Stephen's sword. Someday you will meet your match and then what? You will leave behind a wife and maybe a child or two. What would become of them?"

"And my horse could throw me tomorrow and

break my neck.'' He tilted her chin up, forcing her to meet his stare. ''What is this about?''

''Faucon, please. I cannot marry you.''

''You have said that many times. Explain your reasons.''

She closed her eyes and said in a rush, ''We would not suit.''

He ran the pad of his thumb across her bottom lip. ''I never thought I would see the day when Taniere's lioness avoided speaking her mind.'' His tongue replaced his thumb. ''For every lie you tell me, I will torment you just a little bit more.'' He pushed her onto her back, slid one leg between hers. ''Would you like to try again?''

Like a swollen stream raging out of control, the blood rushed hot through her body. She had two choices: lose a battle she was not equipped to fight, or anger him beyond measure. One would be as bad the other.

Slowly, he slid his hand down her leg. ''We would suit each other.'' He gently stroked and kneaded his way back up her leg. ''Where your temper and passion might burn another man alive, I am more than able to emerge unscathed.''

It was all she could do not to lean into his caress. He might emerge unscathed, but what about her?

His heated caress continued up her thigh, over her hip, pausing at her waist. ''Where another man might find your wayward manners irritating, I find them interesting.''

Lyonesse caught her breath long enough to ask, ''If you find them so interesting, why am I chained like an animal?''

Her stomach burned under his roving touch. ''Because I want you alive.''

''My father would never give his consent.''

He traced the valley between her breasts. ''To retain Taniere, your father would marry you to the first man who requested the honor of his daughter.''

''I do not want a husband who sees me only as a way to gain a piece of property.''

''Property? What need have I for another keep?'' He laced his fingers in the front opening of her tunic. ''I have plenty of land of my own.''

His knuckles burned through the thin shirt beneath her tunic. She grasped at empty reasoning. ''You would treat me as little more than a servant.''

Faucon's eyebrows rose in a look of surprise. He sat up and ripped the tunic apart. ''I have never treated you thusly.'' Before she realized what else he was about, he pulled her up and eased the torn garment from her. ''I would not drop to one knee and swear allegiance to a servant.'' He tossed the useless fabric across the tent, then paused. ''Do I remove the rest, or would you care to try the truth?''

Determined to retain the thin shirt separating her skin from the night air and his touch, she crossed her arms in front of her, praying that he could not see the heat filling her face. "Faucon, stop. I am afraid of you."

"At this moment, you would rightly be afraid of any man." He pushed her back down onto the pallet and pulled a blanket over them. He rested his hand on her leg. "Let us start over."

"You have killed many men."

"Yes, I have." He didn't move his hand. "Whether I liked it or not, in the name of my king and my God, I have always done my duty."

"They call you Satan's Servant."

"Only those who have reason to fear, or hate me. 'Tis part of my reputation. They are nothing more than words put about to scare off unwanted attention. As long as the stories work I will use them to my advantage."

"It is more than that. No mortal man can tame a wild bird like you have that eagle. You must have the devil's power."

"Nonsense." He slipped his hand up her thigh and stopped. "I am a Faucon. What do you think I did when not serving the king?" When she didn't answer, he continued, "I raise and train falcons, hawks and eagles. 'Tis what my father and his father before him have done."

"I've been told that Satan rides with you and your men in battle. That you are without mercy."

"Mercy? In battle? I have ridden at your father's

side. Have you ever seen him fight?'' He laughed softly. ''Your father fights like a demon himself.''

She searched for an argument that he could not answer. One that would convince him of the foolishness of a marriage between the two of them. Any man who could so brutally murder his own wife and child could easily fly into a rage and kill her.

He slipped his hand beneath her shirt, stroking first the flesh of her hip, then her stomach. ''Think faster.''

She could barely breathe, let alone think. Nobody but her maid had ever touched her naked skin. His hands were callused, but his touch was gentle and warm. Mind stealing. She sucked in a quick breath when he glided his hand across her rib cage, his knuckles barely brushing the underside of her breasts.

''Faucon, stop. I will not be your whore.''

''I asked you to be my wife. There is a difference.''

Lyonesse shook her foot, clinking the links of the chain together. ''You have done so in the most chivalrous way.''

A slow smile curved the corners of his lips. ''Ah, now that sounds more like the Lyonesse I have come to know.''

''You know nothing about me.''

''No? You think not?''

''I *know* you do not.''

"You are wrong." Faucon pulled his hand from beneath her shirt. He knelt over her, trapping her between his legs. "I know you are pleasing to the eye."

"Pleasing?"

He leaned forward, resting his weight on his elbows, then stroked her cheek. "If I say you are beautiful beyond compare, will that satisfy your vanity?"

Lyonesse rolled her eyes. "Beautiful beyond compare?"

"And your eyes shimmer more than any chest full of jewels."

"Faucon, cease your foolishness. You will never be known as a minstrel."

He shrugged. "No. I will be known as the great warrior who let a wisp of a girl capture him."

"If you let me arrive at Ryonne unescorted I can quell the rumors before they grow. None would ever know what I did."

Faucon frowned a moment. "You do not wish your father to learn of your actions."

He was right, but this was her problem to solve. "Faucon, I beg you, please. I released you. I did you no harm that cannot be undone. Let me go. Remove these chains and let me find a way to right what I have done."

"Eventually your father will discover the truth."

The thought terrified her, but she'd not let him

know. ''I will face that when the time comes. He will rant and rage, but then it will be over.''

''You think it will be that easy? You kidnapped the Count of Faucon. You imprisoned a loyal supporter of King Stephen without just cause. You prevented a king's man from doing the king's bidding. How will you defend yourself against treason? What pretty words will you use to clear your father's good name?''

Her stomach rolled. She swallowed hard before replying, ''I kidnapped a murderer. I imprisoned a man who ruined my life. I lost my common sense due to grief. They will believe me. There are plenty of people who will say I was not fully rational.''

''And how will you explain spending the night in this same murderer's tent?''

Lyonesse froze. ''You forced me in here. All saw that.''

He leaned forward, his lips barely brushing her cheek. ''None have heard any screams of outrage, nor a single shout for help. You know what they will think and say.''

''I have done nothing.'' Her whisper ended on a soft groan when his mouth covered hers. Her thoughts fled as he swept his tongue across hers.

He whispered against her lips, ''I know you better than you think I do.'' Before resuming his assault on her senses, he threaded his fingers through her hair and stretched the length of his body against her own.

Her soft curves melded against his hard muscles. As if made for each other, their bodies fit together.

Lyonesse gave up on a silent cry, winding her arms about him.

Rhys held back his sigh of relief at her surrender. In a battle of words and wits, this headstrong woman kept him constantly jumping to stay one step ahead. But in his arms, he was the master in control. With his lips on hers, she was out of her element, lost and ready for him to lead the way.

What would it take to make her realize that while love would never enter their realm, in all other ways they were right for each other?

He slid his hand under her shirt, brushing his palm lightly across her sinfully soft flesh. Her heart pounded fiercely beneath his touch. Attempting to calm her nervousness, he whispered meaningless words of comfort and encouragement as he steadily increased the pressure of his caress.

He wanted to see her, to taste her. Rhys wanted that infernal shirt anywhere but covering her body. Before he completed the thought, he pulled it over her head and tossed the garment across the tent.

"Lyonesse, my lioness, don't you see? It would solve many problems."

She tried keeping them apart with the palms of

her hands against his chest. "No. It would solve nothing."

Easily brushing aside her hands, Rhys cradled her beneath him. This is where he wanted to be—stretched out above her, nestled between her thighs. "Yes, it will solve everything." The pulse in her neck beat wildly beneath his lips. "My capture, the ransom demand, your father's good name, your own reputation. When you marry me, none of that will matter. All will be looked upon as nothing more than a lover's quarrel."

Not a sound stirred within the tent. No noise reached his ears from outside. All he heard was the reckless pounding of his own heart echoing hers and their ragged breaths.

When Lyonesse closed her eyes on a softly gasped sob, a twinge of guilt flitted across his reasoning.

Silently, he vowed not to take her as his body demanded. But he would see to it that by the time this night was over, Lyonesse had no room in her mind for any other man.

"Rhys, I..."

"Hush, Lyonesse." He cupped her breast and stroked his thumb across the already pebbled nipple. His caress startled her enough to stop her words. The time for listening to any more of her weak arguments had passed.

Slowly trailing his lips down her neck, across her shoulder and toward her breast, he ran his hand across the smooth flesh of her stomach. When his fingers brushed the fabric of the braies she wore, he swallowed his curse. While the thought of a woman wearing braies was offensive, at this moment he was grateful for the protective barrier they provided.

The strangled gasp that tore from her throat stopped him instantly.

Rhys closed his eyes and took a deep breath, clearing thoughts of desire from his mind. The woman beneath him did not tremble with lust. He lifted his head and looked down at her.

Her bottom lip was caught between her teeth. She held her eyes tightly closed. When he gently stroked her wet cheek, she shuddered—with fear.

Quickly rolling over onto his back, barely touching her, he cursed himself, then asked, ''Lyonesse?''

She opened her eyes, blinking away the tears before taking a breath that shook her chest. ''Why me? Of all the women you could choose, why me?''

''Because you are unlike any other woman I have known. You have shown more bravery, loyalty and honor in the short time I've known you than some men of my acquaintance.''

He waited for her to say something in response. When she did not, he continued, ''When you are not fighting yourself, we share a mutual desire for each other. You are as bold as your name implies, Lyonesse, and usually forthright with your words.

These are not bad things for the woman I would take to wife.''

''Forthright and bold.'' Lyonesse turned her head away. ''Is that why you killed your first wife? She was not forthright?''

Had someone tossed him into an ice-cold stream, his blood would not have frozen as quickly.

''And your son. Did you not want to wait to see if he would be bold? When you tire of these things in me, will you kill me as easily?''

She didn't turn back to face him, but he heard each word. Like a knife slicing down his chest—one stroke for each utterance. He thought her honorable, yet she believed he truly was a murdering monster. He thought her forthright, yet instead of asking, she'd accused him of absolute vileness. Somewhere in the back of his mind he heard laughter.

Jumping to his feet, Rhys tore at the chain around his neck. It broke free with a snap. He pulled a key from the chain and unlocked the shackle around his ankle.

He paused at the tent flap, turned and stared through a haze of rage at the woman cowering on his pallet. Good. Let her cower. If she thought for one instant that she knew what it was to fear The Faucon, she needed to think again—she knew nothing of fear.

But she would. He had once told her that she would pay for capturing him. She would pay, not just for his capture, but for bringing dreams and wasted emotions back into his life.

He tossed the key on the pallet. ''You can leave if you wish. I care not. But hear me well, lady, your enemy roams these woods and I've no time, nor desire to seek them out. I will escort your servants the rest of the way to Ryonne. It is of no concern to me if you are in their company or not.''

''I—'' Unable to keep his building temper under control, he shouted to drown out her response. ''Cease. Do not speak to me. Do not come near me.''

Chapter Nine

Lyonesse twirled a blade of grass. Faucon had done better than his word. After escorting them to Ryonne, he'd left.

Her fears of her father discovering what she'd done were unfounded. In the many days since her arrival, he'd spoken not one word of Faucon. For that Lyonesse was grateful.

However, she was not grateful for the dreams that filled her sleep. Long nights filled with nothing more than memories of Faucon's hands and lips on her body, leaving her aching for his touch. She heard him whisper her name and felt his heated breath brush against her ear.

''Stop!'' She jumped up from the stone bench and paced the small flower garden.

The garden was a misplaced oddity in this fortress called Ryonne. Her father, and his before him, had spent many years and much wealth rebuilding what began as a small wooden outpost into a solid stone keep.

The sound of hammers and axes in the distance reminded her the work was not yet completed. Each time her sire traveled abroad, he returned with more improvements to be done.

Kitchens were now attached to the main keep by an enclosed passageway. Family quarters had been added above the great hall. An improvement she'd implemented at Taniere.

Ryonne's high surrounding walls were thick. Built against their support were barracks and storage huts. The six guard towers were equipped to protect Ryonne from a siege of any magnitude. With strong walls, a water source and stores aplenty, not much would topple this keep.

Her mother had not lived to see all these marvels. Yet she had been the one to create the greatest one of all. Long ago the Lady of Ryonne had planted this tiny plot in a rear corner of the bailey. Her father had enclosed it with a high wall and even after her death, had kept the garden flourishing.

Her parents had spent many afternoons hidden in this secret place. Lyonesse had not understood why. Now she did and a part of her envied the love and passion they'd shared.

Once she thought to find a love like theirs. She would never have a marriage like her parents.

It mattered little. The time allotted her was up. In desperation she'd agreed to wed whomever her father could find. She'd not expected him to act so quickly though. Nor had she expected him to be so secretive.

Tonight she would pledge her troth to a man whose name she didn't know. This very night she would become like so many women before her—a stranger's betrothed. This night she would save Taniere by condemning herself to an uncertain future. Soon, she would give herself to a man all the while thinking of Faucon and wishing she shared his bed.

''Dear Lord, what is wrong with me?'' She hated Faucon. He was naught but a butcher of women and children. She feared him. She feared his strength and determination.

Lyonesse sighed. She deluded herself. She feared the power he held over her senses, her will and her traitorous body.

His touch made her flesh sing. His nearness set her blood soaring. The sound of his voice made her heart pound.

Lust. Nothing more than sinful lust. And hadn't she proved how easily she could withstand his assault of passion?

After snatching a bright green stem of lemon balm, she crushed the newly grown herb between her fingers. Its scent filled the air, but did nothing to calm her.

She needed to concentrate. To forget this foolish desire for Faucon's touch. She could not let her husband-to-be perceive even a hint that she longed for another's kiss. Especially not tonight.

Her father's keep was overflowing with guests. His peers and the king had arrived to attend this formal ceremony. Since King Stephen issued this decree, she should have expected his arrival.

Lyonesse bent to run her hand over the new shoots of lavender, sending the pungent aroma drifting into the air. The wooden gate creaked open and closed with a solid thud. Without turning, she waited for Helen to tell her it was time to dress for the evening's event.

But the approaching footsteps were too heavy and the stride too purposeful to be Helen's. Spurs clinked with each footfall.

A cool breeze ruffled her hair, filling her with trepidation. Lyonesse rose slowly, turned and stared in shock.

''What...'' She swallowed hard. ''What are you doing here?''

Rhys put one foot up on a boulder and rested his arm across his knee. ''Was not every noble of the realm ordered to attend this event?''

''Well, yes, but—''

Faucon spread his arms wide. ''What is wrong, Lyonesse? Are you not glad to see me?'' He straightened and walked toward her. ''Have you not missed my company?''

She could feel the heat of his anger on the breeze.

To save herself from being scorched, she backed away and clasped her hands before her. ''I—''

''Oh, come, come. Are we not dear friends? Is this the way you greet a long-lost acquaintance?''

Dear friends? Every muscle in his face was drawn as tightly as a bowstring. His lips curled sardonically. He was but a step away. Too close. Too near for comfort. She put a hand out before her and ordered, ''Stay right there, Faucon.''

To her amazement, he did. From head to toe, he wore nothing but black. Lyonesse wondered if anyone could ever appear as imposing as Faucon did.

Even dressed formally in a long surcoat with a tightly pleated shirt beneath, he looked like a warrior. His hair was damp. He'd combed it back, but the undisciplined waves already fought to escape. She caught the heady scent of sandalwood. From a recent bath perhaps?

He wore no rings on his fingers and no gold adorned his neck. The only relief from the darkness of the finely woven silk would be the flecks of gold in his eyes.

She lingered over her perusal and realized that once again, he'd caught her eyeing his form. Heat rushed to her cheeks.

He laughed. ''You *have* missed me.'' He slapped a hand to his chest. ''The knowledge gives me such joy.''

She ignored his sarcasm. ''What do you want?''

The half smile left his face. His brows formed a wicked-looking line over his flecked eyes. Faucon brushed his knuckles against her cheek. ''Only you, my love, only you.''

''Oh, dear God.''

''I am not certain even He will save you this time.''

She'd not realized she'd spoken aloud. Moving back from his touch, she chewed on her bottom lip. It'd be useless to beg. However, if it would work, she was not above trying.

His soft chuckle floated across the distance separating them, sending another blast of cold down her spine. ''Do not tire your mind by concocting a useless plan to save yourself.''

''Faucon, please.'' She despised the tremor in her voice.

''Please?'' He closed the space between them with one step and pulled her roughly against his chest. Before she could protest, he locked his mouth over hers.

Lyonesse knew she would faint. But she didn't know if it would be from dread or the torrent of pure lust that weakened her knees and turned her limbs liquid.

He caught her lip between his teeth. She welcomed the brief stab of pain that helped clear the fog of desire.

"Please?" He whispered hoarsely against her mouth. "I will make only one deal with you."

She pushed against his chest. "Let me go. I will not deal with the devil."

He laughed at her struggles before resuming his assault on her senses. As his tongue swept across hers, Lyonesse clung to his tunic. When he lifted his head, she asked, "What?"

His gaze bore into hers, peering into her soul, seeking some kind of answer to an unasked question. His heart thudded in unison with hers. He caressed her back, chasing away the desire to flee. She held his gaze, certain he'd ask only for her life in exchange for his silence.

"Marry me now. Willingly. Or live the rest of your life in hell."

For one small heartbeat she was tempted to say yes. But common sense overruled her baser thoughts. "I cannot. Oh, Faucon, you know I cannot marry you."

He released her so abruptly that she stumbled. After stepping back from her, he bowed. "Then, milady, prepare to meet Satan himself."

He spun around and left her standing there.

Oh, Sweet Jesus, what had she done?

Lyonesse nearly fell down onto the nearest bench and buried her face in her hands.

Would he go to her father now, or would he wait until after the betrothal ceremony and seek out her betrothed? Which would be worse? For indeed, that is what he would do.

She dashed the building tears from her eyes, stiffened her spine and sat up straight. She wanted to cry, or beg for mercy. She wanted to prostrate herself at her father's feet and confess all. But Lyonesse would do none of those things.

She was the Lady of Taniere—the Lioness and she would not cower in shame and fear. Aye, she'd brought this upon herself and she would see it through.

Somehow.

''Milady?''

Lyonesse turned toward the softly spoken question. It took a moment for the fog of indecision to clear, enabling her to see her maid. ''Helen, is it time?''

A senseless query, one she already knew the answer to. Of course the time to prepare for the evening's event had arrived.

Helen glanced toward the gate. ''Lady Lyonesse, did I see milord Faucon?''

''Yes.'' Lyonesse rose. As if nothing was out of the ordinary, she shook the long skirt of her gown and brushed an errant lock of hair from her face. ''Yes, you did.''

''Child, what did he want?'' The worry etched on Helen's face would have been comical had the last few weeks not happened. Before taking Faucon captive, there had been little for Helen, or anyone else, to worry about.

Lyonesse rubbed her throbbing temples and tried not to laugh hysterically. Finally, she admitted, ''He asked me to be his wife.''

''Again?'' The look on the maid's face told all. Helen thought her charge had lost all ability for reasoning. She'd made that clear when she'd learned that Lyonesse had turned him down the first time. ''And, of course, you said no.''

Lyonesse pinned Helen with a stare that hopefully conveyed her unwillingness to discuss this topic. ''Of course.''

''I still say you are wrong. It would solve a great many problems.''

Obviously, Lyonesse needed to work on her stare. ''I am not discussing this again. I will not marry him.''

Helen shook her head. ''I do not see why you simply do not ask the man what happened to his first wife and child.''

''You know what happened as well as I do.'' She crossed her arms before her and hugged her rolling stomach. ''Everyone cried murder. But she was just a woman, so Faucon went unpunished.''

''Nothing more than gossip, Lyonesse. After all that has happened, I cannot believe you lend credence to any rumors told about Faucon.'' Helen turned and headed toward the gate. ''Regardless, what is done is done.'' When her charge did not follow, the maid paused and beckoned, ''Come, child, 'tis time to ready yourself.''

Lyonesse left the private garden and stepped into the courtyard. It was like walking into another world. There were so many people milling about that she could barely move, let alone make her way to the keep.

Vendors' stalls lined the courtyard, selling wares of all types. Musicians, jugglers and all manner of entertainers practiced their craft. While children raced to and fro, men-at-arms stood about in groups and women kept their eyes on both.

She glanced about at the faces of strangers and those that were familiar to her, until one caused her to stumble.

A strong hand gently grasped her arm and helped her find her step. ''Milady Lyonesse, you need be careful on this uneven ground.''

She stared in horror at the dark, brooding face before her. ''Sir Melwyn.'' She pulled her arm free, scoured the bailey. Men dressed in nothing but black milled in and out of the crowd. All but Faucon's captain kept their distance, but they were there—wherever she looked.

''Do you seek someone, milady?''

''No. Of course not.''

His silky, sly voice put her more on edge. What was going on in her father's keep? What were

Faucon's men doing here? More importantly, why were they acting as if they were guarding her? Her heart skipped again. Or where they hunting her?

Hurrying to catch up with Helen, she kept track of the dark figures. They moved as one. For every step she took forward, they stepped forward. She looked over her shoulder and gasped when Faucon's captain touched his forelock and nodded.

She was *not* imagining things. They *were* dogging her every move.

Lyonesse quickly gained the safety of the keep by bolting past her surprised maid.

The time was nigh. Lyonesse stood at the top of the stairs that would lead her down to her future and took a long, slow breath.

She ran her hands down the rich fabric of her new gown, knowing how fine she looked this night. The golden fabric of the bliaut clung to her hips and legs as she walked. The thin undergown of the same color did little to conceal any of the curves beneath. Never had she owned such a wondrous garment.

Absently, she touched the gem-studded girdle about her hips. Heavy with jewels, it rode low about her. Gold and silver threads sparkled in an intricate pattern on the bright green of the fabric. The embroidered free-flowing design matched the neck and hem of her gown. The same colors and pattern matched the thin metal circlet holding her golden tresses in place.

Her father had gone to great expense to ensure her appearance would be unrivaled by any. She was grateful. She knew not what this night would bring, but the richness of her clothing gave her a small measure of confidence. She did indeed look like the Lady of Taniere. If she could hold on to that image, all would be well.

Boldly descending the stairs to the great hall, she kept her head upright and tried to ignore the fact that again, everywhere she looked she saw Faucon's men.

They stood by the raised dais at one end of the hall, their black clothing a sharp contrast against the freshly whitewashed walls. They lingered by each of the four ornate arch supports. They gathered by both fires and they conversed with Ryonne's guards at the great double doors.

She crossed the floor toward her father's outstretched arms, fighting desperately to ignore the man standing next to him. Her boldness fled. She beat back the sudden urge to throw herself at her father's feet and beg for mercy.

Instead, she walked silently into her sire's warm embrace, rested her cheek on his chest and felt safe. She felt loved. She felt like crying. Would she ever again feel this cherished?

The scents of cinnamon and cloves filled her

senses. Like a warm, mulled wine on a cold winter night, the scent always reminded her of her father and home.

His heart beat strong and steady beneath his burly chest. He kissed the top of her head. ''Ah, child, are you ready?'' His rumbling voice helped calm her worries.

She nodded her head. The soft wool scratched lightly against her cheek. ''Yes. I think I am.''

''Know this, Lyonesse, you are the jewel of my life. Never would I give you to any I would not be proud to call son. Worry not, your husband will cherish you as much as I always have.''

She wanted to ask him who this paragon was, but knew it would be useless. She'd spent every moment in his company these last two days plying him with questions he refused to answer. Her father loved her. He did cherish her. But no one had ever been able to sway him when his mind was set on something.

Instead, she smiled and nodded. ''I know, Father.''

He moved her around to his side. ''Come, let me introduce you to—''

''Milady Lyonesse,'' Faucon bowed, then rising, he took her hand briefly, in his own. '''Tis a pleasure to meet you at last.''

Her father's chuckle surprised her. What was so humorous about Faucon's interruption? ''Ah, yes,

Lyonesse, this is Count Faucon. Surely you have heard me mention him a time or two?"

Forcibly smoothing the frown from her brow, she looked up at her father. "A time or two, yes." She met Faucon's mocking gaze and had the sudden urge to rake her nails across his face. Unladylike, true, but nevertheless it would serve him right.

A page skidded to a stop at Lord Ryonne's elbow and whispered something Lyonesse could not hear. Her father nodded, then instructed the lad, "Tell him I will join him momentarily." He turned back to Lyonesse. "Then Rhys is not a complete stranger to you." He placed her hand on Rhys's arm. "I am certain he will not mind accompanying you until the meal is served."

"Father?" His announcement caught her unaware. There were dozens of people in attendance who would make a better companion than Faucon. He would torment her unceasingly until they broke company for the evening meal. A wary glance at the still empty and unset tables informed her that it would be some time before she could escape.

Ryonne patted her hand. "You are in capable hands." He waved to someone across the hall. "I will rejoin you anon."

"This cannot be." Her breathless whisper left her lips in a rush as she watched her father cross the hall.

Rhys tucked her hand securely into the crook of his arm.

"Faucon, release me."

He reached across with his free arm and grasped her wrist. "Do you never tire of those words?"

"The only thing I tire of is you." A trail of fire raced up her arm. Dear Lord, the man was stroking her wrist. She sought to free herself, to no avail. "Do you never tire of tormenting me?"

"I?" He lifted his eyebrows in a mockery of innocence. "Why, milady, devising new ways to torment you is what keeps my blood flowing."

"Well, praise be to God, that will soon end." The sooner she was pledged to someone, the better. Even if Faucon took it upon himself to inform her betrothed of all her misdeeds, there was a chance that she'd escape unscathed. After all, she was bringing much wealth and property to this marriage. That had to account for some measure of forgiveness.

A devious smile twitched at his lips. "Oh, how so?"

She looked deeper into his gaze and realized that Faucon's sarcasm was a ruse to cover his rage. At this moment he was angrier than she'd ever seen him. The golden flecks nearly glimmered in the dark pupils. That explained his softly spoken cockiness. He was prepared to strike without notice and thought to cover his attack with words. She narrowed her eyes and looked about the hall. He would hardly lose his temper with this many people in attendance. And if he did, he would look the fool, not she.

Lyonesse smiled as she turned back to look up at him. He glared in return. She bit her lip to keep from laughing. "How so, you ask?"

He only nodded.

"'Tis simple, milord. Once I have a husband, you will no longer have the freedom to torment, or threaten me any longer."

A tick in his cheek pulsed once—twice—before he broke out with a laugh that literally terrified her. An unsettling dread uncoiled in her stomach and raced to grasp her heart.

His laughter stopped as quickly as it had begun. Before she knew what he was about, Faucon tugged her toward an alcove. When she resisted, he only tugged harder, forcing her along.

Lyonesse knew not whether to scream or cry. He pulled her into the small room built into the wall for privacy and yanked the curtain across the opening.

Rhys pressed her against the wall, looming above her. "Do you really think this husband of yours will care what I do, or don't do?"

His tone was deep and very mocking. Lyonesse swallowed. While it was true that Faucon could not cause a scene in front of all the guests—neither could she. Screaming was out of the question. She knew that if she opened her mouth a scream would find its way free, or worse—he would silence her with a kiss. Her breath caught at the mere thought. Her heart stilled at the realization that she wanted his kiss. She needed this evening to be over quickly. She needed to be promised to someone so she could forget Faucon and what he did to her. Lest she give away her errant thoughts, she remained silent and stared up at him.

''Very good, milady.'' He stroked her cheek with the back of one finger, then ran his thumb gently across her lower lip.

Unable to stop her shiver, Lyonesse closed her eyes. Maybe if she could not see him, she would not fall helplessly into his arms like a wanton strumpet.

She could feel his warm breath as he laughed softly against her lips. Lyonesse silently cursed her now rapidly beating pulse. His tongue followed the path his thumb had just traced. He was like a heady wine that she could not resist. She was stronger than this—more intelligent than this. *Then why could she not act strong or intelligent when he was near?*

The feelings, the want, he aroused in her were wrong. He cared naught for any save himself. She would soon become another man's wife, she had to fight this insanity that came over her at his touch.

Yet she could no more fight it than she could cease breathing.

Lyonesse leaned into him with a groan of self-disgust. ''Faucon, how will I explain this to my husband?''

He stopped his mind-robbing assault. "Explain what?"

"This. You." Unable to meet his gaze, she leaned her forehead against his chest. "That you have somehow bewitched me."

His chest rumbled beneath her touch. "You are twenty times more foolish than I ever imagined."

She sought to free herself, but pushing against the hard plane of his chest proved unsuccessful. Giving in, she asked, "How so?"

"Because, Lyonesse, you are not bewitched. I cast no spell over you. Unless you call lust a spell."

"Spell or no, it is wrong." When she struggled against his hold, he let her pull away. "Lust for any save my husband is wrong. I could burn in hell for the things you make me feel."

"What things are those, Lyonesse?"

Embarrassment rushed to her cheeks. Lyonesse ignored his question, resisting the urge to cover her burning face. She could not tell him how a simple kiss set her afire. Nor could she tell him of her sleepless nights spent wondering what it would be like to lie beneath him—to be consumed by the flames of passion. Instead, she insisted, "I know you care not, but I will spend an eternity in hell."

One dark brow winged high. "Have I not already promised you hell? What is there left to fear?"

The reminder of his threat served well to douse any remaining fog of passion. She stiffened her back, lifted her chin a notch and met his dark gaze. ''Yes, you have. Tell me, Faucon, has my punishment started?''

He shrugged. ''If you have to ask, then I think not.''

''Should I expect it to commence anytime soon?''

''Perhaps.''

No one could be more exasperating than Faucon. Lyonesse forced a smile to her lips, quelling the urge to stomp her feet and scream like a frustrated child. ''You are only dragging this out because you know how it upsets me.''

''Upsets you?'' He widened his eyes in mock surprise. ''I was certain that you enjoyed playing games. Have you changed your mind?''

Lyonesse said nothing. She knew full well that she would only fall into whatever verbal trap he set.

His warm breath rushed across her cheek. ''Or do you only like games that you think you cannot lose?'' His lips, warm and coaxing, briefly teased her own. ''Are you a poor loser, Lyonesse?''

''No more than you.'' She regretted the words the moment they left her mouth.

''I have never lost.'' Faucon raked a hand through her hair. ''Nor do I intend to start now.'' He tilted her head slightly to one side. Lowering his lips to hers, he whispered, ''Ignore my kiss, Lyonesse.''

His breath warmed her lips. He covered her mouth with his own—coaxing her lips to part. It was blasphemous that something as warm and soft as his lips could command so much power.

Faucon pulled her closer to him, molding their bodies together. From chest to thigh, the hard planes of his body supported the soft curves of her own.

His tongue swept across hers. Teasing, retreating, returning for more. Lyonesse thought she'd been kissed before. She'd thought wrong. This was more than a kiss, more than two sets of lips caressing, more than the ages-old duel between a woman and a man.

Even though it was hard, she could ignore her physical reaction to him. The rushing pulse would slow. Her erratically pounding heart would eventually settle back into its normal rhythm. The throbbing low in her belly would ease. The dizziness would pass. Her blood would cool.

But she could not ignore his possession of her mind. Not even marrying another would wipe this man from her memory. Faucon would always own a piece of her soul. The will to fight him disappeared as quickly as a sweet in the hand of a child.

Lord forgive her, she wanted his kiss. Lyonesse leaned more heavily against him. Sliding her arms around his back, she held him tightly.

She felt Faucon's near growl of satisfaction rumble against her breasts. His kiss deepened, setting fire to her blood. He caressed her mouth with his own, beckoning her take as much as she wished and more.

Saints above, this was the hell he had promised her. Desiring his touch while married to another would make her life a living hell.

Yes, her life would be miserable. Why could her heart not fear Faucon as much as her mind insisted she must?

Voices and laughter from the too-crowded hall cut through the haze enveloping her. Faucon's kiss ended as abruptly as it'd begun. Resting her cheek against his chest, Lyonesse thought for a moment that the hand stroking her hair shook. In the same moment she imagined that his breathing was as ragged as her own.

Faucon pulled away, holding her at arm's length. A frown creased his forehead and she knew she'd been mistaken.

''Lyonesse, I...'' His voice was husky, thick with some emotion she could not name.

Before he could continue whatever he was going to say, Lyonesse's father shouted out her name. Faucon ran a fingertip across her lower lip before he slid the curtain aside and stepped out of the alcove and into the crowd.

It took her a few heartbeats before she could follow. She wondered if everyone would be able to tell what she'd been doing and licked her still-tingling lips. Then she realized that they'd not care. Drink had flowed freely for hours. The jugglers and exotic dancers would draw more attention than she. It was doubtful that any would notice anything was amiss.

She walked to her father's side. His arm went about her shoulders easily as he welcomed her with a brief hug. ''You will be glad to know that your wait is at an end.''

Lyonesse glanced about the hall. She did not see one person whom she wished to spend the rest of her life with. Suddenly, she did not want to know who the man was she would marry.

As if sensing her thoughts, her father winked at her. ''Now, now, child. Fear not.''

Her heart tripped painfully in her chest. ''Father, I—''

''No. 'Tis settled. The agreements are signed and approved by the King and the Church.'' The stern expression on his face promised only ill should she decide to argue now.

She swept the hall with her gaze, stopping at Faucon. Her breath rushed out in a gasp when he approached. She closed her eyes, silently praying that he would not add to her misery now. If he touched her, or kissed her, she'd disgrace herself before her husband-to-be and her father.

King Stephen called for silence and when the hall quieted, her father led her to the center of the great room.

Faucon moved closer and Lyonesse fought to douse the fire in her blood.

''Friends, I welcome you to Ryonne for this occasion.'' Her father took her hand and raised her arm in the air. ''You all know my daughter, Lyonesse.'' He turned toward the king. ''King Stephen's decree states, to hold Taniere, Lyonesse must wed.''

Faucon was now only a few steps away. The seductive smile on his face did not bode well. Lyonesse took a deep breath to keep from crying out.

Releasing her hand, her father continued. ''Since Guillaume du Pree's death, I have sought for one worthy to be not only my daughter's husband and protector, but for one who could easily assume the duties and the great responsibilities of Taniere.''

She wanted to scream. Why could he not just end this? By the time he was done making his speech, Faucon would be upon them. He would take great pleasure in angering her husband-to-be and even greater pleasure in disgracing her before her father's allies and friends.

While her father told of the riches Taniere would bring to the marriage, she stared at Faucon. His eyes glittered. His lips were drawn up into that mocking half smile that irritated her so. It had always proved to be a warning that he was up to no good.

''Lyonesse?'' She turned to her father and took his outstretched hand. He drew her in front of him, not more than a step away from Faucon.

Faucon.

Oh, no. No. He would not. He could not. No. Her father would never do anything so unthinkable.

She glanced at Faucon. His half smile grew until she was certain he was about to laugh at her.

The realization of what was about to happen hit her with the force of an ancient oak tree falling on her.

She watched in silent horror as her father placed her hand in Faucon's and announced, "Count Rhys of Faucon, I hereby entrust my daughter and Taniere into your care."

Chapter Ten

Before Lyonesse could sort through the surprise her father had just delivered, Rhys leaned forward and kissed her still-open mouth. Determined to make certain their bargain was well and truly sealed, he drew her close and silently demanded a response.

At first Lyonesse remained frozen, then she leaned into him and returned his kiss. But only for the briefest moment did she yield to the pull of desire. He knew the instant her common sense took hold—her lips tightened beneath his and she pushed against his chest.

A gasp ran the length of the hall. Rhys watched a couple of the women lift a hand to their throat as if to ward off some evil threatening to take their life. A few others covered their mouths and shook their heads. Pity and relief transformed their faces into masks. Both emotions were for Lyonesse. Pity for the horrors she would surely face being married to the devil Faucon. Relief that it wasn't one of them.

The wild tales had done their job well with these

women. This is what he had set out to accomplish. These were the reactions he wanted. Why did their reactions concern him?

Looking down at the woman who would soon be his wife, he recognized the growing fear in her over-bright eyes and the slight tremor of her chin. Disgust and shame for what he had wrought slammed like a fist to his stomach, nearly driving the breath from his body.

In a heartbeat, anger replaced his disgust. Of all the people gathered in this hall, Lyonesse knew better. She knew the type of man he really was—she'd seen him without the mask, behind the facade. Had he not helped defend Taniere? Who had escorted her to her father? Had she not arrived unharmed and unsullied?

He'd had every opportunity to take advantage of her. And it would not have required force. A few more kisses, another gentle touch and she'd have been compromised beyond repair. He could have so easily been the man the tales told of, but he'd not sunk that low.

For what reason had he acted the gallant?

Her cold hand trembled in his. How dare she treat him in this manner? After releasing her, Rhys turned back to Lord Ryonne. ''Gladly do I accept responsibility for Taniere and your daughter. I will protect both with my life.'' He slanted a quick look down at Lyonesse before adding, ''It will be a challenge I shall enjoy.''

Rhys heard her soft intake of air at his remark. Let her think what she wanted. She was no different from all who thought the stories true.

He lifted her hand to his lips for a kiss, and whispered, ''I thought you were smarter than this. Think, Lyonesse.'' He quickly released her, turned to Lord Ryonne. ''Pray excuse me, milord. Your daughter's kiss has taken my breath away. I find I require air. I will rejoin you momentarily.'' He bowed, a mocking look in his eyes.

Lyonesse watched him leave. If his anger wasn't evident to anyone else in the hall, it was to her. His back was too straight, his shoulders held too stiffly, his gait far too strident for a man simply looking for a breath of air. He may have mocked her, but it was naught but a ploy to escape the gasps and whispers of those in the hall.

As much as she wished to, Lyonesse could not escape. Defeat tasted more bitter than any anger or fear she'd ever known. Faucon had the power to seduce not only her body, but her will, her very soul.

She knew his plan. His method of revenge would succeed. He would inflame her sense, he would drug her with his touch, his kiss and then…? She had not yet deduced that part of his plan, nor did she wish to.

The only chance she saw before her was to tell

her sire all. Maybe then he would find a way to negate this betrothal contract. Regardless of how angry he would become at her outrageous behavior of late, he would never withdraw his support of her. In the meantime, she'd have to find a means to hold Faucon at bay.

"He is very angry." Her father nudged her shoulder. When she didn't respond, he repeated, "Faucon is angry."

Lyonesse blinked, hoping to clear the countless thoughts clouding her mind. "Aye." She glanced around the hall. People had broken up into little groups. Obviously, by the way they looked at her and then toward the door, she and Faucon were the topic of the discussions. "Of course he is angry. Look at them."

Lord Ryonne shook his head. "Nay, Lyonesse. He is angry with you."

"Me?" She frowned at her father. "Why would he be angry with me?"

"I thought perhaps you could tell me. Did you say anything to anger him earlier when I left the two of you alone?"

She'd said many things that made him irate—she always did. What difference did it make? She wasn't about to tell her father that, though—at least not yet. Instead, she shrugged and lied, "I said nothing I can think of."

Lord Ryonne's eyebrows disappeared beneath a

shock of graying hair. He placed a hand gently on Lyonesse's shoulder. "Daughter, I know not what you have against this man, but you need make amends. This union is a good match. Regardless of what misgivings you may have, the match will stand. It would be in your best interest to accept what will be."

Accept what will be. How was she to do that? Had it been any other man, every woman here would have envied her.

But it wasn't any other man. It was Faucon. And all pitied her.

Lyonesse stared at her father and contemplated her choices. There was only one slim thread of hope. Maybe if he knew what she had done to Faucon, he would realize the position this marriage would put her in.

Hesitantly, she asked, "Father, may I speak to you for a moment?" She looked around and nodded toward an empty alcove. "In private?"

"Lyonesse, you will not change my mind. The deed is done."

She wouldn't give up that easily. Insistently tugging on his hand, she led him across the hall. "Please, just hear what I have to say."

After ducking into the alcove, she sat on one of the small benches tucked into the corner. "Father, what I am about to tell you will bring you grief and dismay." She looked up at him. Very little light reached into the tiny chamber. Unable to see his face clearly, she could only guess at his reaction by the sudden slumping of his shoulders.

"You carry another man's child."

Speechless, Lyonesse had to swallow and blink twice before finding her voice. "Good heaven above, nay. I carry no child. How could you think such a thing?"

Her father sat on the other bench and sighed heavily. "Thank God. I thought…well, the way you were acting, I thought—"

She cut him off. "Rest assured, you thought wrong."

He leaned forward. "If you are not breeding, then what desperate news do you have to tell me?"

"Faucon is not all he seems." She took a deep breath and rushed on before she lost her nerve. "I kidnapped and held him captive for killing Guillaume. He has been a prisoner in my tower these past few weeks. He is only marrying me for revenge." She grasped her father's hand. "Please, do you not see? He seeks marriage only so he can punish me for what I did to him."

Only the sounds of her ragged breathing and her father's steady breaths broke the silence in the alcove. The shock and rage she had expected did not come. That could mean only one thing—he already knew. Her slim thread began to unravel.

Lyonesse dropped to the floor before him. She

rested her head on his knees, pleading, ''Please, Father, if you care for me at all, you will not force this marriage on me.''

Lightly running his hand over her hair, Ryonne laughed softly before saying, ''Faucon was wrong. He said you would never tell me about what you had done. He does not know you as well as he thinks he does.''

''You know,'' Lyonesse whispered. He knew and yet he would let this happen.

''I greatly resent the fact that both of you think I am nothing but a dottering old fool. Sit up, Lyonesse.'' When she regained her seat, he asked, ''Do you honestly think that eventually I do not learn of everything that takes place at Taniere? Did you believe that Faucon could lead you across my lands and deliver you to Ryonne without my knowledge?''

Lyonesse waved a hand absently in the air before her. ''What matter is any of that now? I will marry Faucon. His revenge will make my life hell. Nothing will matter.''

Ryonne grabbed her shoulders and shook her until her teeth snapped together. ''Stop this nonsense. Dear God, who put such an idea into your head? Faucon will not harm you.''

''He has already sworn revenge.''

''Jesu, child.'' He pushed himself away from her. ''What do you expect from him? You wounded his arrogant pride. You've done something no man has even attempted, let alone a woman. Of course he promises revenge. But he will not harm you.''

Her father would never understand and she could find no way to explain. Lyonesse shook her head. ''You cannot be sure of that.''

''I am as certain of your safety as I am of my own name. He had far too many opportunities to enact violence upon you. Yet he did not. Lyonesse, when he left you and your traveling companions at the crossroad to make your way to Ryonne's gates alone, he protected your back against a force of men following you.''

''He told you that?'' She didn't doubt that Faucon would tell any lie to gain her father's trust.

''No. There was no need. My men and I had been watching him. When I received word from Ryonne's outriders that you were being led here by a stranger, I rode out to see. I watched you and Faucon part ways, assuming it was to keep your relationship a secret from me.''

In a manner of speaking that was the intent. Before she could explain, he continued, ''When he attacked the men following you, I joined in the fight.''

''How did Faucon know you were not with the enemy?'' The question slipped out of her mouth before she realized that she already knew the answer.

Lord Ryonne shook his head. ''''Tis impossible to

fight at King Stephen's side and not know Count Faucon.''

Her cause was lost. In truth, it had been lost the moment she'd kidnapped Faucon. Still, she wanted to hear the details of his explanation. ''And after you defeated the enemy, he told you about being held captive.''

''No. We did not defeat the enemy. They ran before much of a fight could ensue. Afterward, he simply told me he was going to marry Lyonesse of Taniere. And then he explained why.''

''Oh, I would love to hear this.''

Her father laughed. ''Yes, you probably would. But I'm not going to tell you.'' He rose and looked down at her. ''If you would cease angering him at every turn, you might find a completely different man than the one you have fabricated in your mind.''

Lyonesse snorted in disbelief. Her father's sigh made her regret the unladylike response. ''Father, I already know Faucon. I doubt if there is another man hiding behind the face he has shown me. He means what he says and he's promised revenge.''

''And revenge he will have.''

She could not believe that the man who had raised her would do this. ''Have I been such a bad daughter that you care so little for my well-being?''

He patted her shoulder. ''You have been a good daughter. I care deeply for you and always will. You know this. And you know that I would never give you over to one who would bring you harm.''

''Then you are doing this for Taniere.''

''I will not tell you pretty lies. Yes, I do this partly for Taniere. But I also believe that once the two of you work this out between you, that Faucon will make you a good husband. And God forgive me, I know he will be a better master for Taniere than Guillaume ever could have been. Just remember, Lyonesse, you cannot always have things your way.''

''You talk as if my every wish has always been granted.''

''Has it not? Have you not always been given every little bauble or trinket your heart desired? Have you not been educated and groomed for the care of Taniere? Were you not given a force of men already trained to protect you and your property? Were they not placed into your care, instructed to follow your commands? How many other women are as fortunate as you, Lyonesse?''

She hated the hurt tone in her father's voice, but there was more at stake here than his feelings, or her heart-wrenching guilt. ''I know I am fortunate. I am well aware of all I have been given in this life. I realize my duties and I accept them. I only wish to protect Taniere by the side of a man I can trust. A man as kind and giving as Guillaume was to me.''

''By all the Saint's bones!'' Her father stood. He

was so close that she could see the veins in his neck. ''You know nothing of Guillaume du Pree. Do you think a man who is kind and giving would be capable of overseeing Taniere, or you?''

''You'd rather I have a strong, brutal husband whose reputation alone makes men cower?''

Ryonne took a step away. She heard his heavy intake of air before he stepped back to her. ''I'd rather you had a man who was a man. Someone you could not wind around your pretty finger. Someone with enough brains to do what was right, regardless of your opinion. Someone *I* could trust to hold Taniere from any enemy who might approach the gates.''

''Guillaume would have—''

Her father cut her off. ''He would have given Taniere over at the first sign of force.''

''Father, that is not true! Guillaume would never be so craven.''

''Ack. You see nothing except what you want to see. Guillaume...'' He paused, then said, ''This discussion is over. You will marry Faucon.''

Before she could continue the conversation, he placed a kiss on the top of her head and left the alcove. Lyonesse stared down at her hands. Her father believed that Faucon would make a better master for Taniere? Is that what it all came down to in the end? Taniere?

She laughed softly. Taniere, of course. Hadn't that

been *her* main concern of late? Why would she expect her father to think any differently?

What was she going to do? It would prove nigh on impossible to hold Faucon at bay now. Not when her father was intent on pushing her into the man's arms.

Lyonesse rose. She'd figure something out, but in the meantime she could not very well remain in this alcove forever. People would talk. Worse than that—they'd think she was hiding. Lyonesse of Taniere hid from no one.

After straightening the long skirt of her gown, she stepped out of the alcove and into Faucon.

He grasped her arms to prevent her from sidestepping him. "So, you have decided to rejoin the celebration?"

"Celebration?" Lyonesse wanted nothing more than to laugh in his face. "'Tis more like a wake, is it not? Perhaps a little premature, but still a wake."

He ignored her sarcasm and asked, "I would be right in assuming that you have finally realized you will not be released from this betrothal? You will be my wife."

Lyonesse shook her head. She couldn't admit it. She wouldn't admit it. Doing so would only make it real.

"Taniere's vicious kitten has suddenly lost her tongue? What a surprising occurrence." Faucon paused, giving her time to respond. When she didn't, he continued. "'Tis fine by me if you say nothing. The night will only proceed more smoothly."

Her gaze sliced clean through him and he realized that she was plotting and planning still. Amazing. Cornered and well trapped, yet the woman still sought a way to elude the snare.

Taking advantage of her distraction, he ran his thumb across her lower lip and watched the shiver race through her.

"Stop that." Lyonesse turned her head to escape his touch.

Easily catching her chin, he brought her back to face him. "Nay, I think not." He traced the shell of her ear. "Your mind may as well learn to enjoy my touch as much as your body already does." He stroked her neck, waiting until her shoulders sagged slightly before adding, "As soon as we are wed, I have every intention of keeping you naked in my chamber until I've tasted enough of your passion to drive this desire for you from my blood."

Even though a blush of embarrassment reddened her face, she glared up at him. "And what then, milord? Once you have sated your lust, what becomes of me? Will I then be another wife you no longer require?"

Rhys had sworn he'd not let her goad him into an inhuman rage. He'd never broken a vow yet, but she seemed bound and determined to change that.

He brushed the pulse in the soft spot on her neck.

''I hadn't thought that far ahead. I assumed it would take quite a while to...what did you call it?'' The steady beating beneath his fingers quickened. ''Ah, yes, now I remember. I expect it will take a very long time to sate my lust. Many days and even more long nights. After that, who's to say.''

Lyonesse grabbed his wrist and pulled his hand away from her neck. ''Are you threatening me?''

''Am I?'' Rhys didn't know whether he should laugh or roar. The urge to do either, or both, was strong. This woman drove him insane. Whenever he was near her, he wanted nothing more than to kiss her into silence. Why he had to have her to wife was more than he could understand—or wanted to understand. It would be much easier to take her to his bed and keep her there until he'd sated this rampant lust. But something kept him from doing just that. What? He hoped he figured it out before he lost every bit of sanity he possessed.

''Yes, you did and I will not stand for that.'' She nodded toward the hall. ''People are staring.''

''Let them stare.''

''No. I will not be made a fool of in my father's keep.''

She moved as if to join the crowd. Rhys grasped her arm. ''Neither will *I* be made to appear a fool. You'll leave when I say you can.'' He tightened his hold when she tried to pull away. ''Lyonesse, do not. You will not win.''

She stopped her feeble struggle against him. Rhys released her and held out his arm. "Shall we join our company?"

Lyonesse placed her hand on his arm. "Oh, yes. Let us make merry."

He gritted his teeth against the sharp pain of her fingernails biting through the fabric of his sleeve and into his arm. He'd never imagined that he would need his armor this night. Rhys smiled down at her, warning, "You only add to the list of grievances I hold against you."

She smiled back and whispered loud enough for him to hear. "I am sure the list will grow daily."

"I doubt that not." He reached across with his free hand and pried her fingers from his flesh. "Sheath your claws, hell-cat."

Lyonesse relented and plastered a smile on her face before looking at the expectant crowd. "If you are still eager to join this gathering, let us be on our way."

How Faucon could enjoy conversing with those who feared and despised him was beyond her understanding. Perhaps her father would see how others felt and finally agree with her. She relaxed. This evening could yet turn her way.

Rhys peered down at her. A frown flitted briefly across his forehead before turning into a look of amusement. "I wonder what you plan now."

Lyonesse blinked up at him. "Nothing, milord."

He threw back his head and laughed.

Lady DeJette tapped him on the arm, bringing his humor to a sputtering halt. "Child, what do you find so amusing?"

Child? Lyonesse wondered if the old lady had finally gone daft.

Rhys winked at Lyonesse before leaning forward briefly to kiss the woman's wrinkled cheek. "Life, Hawise. I find life full of amusement."

"'Tis a good thing, my lad." Lady DeJette encompassed both of them in her watery stare. "If you can laugh together now, you will have a full life ahead of you."

The one side of Rhys's cheek sunk in as if he bit the inside of his mouth. Lyonesse hoped the fool drew blood. She kept the wish to herself out of respect for Lady DeJette.

"I will not delay you long." The lady addressed Rhys. "I wished only to thank you for the merlin."

At just under a day's ride to the west, Lady DeJette and her husband were Ryonne's closest neighbor. It was well-known that the woman's greatest joy was riding out with her small hunting merlins. Although it amazed Lyonesse that the woman still did so at her age. Lady DeJette was ancient. She had to be well beyond fifty years. More than twice Lyonesse's age.

"It was nothing. I was happy to replace the one

you lost.'' Rhys then asked, ''Does she do well for you?''

''Oh, my, yes. She has supplied many a sparrow for the table.''

While the two discussed the merits of the new merlin, Lyonesse studied Faucon. His manner and tone appeared to be sincere. He took every care with the older woman, leaning forward so she could hear him better, nodding or gesturing to make his responses easier to understand.

This was a side of him that she'd not witnessed before. She thought back to the first week she'd held him captive and remembered his teasing of Michael when the boy had brought him food in the tower. The same day he'd held her while she'd cried. A few days later he'd protected her keep.

A vision of his face the night Sir John had been killed floated before her. Faucon had been angry, but had the tightness of his jaw and the catch in his voice also been caused by concern?

Her heart raced. She labored to draw breath. Lyonesse took a step away, seeking to clear the conflicting images from her mind.

Something was not right. What she'd heard of the man did not measure up to what she'd seen.

Before she could sort through the confusion, Lady DeJette drew her back into the conversation. ''Lyonesse, I bid you God's good grace and many happy years in your coming marriage.''

Lyonesse stepped back to Faucon's side. "I thank you, Lady DeJette."

Just as the woman took her leave, Rhys touched Lyonesse's arm. "You father awaits us at the table." He paused for a long moment before asking, "Are you ready?"

"Do I have a choice?" She knew what he meant. Father Joseph had arrived and before they ate, he would bless this union between her and Faucon.

Rhys looked up at the ceiling before facing her directly. "Yes, you have a choice. You have always had a choice. You can marry me, or you can lose Taniere."

The decision was hers? She did not want to marry Faucon. He confused her. He frightened her, but to be honest with herself, she had to admit her fear was not the same as it had been only days ago. This fear went deeper.

No other man touched her the way he did. He made her lose control. With a single touch he stole her thoughts and her own will. He made her blood burn, her mind numb and her tongue too heavy to find words.

Could she live with that? Could she spend a lifetime unable to think clearly? Could she spend that many days and nights on fire?

Faucon would accept nothing less than everything from her. He would demand her passion, her desire.

He would want her heart and her soul. Could she give all to him?

Could she give up Taniere?

He extended his hand toward her and waited.

Faucon and Taniere or lose all? There was no choice. She needed more time to think, but that option was gone. Too many people depended on her lands for their livelihood. She could not let them or her father down.

She offered up a silent prayer. "Lord, give me strength and bless me."

Then, looking up at Faucon, she stared into his dark eyes. The anger she searched for was not there. Instead, just beyond his usual arrogance, he looked almost...hopeful.

A loud crash as the large door to the hall burst open drew her attention away from Faucon.

Too many people blocked her view, but their cries of surprise and shock reached her ears.

She took a step forward to see what the commotion was about. Faucon held her back. "Lyonesse, an answer first."

After turning back to him, she placed her hand on his arm and nodded. "Yes, Faucon, I will marry you."

"Like hell you will!"

Lyonesse froze. Nay. It could not be. Impossible. She stared at Faucon and watched in confusion as a mask of fury dropped down over his face.

She stepped away. Slowly turning around, Lyonesse lifted a hand to her mouth. The action did little to stop her cry.

"Guillaume."

Chapter Eleven

"Guillaume." This time it came out as little more than a ragged whisper.

All the voices merged into a single incoherent mumble. The hall spun—walls moved faster and faster until they were but a blur. The floor buckled beneath her feet. Then darkness enclosed her within its confusing hold.

When the world came back into view, she found herself in Rhys's arms. *How had she come to be there? Had she fainted?*

Uncertain, Lyonesse looked up into his eyes and was taken aback by the concern she read there. Concern and something else, something stronger—what?

Before she could question the strange emotion, another's hand gently grasped her wrist as if to pull her from Rhys's hold.

"Release my betrothed."

Blood rushed through Lyonesse's veins. *Guil-*

203

laume! It had not been a trick of Satan. He was truly here.

She struggled to regain her footing and pulled out of Rhys's arms. Before reaching for Guillaume, she took one look back at Rhys and nearly gasped at the pain tearing through her chest. There was no time to question these reactions, no time to sort out the emotions ripping through her—not when Guillaume stood within sight.

She stared at him, seeking to reassure herself it was truly Guillaume.

Blond hair reached beyond his shoulders without one curl falling out of place. The facial hair he'd grown to hide a birthmark on his cheek had begun to take on a reddish hue, but its precision cut—ending three fingers below his chin—was the same.

His long, lean frame, a little thinner than she remembered, was clothed in brilliant blues and reds that he'd always loved.

When he reached toward her, Lyonesse noted the spotless, trim fingernails and knew for a certainty she saw Guillaume.

She reached out to touch the vision before her. Certain the moment her trembling fingers found what she sought, the apparition would disappear. She would be left touching nothing but air, nothing but the memory of a dream.

Instead of a formless mist, her fingers met flesh and bone. He grasped her hand and at his touch,

Lyonesse nearly fell into his arms with a cry. "Guillaume."

"Yes, Lyonesse, 'tis I."

She stroked his familiar face, staring into the blue eyes she'd thought never to see again. "You were dead, lost to me forever."

"Never dead, but lost for a long time." He held her hands and dropped to one knee. "Tell me I am not come too late. Tell me you have not given your heart or pledge to another."

"Du Pree." Before she could respond, her father pushed his way through the crowd and pulled Guillaume to his feet. "What is the meaning of this? What trickery is afoot?"

"Father!" Lyonesse wanted to shake her sire. "I am certain he will explain all." Still clinging to Guillaume's hand, afraid he would again disappear if she let go, she asked, "Can you not be happy that he is alive and with us now?"

King Stephen stepped through the people gathered about them. "We are all gladdened to see Master du Pree breathing, child."

Lyonesse knelt before the king. "Thank you, Sire."

Guillaume released Lyonesse's hand. He hugged Lord Ryonne. "Have you not a welcoming hug for a returning son?"

The embrace was returned, but Lord Ryonne said, "Do not presume too much."

Outraged, Lyonesse sprang upright and tripped on the hem of her gown. Faucon grasped her elbow and steadied her. His touch burned through the layers covering her arm. She frowned at the sensation. ''Thank you.''

''Yes,'' Guillaume took her other arm, ''and I thank you to take your hand off my betrothed.''

''*Your* betrothed?'' Faucon's smile covered only half of his mouth. His eyes glittered. ''That is yet to be determined, unless the lady is willing to take two husbands.''

Lyonesse ignored his words, forcing herself not to cringe at his smooth tone. A battle was brewing and Faucon was more than ready to fight.

Guillaume laughed, tugging her toward him. ''My suit for the lady's hand was first. I am certain the king and the church will uphold the arrangement.''

Faucon tightened his hold. ''Mine is the most recent and therefore the most binding.''

Caught fast between the two men, she looked to her father for help, but he was deep in conversation with King Stephen and did not notice the building argument.

''Nay,'' Guillaume insisted, with another tug, ''we were betrothed as children. Lyonesse knows who she will serve.''

Serve? Is that all Guillaume thought a wife did— serve? Nay. She banished the uncharitable thought.

She'd known him almost her entire life. Guillaume would never treat her so.

When Faucon's grip tightened another hair, Lyonesse jerked her arms away from both men. ''Cease! I will not stand here and listen to you argue as if I matter not.''

At her shout, King Stephen directed them all toward the stairs. '''Tis plain this will not wait. Come, let us discuss this in private.''

Lyonesse nearly laughed when Guillaume and Faucon each offered her an arm as escort. She turned her back on both of them, clung to her father's side and followed the king up to the solar.

Lyonesse could not tell who was angrier. Her father, who paced the small chamber with his hands clasped behind his back?

Or King Stephen who sat by the fire in the only chair, his scowl speaking volumes about his displeasure?

Perhaps the ever-mild Guillaume, who mimicked her father's pacing and appeared as bewildered as she felt. Lyonesse could not fathom what horrors kept him from her side. She was certain, however, that those tribulations wrought the hate she saw in his eyes. A hatred he turned full force on Faucon whenever the man crossed his line of vision.

Or maybe the angriest man in the room was the one who lounged against the wall by the arrow slit acting as if nothing were amiss. His nonchalant manner and easy smile may have fooled a stranger, but she was no stranger to Faucon's temper.

The relaxed appearance was nothing but a well-practiced disguise affected to conceal the predator ready to strike.

"Well?" King Stephen broke the heavy silence.

Guillaume stopped pacing long enough to say, "I demand my suit for marriage be upheld."

Lord Ryonne grasped Lyonesse's hand and pulled her next to him as he took a seat on a small stool. "Before I give you my daughter, I think an explanation is in order."

"I would be interested in hearing this myself." Faucon barely whispered from across the room.

Guillaume turned a hot, blazing glare on Faucon, pointed at the door and ordered, "You may leave us, Count Faucon. This has nothing to do with you."

King Stephen cleared his throat. When he had the attention of all present, he leaned forward and stared at Guillaume. "Faucon stays. Since he stood accused of your murder, it does concern him." He sat back in the chair and drummed his fingers on the wooden arm. "I am waiting."

Guillaume frowned and pursed his lips. Lyonesse recognized the familiar habit and wondered what he had to consider before speaking. Why would telling what happened require any thought? Guilt assailed her. He fought for their future together, of course he would carefully choose his words.

A future she had longed for rested on his explanation. She looked at Rhys. He stared back at her. Unable to read his closed expression, she could only wonder at his thoughts. What would he do when she was beyond his grasp?

"Lady Lyonesse." Guillaume walked across the floor and addressed her. "I do heartily beg your forgiveness."

Eager to grant his wish, she gazed up at him. His eyes reminded her of winter's ice covering a frozen pond. She held back the words that would offer him the forgiveness he sought. What had happened to him to cause such a glacial look?

Thankfully he did not wait for her to speak. Instead, Guillaume turned to her father. "When last I saw you, I was riding north to help protect my uncle's lands from an encroaching enemy."

Lord Ryonne nodded. "This much I remember."

"I arrived outside his demesne lands and found that the attacking force was larger than expected." Guillaume shook his head. "There was slim hope for victory, but I had to try."

The disbelief on her father's face surprised Lyonesse. She glanced at Guillaume and caught a glimpse of a snarl he quickly concealed. Obviously, he had seen her father's expression, too.

Before any of this happened, before Guillaume

had left to help his uncle, her father had oft-times called Guillaume ''son.'' He'd seemed proud of the man she was to marry.

Had something changed? Had he heard something she was not privy to? Would he not have said something to her, or at least to the king? Even so, who would dare besmirch her beloved in such an odious manner? Who would have anything to gain by such a brazen act?

Lyonesse's questioning glare flew instinctively to Faucon.

Rhys felt her sharp, piercing stare before he turned to meet it, face-to-face. What was she incensed about now? At this moment, Lyonesse should be the happiest woman alive. Here was her beloved Guillaume. The path to her bright, happy future lay open before her. How did anger have any room in her thoughts?

Her heart and mind should be so full of gladness— and relief—that she should be a besotted fool. So why wasn't she?

Unable to fathom an answer, Rhys turned his attention back to Guillaume. He listened closer to the biggest tale of woe he'd ever encountered.

King Stephen looked bored to tears. If Ryonne's reddening face was any indication of his anger the man appeared ready to throttle someone.

Yet du Pree appeared not to notice. He continued spinning his story.

"We were quickly outnumbered. I fought off as many of the enemy as I could." He petitioned Lyonesse. "My love, I fear that I lost your grandfather's sword in the melee. I know how you cherished it so, but I was hit so hard in the back of the head that I lost consciousness." He took a step toward her, holding his hands out as if begging. "I am most truly sorry, but I know not what happened to my weapon or armor."

Rhys swallowed a snort of disbelief. The king gazed out the arrow slit. Ryonne's face deepened yet another shade. Good. Such reactions from these two men let Rhys know that his instant misgivings about du Pree were not wrong.

Lyonesse reached out and took du Pree's hand in her own. "Worry not about the sword. 'Tis safely in my possession."

Guillaume encircled Lyonesse in a quick embrace. "I am relieved to hear that. Losing your grandsire's sword made me sick at heart."

The hairs on the back of Rhys's neck rose. While du Pree's words may have expressed concern and sorrow, his tone and expression did not. His smile, over Lyonesse's head, was not one of relief, gladness or thanksgiving. Rhys narrowed his eyes at the self-satisfied smirk.

Guillaume met his direct look. The smirk turned to a near snarl as he shot Rhys a look of pure hatred. A hatred Rhys could not remember earning.

Something was afoot and he was determined to find out what.

His attention darted to Lyonesse. She had eyes only for du Pree. She leaned back in his arms, her gaze never wavering from the man's face. Maybe she did truly love Guillaume. A knife twisted in his gut. Why did he care that she loved Guillaume?

Did she not realize more than love was needed to control Taniere? Had no one ever explained to her that love was fleeting and not enough on which to build a marriage? Love was an emotion suited only for the troubadour's tales.

It mattered little, since she would become the next bride of Faucon. The arrangement was signed and sealed between himself and Lord Ryonne. She would learn soon enough that love was not required for life or marriage. He would add Taniere to his possessions and rule it well enough that one of the many sons he would soon give her would some day rule in his stead. That would give her fair du Pree reason for his hatred.

King Stephen shifted in his chair. ''This is all very well and good, du Pree. But why did you not return home?''

Guillaume stepped away from Lyonesse and faced the king. Rhys moved along the wall, circling the chamber until he stood in the archway of a shadowed alcove behind Lord Ryonne. From this vantage point he couldn't see Lyonesse's, Stephen's or

Baldwin's face, but he could more closely watch the one person he didn't trust—du Pree.

"Sire." Du Pree wiped the sweat from his brow. "'Tis a tale you will find nearly unbelievable." His gaze swung from Lyonesse to the king. "But I swear to you all I say is true."

Did the imbecile not realize that statement alone would make any thinking man doubt everything else he said?

"I remember little of what happened after the blow that left me unconscious. I awoke in the hovel of a farmer and his wife." Guillaume shuddered. "When I could finally perceive my surroundings, I realized I was lying on a flea-infested pallet on the dirt floor of their abode."

"You were alive," Ryonne interjected. Rhys wanted to laugh. If du Pree thought to belittle the farmer and his meager possessions, he did so in front of a man who would not like the attempt. From what Rhys had seen, Ryonne cared for and appreciated those on his lands. Du Pree should know that.

"Well, yes, I was as alive as I could be at the time."

King Stephen sighed heavily, then asked, "And why is that?"

Rhys hid his smile. Guillaume was boring Stephen by dragging this tale out. Soon the king would lose his temper.

Guillaume turned a pleading look to Lyonesse.

"Forgive me, but I did not stay away from you out of choice. I could not remember who I was. Nor did I have any memories of you, Ryonne or Taniere. I did not even remember my own name." He took a step toward her. "As God knows, I came back to Ryonne the very moment I regained my memories."

Lyonesse heard Rhys's half-concealed snort. Amused? How dare Faucon be amused by the terrible things that had happened to Guillaume? She stepped away from her father and took Guillaume's hand. "I do forgive you. You are home now, and that is all that matters."

"Oh, nay. You are wrong. My return is not all that matters." He stroked her arm. "What matters the most is that now our wedding can take place."

His eyes sparkled with unshed tears. He grasped her hand and she felt the tremors coursing through him. "Guillaume—" She paused when a hard stare pierced her back. "I—" Again, she stopped the words from leaving her lips.

She glanced down at her hand. Her fingers entwined with Guillaume's.

He whispered, "Lyonesse," before running his hand up her arm. He squeezed her shoulder. "Oh, my beloved."

The stare piercing her back sent shivers of fire down her spine. She resisted the urge to return Faucon's stare. Without turning around she knew that he stood on alert. She did not need to see him to know that his back was rigid, his shoulders squared and his hand rested on the sword at his side.

She did not need to see his face to know that his brows were drawn into one line, his jaw was clenched, or that his eyes shimmered with golden flecks of fire. Tiny flames that had already ignited a warmth low in her belly. Her lips tingled anew with thoughts of their last kiss.

Lyonesse took a breath, hoping to put out the flames, and lifted her eyes to Guillaume. The look of tenderness on his face made her feel—nothing except sympathy for his recent plight. She wanted to shake his hand from her shoulder and pull her hand away from his.

Dear Lord, what is wrong with me?

These feelings were wrong. They were in direct opposition to what they should be. Guillaume's touch and loving looks should set her afire. Yet she was being singed by nothing more than a stare from Faucon. What had the devil done to her?

Guillaume interrupted her thoughts by quickly squeezing her shoulder. ''Lyonesse, our wedding can take place as soon as you wish.''

Rhys stepped out of the alcove. ''My pardon, but she is betrothed to me.''

Relief at Faucon's statement gently pricked at Lyonesse's heart. She closed her eyes against the steady current of guilt that now coursed through her. Surely she had lost her mind.

Guillaume released her hand and stepped toward Rhys. Thinly veiled hatred rippled across his features.

Rhys gripped the pommel of his sword and cleared the distance between himself and Guillaume in two steps. King Stephen nearly bolted from his seat while ordering, "Faucon, do not."

Lyonesse breathed a short prayer of thanksgiving that Faucon followed orders from his liege lord so quickly.

Stephen stared at both men and then at her. "Lady Lyonesse, you have two men before you. Both are apparently ready to attend a marriage ceremony on the morrow."

Lyonesse looked at Guillaume. He smiled and nodded at her.

She looked at Faucon. He didn't smile. Nor did he nod. But those golden sparks from his heavily lidded eyes nearly knocked her off balance with desire.

Guillaume made her feel comfortable. They would lead a simple, quiet life. The many times they'd discussed their future, he'd always assured her that together they would hold Taniere and see to its prosperity. She trusted him. She loved him. She'd made a vow to him first.

She'd made no vow to Faucon. But he had made one to her and Taniere. In truth he had already upheld that vow by protecting her and Taniere. Could she trust him?

"Sire." Lyonesse returned Guillaume's smile before turning back to King Stephen. "Sire, I am more than ready for my long-awaited wedding to take place."

"Nay!" Her father lunged from his seat. "You will not make this decision in haste."

"In haste? 'Tis not made in haste." She gaped at her father in disbelief. "This has been planned for many years."

"Daughter, listen to reason." Ryonne moved Guillaume aside with a thunderous look. "Let me at least get to know du Pree again before this decision is finalized."

He motioned Rhys closer. "And give yourself a chance to come to know Count Faucon before turning him down out of hand."

If the king had not been present, Lyonesse would have screamed. Get to know Faucon? How laughable. She already knew more about Faucon and his effect on her than she wanted to know. It would take more than one lifetime to sort through all the contradictions she had seen and heard of late.

King Stephen pounded on the arm of his chair. "My God, this situation is better suited to my wife than I." He pinned each occupant in the room with a hard stare. "It seems we have a difficulty. Both suits are valid, yet I've no wish to involve the church in this matter. I value Lord Ryonne's assistance in our ongoing struggles with my cousin, the Empress Matilda, and must take his hesitation into careful consideration.''

A smile broke his frown and Lyonesse dreaded hearing what solution he'd devised. ''Since we are at an impasse, let us do something out of a minstrel's song.''

''My lord?'' Ryonne found his voice first. ''What do you suggest?''

''Nay!'' Guillaume's angry shout made Lyonesse want to hide behind her father. ''This is no matter upon which to play. The decision was made long ago. Let us fulfill that decree now.''

Faucon slammed the tip of his sword into the floor and leaned on the pommel. ''We could decide this with a weapon.''

Lyonesse gasped at his audacity. Ryonne laughed. Guillaume turned three shades lighter.

Stephen held up his hand. ''Enough!'' He turned his renewed attention on Lyonesse. ''I will return here in a sennight. At that time a marriage ceremony will be held. I care not who you choose, as long as you have your father's approval.''

He looked back at Rhys and Guillaume. ''The both of you have seven days to convince the lady of your worthiness.'' He paused and ran a hand down his short beard. ''You will do so without bloodshed.''

Guillaume dropped to one knee. "Sire, I—"

"Cease!" King Stephen's shout could have been heard below, in the hall. "A sennight, du Pree." He looked at Rhys. "No bloodshed. Is that clear?"

Faucon nodded. "Aye, milord."

Stephen then turned his impatience to Ryonne. "Make certain all three of them follow my orders."

"I will."

"Good." Stephen headed toward the door. "Now, let us leave Ryonne and his daughter alone."

After the three men left the chamber, Ryonne turned to Lyonesse. "Choose wisely, daughter. If you pick the wrong man, I will be able to do little to save you."

"My choice was made long ago."

He grasped her shoulders. "Listen to me. Something does not seem right about Guillaume."

"Father—"

"No!" He shook her, stopping her defense of Guillaume. "Lyonesse, I know not what is different, but something is and one way or another I will discover what is bothering me. Until then you will forget everything you know about either man."

"Forget?" How could she forget anything about Faucon? "'Tis not possible."

"'Tis possible." He stepped away, dragging a hand down his face. "Lyonesse, I can only imagine the things that were done and said between you and Count Faucon."

Her face burned. She looked away. This was not a proper discussion to have with her sire.

He tilted her chin up with the side of his hand. Her face burned hotter under his penetrating stare.

His low laugh made her close her eyes tightly. He stepped back and studied her for a moment before stating, ''You are afraid of what Faucon makes you feel.''

''You are mistaken.'' When did her sire become so observant?

''Heavens above, I wish your mother was here. I cannot hold this conversation with you, Lyonesse. You would think me daft.''

Aye, she did, but wisely held her tongue.

''Do you think I do not see? Do you think me so old that I do not remember?''

Now he spoke in riddles. ''See what, Father? There is nothing to see.''

''You, a mere woman, captured the mighty Falcon and held him captive in your keep.''

''I am well aware of what I did. You need not remind me.''

''Yet here you stand. Alive. Untouched. Unharmed. Can you give me an explanation for that?''

She didn't know the answer. She could only think of one reason. ''He swore an oath to me and Taniere.''

Ryonne coughed. Then he sat down in the chair

King Stephen had just vacated. "He swore an oath to you?"

"Yes. The night Taniere was attacked, we were on the wall waiting and he swore an oath to protect me and Taniere."

"He did this in front of others?"

Why did his voice sound so odd? Why did he look at her as if she'd grown another head? "Aye, of course he did." She smiled at the memory. "He even knelt to do so."

Ryonne burst into laughter. "This is rich." He struggled to catch his breath. "Faucon swears to no man, yet he kneels to my daughter." His uncontained laughter filled the room.

"Oh, for heaven's sakes, Father. 'Tis nothing. I was frightened of him. Scared that he and his men would turn on Taniere and attack us. He only sought to banish my fears and those of my men."

The laughter grew louder. After long moments, Ryonne wiped the tears from his face and cleared his throat. "And you are frightened of this man?"

Lyonesse crossed her arms in front of her. She was not going to stand here repeating herself over and over. Not even for her father.

He pushed himself out of the chair and stood before her. "Lyonesse, if your mother were alive she would be more able to talk sense to you. I am just a man. A father who has not been here when you sorely needed him." He lifted his hand to stop her denial. "But I am a man. One who has desired women. Do not be afraid of Faucon and what he makes you feel." He pulled her into his embrace. "Daughter, upon your mother's grave I swear, he will not harm you."

"Oh, Father, if I could believe you things would only be more difficult. I would then truly need to make a choice."

He held her away from him. "Again, I order you to forget what you know, or think you know, about both men. From this moment on, they are strangers. Strangers you must come to know and trust, quickly."

Weary of arguing with him, she agreed. "I will try."

"You will do more than try. You will determine of the two who will be the better master for Taniere. The man who will make a good master for your keep and your people will also make you a good husband."

"What about love, Father? Will not the man who loves me also make a good master for Taniere?"

"No. The man who claims to love you without having lived with you, shared your bed, or shouldered your burdens, is a man who lies, Lyonesse. To you and to himself."

What he said made sense in some strange way.

Her father stroked her hair. "Dwell on what I have told you and choose wisely. You have been given a rare gift, Lyonesse. The king himself has given you the gift of choice. Once you have made your choice and once you and Taniere are in your husband's hands I can do little to help you if need be.''

His words were true. Once wedded to either man, the king would give complete control of Taniere to her husband.

It would take little less than her death for Stephen to give her sire permission to attack Taniere. The king's excuse for not granting permission would always be close at hand—he'd permitted her the rare freedom of choice.

''I will think well on what you have said, Father. I swear it.''

He kissed her forehead. ''I know you will, daughter.'' He stepped away and stopped. ''Just remember, Lyonesse, that they are men and they will use every wile they know to convince you to choose them.''

Guillaume's pleading would not bother her. While she felt much sympathy for his plight, it was over and soon he would cease his complaints and settle into his old self.

However, Faucon knew how to cloud her mind and make her unable to think. Of the two, he would be the most dangerous.

''They will not best me at this, Father. I am well

able to look beyond their games and choose wisely.''

Ryonne opened his mouth, but quickly closed it. Instead, he simply nodded and said, ''If at anytime you need discuss their—'' He looked to the ceiling and then back at her. ''If you are confused by whatever wiles they employ, please, do not hesitate to seek me out.''

The day would never come when she sought out her father to discuss any man's wiles. She could not imagine going to him and asking why her heart beat so hard at Faucon's look, or why her thighs trembled at his touch, or why her belly rolled or her mind fled at his kiss. No. She'd not do it.

Lyonesse smiled and nodded back. ''Of course I will, Father.''

Chapter Twelve

Rhys's lance hit the quintaine dead center, splintering the wood and sending the tilting dummy spinning on its post. He'd much rather be riding the lists with another man as an opponent. But Melwyn was tired of being unhorsed and had left Rhys to his own devices.

In truth, he'd rather be doing anything besides amusing himself on the practice field. However, it was the safest place to meet with his men in private. Two groups had been out for three days searching for the impostor who'd attacked Taniere and they were due back this morning. His next move depended on their report. Rhys would either stop the search until he could leave Ryonne to investigate himself, or send out two different groups.

Either way, eventually he'd find the knave and make the bastard pay. In the meantime he had enough to occupy his mind.

The choice was hers. He slashed out with his sword, emptying the sandbag onto the well-trampled ground. Even if she did have to have her father's approval, it was unheard of to give a woman that much power.

Her father should simply order her to do his bidding, instead of agreeing to what she decided. It would take little pleading on her part before Ryonne gave in to her desires.

Sweat dripped down Rhys's forehead, stinging his eyes. Was he the only one who thought du Pree's explanation nothing but a fabricated tale of woe? He spun his horse around and slashed down with his sword, cleaving the quintaine from its post.

While King Stephen might not be the strongest leader of all time, he was not a simpleton. If Rhys, who did not know du Pree, could see his duplicity, surely Stephen could, too. It made no sense—but then very little made any sense of late.

Rhys sent his horse charging down the list. When he reached the end, he turned the beast and charged back. He needed a good battle, a fight or a challenge upon which to expend this restlessness eating at him.

''Faucon.''

Rhys lifted his sword to herald Lord Baldwin of Ryonne's approach, but the older man shook his head. ''Nay. You already sent your man running for cover, I'll not take his place.''

Ryonne looked up and down the jousting field. ''There are dozens of men at the keep who would relish the opportunity to meet your blade. Yet you tear up my field instead.''

''A mock battle sword to sword would not be fast-paced enough.'' Rhys inspected the damage he'd done to the area and grimaced. ''I will see this put to rights.''

Lord Ryonne nodded. ''Of course you will.'' Then he leaned back on his saddle and considered Rhys for a moment. ''If you have a great need for fast-paced activity at this time, why are you out here and not in the hall? A sennight is not a great deal of time in which to woo a wife.''

Rhys sheathed his sword, it rasped against the wooden scabbard like a hissing snake. A snake that would lie to his host. Better that he appear a fool, than involve Ryonne in his quest. ''I have no soft words, or minstrel's tales with which to woo Lyonesse.'' He had no intentions of wooing her with mere words.

''Then you need find some.'' Baldwin tried staring him down. ''Unless you wish du Pree to win this challenge the king has set between you.''

Rhys met the man's stare without flinching. Du Pree win the challenge? Not likely. ''I have had little opportunity to learn fine courting skills while pledging my sword arm to the king.''

''Come now, Faucon. Surely you don't expect me to believe you are going to surrender without participating in the battle?''

"Surrender?" Rhys reared back as if he'd been slapped. "Surrender to du Pree?" He shook his head. "Lyonesse will not marry him."

"What makes you so certain? I see her with him at every turn, while you...you battle your frustrations on an empty tourney field."

"It is better I battle my frustrations on a field than in your hall."

Ryonne narrowed his eyes. "Tell me, Faucon, how do you intend to fulfill our bargain?"

"Do not fear, milord, I will ensure that your grandchildren rule Taniere."

"I know they will. What I don't know is who will sire them." Baldwin brought his horse closer. After looking about, he lowered his voice. "I do not wish that man to be du Pree."

"That will not happen."

Baldwin cursed before ordering, "Get off this field and do something about it before it does happen."

Three steps brought his beast level with Ryonne's. Rhys stared down at the man. "This challenge seems to upset you more than it does anyone else. What are you so worried about? What are you not telling me?"

Ryonne frowned, as if considering his words. Finally, he said, "Taniere needs a strong hand, not one that will fold or run at the first sign of trouble."

This was a topic they had discussed before. Why

did Ryonne not want to discuss his misgivings about du Pree? Rhys scanned the line of trees looking for his men. If none wished to explain their reservations about du Pree, then Rhys would set his men to see what they could ferret out. In the meantime, he'd follow Ryonne's lead. ''A strong hand for Taniere? What about Lyonesse? Is she not your daughter? Do you not care about her wishes?''

''Yes, Lyonesse is my daughter and while I wish to see her choose wisely, I know her. She will pick the man who will be easily controlled by her whims.''

The man did not know his daughter at all. ''No. You are wrong and you above anyone else should know that.'' He leaned forward on his saddle. ''You taught her the importance of Taniere very well. She will honor her responsibilities. She lives and breathes for the welfare of that keep and its people. She will choose the man who will be the better master for Taniere regardless of her own wants.''

''And you think you are that man?''

''I know I am and before the sennight is over, so will she.''

Ryonne rolled his eyes to the sky, then pinned Rhys with a hard stare. ''You are forgetting one thing.''

''And what is that?''

''She fears you.''

Rhys wanted to laugh. She didn't fear him. She

feared what he did to her senses and body. Had she not already admitted that more than once? He certainly couldn't explain that experience to her father. Instead he tried to ease Ryonne's concerns. "I will set that mistaken idea from her mind."

"See that you do." Baldwin tugged on his reins and wheeled his horse around. Before he left, he looked back at Rhys. "And see that you do not fail me, or Lyonesse."

Behind Baldwin's back, the sun bounced off a flash of metal from the line of the trees at the edge of the forest. Thankfully, Ryonne did not turn in time to see it. Before joining his men, Rhys watched Ryonne leave the field. His earlier question was answered. Obviously, he was not the only person who did not trust du Pree. Why?

From the tower roof, Lyonesse could see forever. Ryonne's fields looked like ribbons, the bright greens of the planted fields contrasted sharply with the barren plots of land. They ran in streamers from the ever-growing village to the river.

"Do you miss Taniere?" Guillaume leaned on the parapet alongside her. "'Tis not good for you to be away from your keep for so long."

"Taniere's steward is a capable man in my stead."

"I am certain he is, but no one is more capable than the lord of the land."

Lyonesse glanced sideways at him. "Even if the lord is a lady?"

"Beloved, put your mind at ease." He rested his hand atop hers. "I am here and Taniere's concerns will be lifted from your shoulders."

She pulled her hand away. "We are not yet married." It mattered not which man she married, her keep's concerns would always rest on her shoulders.

Guillaume turned around and leaned his back against the low stonewall. "Ah, but we will soon be man and wife." He brushed an errant strand of hair from her face. "Did you miss me while I was gone?"

"Of course I did. There were times I thought I would go mad with despair."

"Surely you did not grieve so over my premature death?"

"Would it not have been odd had I not grieved?"

"Yes, well then, perhaps it is a good thing."

Lyonesse laughed bitterly. "How so, Guillaume?" With all that had taken place during his absence, she could not think of many good things that had happened.

"You had an opportunity to discover how difficult running a keep was without a strong hand to help you. Our separation gave us a chance to realize how much we loved each other."

"And is that what you feel for me? Love?"

"You question me?"

She studied his face a moment. He stood here talking to her about matters of feelings, yet he appeared to be lost in thoughts of his own. ''No. I do not question you. I question this love you profess. 'Tis not how I imagined love felt.''

''What did you imagine?''

The memory of Faucon's last kiss brushed her mind and set her stomach to tighten. Lyonesse focused on Guillaume. ''I truly am not certain.''

''Lyonesse, love is nothing more than a man willing to take on his wife's responsibilities and a woman willing to follow her husband's will.''

Luckily she had no interest in the troubadours' romantic love. Faucon was certain love didn't exist and what Guillaume described sounded more like a master and serf.

He straightened her cloak about her shoulders. ''Lyonesse, you have ever been headstrong. Your greatest needs are simple. You need a man who is capable of seeing to Taniere and at the same time can provide the strong guidance you require.''

Guidance? What about desire and passion? She wished Guillaume would cease his inane explanation, pull her into his arms and kiss her senseless. Could he? Would his touch or kiss steal her mind and breath the Faucon's did? She had to know.

Lyonesse attempted to pull his mind away from thoughts of his responsibility as a husband. ''Guillaume, it is a beautiful day. The sky is clear. The sun is bright. It has been a long time since we could share a day this fine. Let us sneak off to the river for a picnic, just the two of us.''

He pursed his lips and stared out over the wall a few moments before turning his familiar smile on her. ''Aye, that would be a fine idea.''

While Guillaume gathered a blanket and had the horses saddled, Lyonesse searched for Helen and her father. Soon, she and Guillaume had everything ready and met in the hall.

They left the keep and strolled toward the stables. Hip brushing hip, thigh touching thigh, they walked across the bailey. Nothing. Lyonesse felt nothing and fretted over the lack.

For her whole life, she had dreamed of these days, longed for them. Had impatiently waited to grow up so that she and Guillaume could finally share everything together. And now all those dreams and wishes seemed so far away. The distance and loss of that longing brought a sharp pain to her heart.

The rain-swollen river roared past the bank. Lyonesse tossed a stick in the current and watched it speed downstream.

''Lyonesse, step back from there.'' Guillaume's concern turned his voice harsh.

Not willing to argue, Lyonesse did as he bid and rejoined him on the blanket they'd spread under a gnarled apple tree.

Curling her legs beneath her, she sat next to him. With his legs stretched out before him, Guillaume propped himself up on his elbows. ''That is better.''

She agreed, not realizing until now how she'd missed these sights. The rushing river, with its steep rocky bank. Wildflowers dotted the lush rolling hills. Petals flittering like butterfly wings, swayed in the gentle breeze.

Later in the summer the open fields would be sprinkled with families enjoying the day. They'd spread covers on the ground in the sun, or in the dappled shade provided by the fruit trees in the small orchard. But today they were alone.

It had taken Helen no time at all to have a small meal put together for them. While Helen was there to make certain nothing untoward occurred, so far she'd obeyed Lyonesse's order to keep her distance. She sat under another tree, close enough to see her charge, but not close enough to hear what was said.

''Are you pleased that we came?'' Guillaume's question brought her out of her silent musing.

''Of course I am. Why would you think otherwise?''

''You are so quiet.'' Guillaume shrugged his shoulders. ''I get the feeling that you are not all here. It is as if your mind is elsewhere.'' He studied her. A frown marred his face. ''Is there somewhere else you would rather be?''

Lyonesse glanced quickly toward her maid.

Helen's head bobbed down, her chin hitting chest. She appeared to be napping. "Yes, there is some-place else I'd rather be."

The desperate need to know what his touch would do to her, made her brazen. She leaned closer to him, her lips mere inches from his cheek. "I would much rather be in your arms."

Surprise and shock registered on Guillaume's face. He shook his head. "I do not think—"

Certain that boldness was required to get him past his hesitancy, Lyonesse placed her hands on his shoulders. "Do not think. Just kiss me, Guillaume, that is all I ask."

Still leaning back on his elbows, and not touching her, he allowed her to place her lips against his. This wasn't exactly what she had in mind. Lyonesse pulled back a hair's breadth. "Please, Guillaume, kiss me."

After another moment's hesitation, he slid one hand behind her head and drew her to him.

Lyonesse wanted to scream in frustration. While his lips were warm, it was like kissing her father farewell.

Uncertain how to coax him further, she ran her tongue across his lips. Instead of following her lead, Guillaume tightened his lips.

Had he never kissed a woman before? Did he not know what a kiss of passion was? Heaven help her,

Lyonesse knew not how to teach him without insulting his feeble attempt to please her.

"Milady Lyonesse!"

Helen's cry tore Guillaume away from Lyonesse. He jumped up from the blanket like an arrow being loosened from a bow.

Lyonesse looked up at him. His face reddened in what she first thought was anger, but his sudden fidgeting led her to realize it was embarrassment. "Guillaume, 'tis all right. You did nothing."

What was she going to do? She'd sworn a vow to him. Could she honor that vow with a man who made her feel nothing? A man who had no desire to be intimate with her?

Helen reached them, breathless. "What are you two doing over here?"

"Nothing." Guillaume's expression was unreadable.

She held back a groan. His hasty response would make Helen think he lied. To stop Helen's queries, she said, "If you had not been asleep you would not have to ask that question."

Asleep? Her maid *had* been asleep. Once Helen slumbered, you could hardly rouse her. Usually someone had to physically shake the maid awake. Lyonesse peered at the spot where Helen had been resting. Rage took her breath away.

Faucon sat atop his horse by the tree. His shoulders shook with laughter. He'd seen them and had awakened Helen.

By all that was unholy how did Faucon do it? How was he always in her shadow? How did he always hear everything that went on? Perhaps he truly was one of Satan's helpers. No. She knew that wasn't true, but he certainly did seem to have the ability to be everywhere at one time.

Guillaume turned, following her line of vision, and cursed before asking, ''How did he know we were here?''

Lyonesse leaned away from the anger in his tone. ''I certainly did not tell him.''

Guillaume's voice rose in disbelief. ''Then who did?''

He was making her angry. Good. At least it was some kind of emotion. ''What are you asking, Guillaume? Are you accusing me of something?''

His glare contorted his fine features into a mask of near evil. ''Nobody knew we were coming here. It only makes sense that you told him. Had you planned on sharing this fine day with both of us? Will you now seek to force a whore's kiss on him, too?''

Lyonesse rose. She curled her hands into fists at her side. ''That is uncalled-for. You will apologize.''

''Apologize?'' He stepped toward her, lowering his voice, ''I will not apologize for your unseemly behavior.'' He nodded toward Faucon before adding, ''We will discuss this in private.''

Lyonesse stared at him. Who was this man? What had happened to so change him? First he thought she needed a firm guiding hand. Then he refused her advances and accused her of acting like a whore. Now he thought to chastise her?

She unclenched her jaw. ''We will discuss nothing in public nor in private.''

''Pardon me. I hate to break up this touching scene,'' Faucon called out as he rode toward them, ''but, du Pree, someone from your keep is looking for you.''

''And they sent you out to find us?'' Venom colored Guillaume's words.

Faucon leaned back in his saddle and studied his fingernails a moment before spearing Guillaume with a look that forced the unmounted man to take a few steps backward.

Lyonesse shook her head. Now how did he do *that?* With just a simple look no less.

''No, they did not send me.'' Faucon kept his stare pinned on Guillaume. ''I volunteered to come.''

Guillaume broke eye contact first. He glanced to Lyonesse, anger still etched on his face. ''I must return.'' Without another word he turned on his heels and strode to his horse.

Until Guillaume rode out of sight, nobody moved.

Nobody breathed. The very air around them cracked with silent anger until Faucon dismissed Helen with nothing more than a nod.

Lyonesse gasped. ''How dare you.'' She called after her maid, ''Helen, stay.''

Over her shoulder the maid answered back, ''I will be right over by this tree, milady.''

Before Lyonesse could act, Faucon dismounted, grasped her arm and tugged her toward the river.

''Unhand me.'' Her order was lost in the river's roar.

Faucon pulled her against his chest and slid a hand up her neck, threading his fingers in her hair. With a firm tug, he tipped her head back.

Lyonesse's heart flew against the inside of her chest with a driving force so hard she feared it would burst free.

He lowered his lips to her exposed neck and stroked his tongue across her flesh, chasing away her breath.

Faucon nipped the lobe of her ear. Her mind hazed over. His breath was hot, but not as hot as the blood setting fires in her veins.

''If you wish to kiss someone, this is how it is done.''

She heard his near growl clearly over the raging river. Before she could form a reply, he slanted his mouth over hers.

No. She would not give in this time. But the turmoil in her heart would not be denied. She swallowed hard, trying to force her body to listen to reason.

He tripped his tongue against her lips. Taking a lesson from Guillaume, she tightened her lips.

Rhys paused for half a rapid heartbeat before lifting his mouth away from hers. He stared down at her.

She was lost in the intensity of his gaze. Even someone blind could read the desire and passion there.

"Tell me to leave and I will."

Did she want him to leave? Her heart skipped a beat. Nay. Lord help her, she did not. But if she begged him stay, what then? "Faucon, I..." What did she want?

"Bid me stop and I will go."

That was the last thing she wanted to tell him. She wound her arms around his neck. "No. I—"

He swept away her words with his lips and tongue. Lyonesse clung to him tightly, seeking safety from the waves crashing over her, threatening to drag her away in passion's current.

Rhys deepened their kissing, teasing, tormenting, beckoning her to do the same. Senses already heightened by his demanding touch, she thrilled to every movement. He smelled of sandalwood and tasted of mint. Lyonesse moaned, unable to get close enough to satisfy her body's rampant need.

He tangled his fingers in her hair, sending shivers cascading from her scalp down her spine. He slid his hand down the small of her back and drew her yet tighter against him. The heat of his body set hers on fire.

Molded together, tongues entwined, Rhys could not have hidden his desire for her if he'd tried. The length of his arousal pressed low against her belly, creating a maddening pulse between her thighs that begged for more. She moved against him, seeking to obey the cry of her heart.

He broke the kiss with a ragged groan. When she would have fallen, Rhys held her close and coaxed her to rest her cheek against his chest.

Lyonesse laughed weakly at her shaking limbs. ''What are you doing to me?''

His answering chuckle was deep. It whispered softly against her hair. ''Nothing that you do not do to me.''

She turned slightly and rested her forehead against his chest. ''You do realize that someday we will not stop?''

''Then perhaps we should have the benefit of the church's blessing.''

Lyonesse pushed away. ''You will not wring a promise from me that easily.''

Rhys pulled her back to him. ''Maybe not. But neither will you run about the countryside seeking kisses elsewhere.''

His audacity was amazing. "You think to stop me?"

"Think?" Rhys held her away from him. His stare froze her in place. "No, Lyonesse, I will not permit it to happen."

Why did a thrill run through her? How was it possible that ire did not fill her heart? Instead of raging at him, something mischievous prompted her to ask, "And how will you stop me?"

Rhys lifted one eyebrow before gracing her with a smile that caused her heart to trip over itself. "Easily." He brought his mouth closer to hers. "I will give you enough of my kisses every day. Then you will have no desire for any others."

Lyonesse moaned at his sinful threat. "Every single day?"

He whispered against her lips, "Aye."

The thought made her burn. Through the haze and heat of desire, a small voice whispered inside her head. *Why?* What prompted Faucon to go to so much trouble? What convinced him that he had the right to do with her as he pleased? After all she'd done to him it would have made more sense for him to leave Ryonne without a backward glance.

After all she'd done. Lyonesse stiffened. She remembered his promise in the garden. "This is your revenge on me." She squared her shoulders, letting anger fill her chest and fire her words. "This grand passion is nothing more than your way of making me pay for capturing you.''

Faucon looked down at her. The desire had fled in the wake of his ire. ''Have I not always promised you revenge?'' He hauled her back to his chest. ''What did you think I meant?''

She couldn't think. She did not know what he meant. Her mind swirled faster than the river's currents. One thought after another, each darker than the last, whirled from her head to her heart. ''You play these games of lust with me? Why? So that when you set me aside I will be little more than whore?'' Lyonesse filled her lungs, then continued, ''You care nothing for me, nothing beyond what you can take in return for what I did out of grief.''

Faucon gripped her hair, jerked her head back and shouted at her. ''By all the Saints! Woman, you are a fool.''

Lyonesse beat her fists against his chest. ''Let me go.'' She struggled to pull out of his hold.

He stopped her by tightening his fingers. The pain brought tears to her eyes, but she refused to let them fall. ''Damn you, Faucon, release me.''

''Never.''

She willed herself to ignore the pain and tried again to pull free.

''Lyonesse, cease this now!'' His shout reverberated off the boulders along the river's bank. It cut through the murky fog clouding her mind.

The tears she had been holding back began to slip, one by one, down her cheeks. Mortified, Lyonesse dashed them away. She did not want this brazen churl to see her pain—only her anger.

In one fluid movement, he released her hair and slid his hands down her back. Before she knew what he was about, he pulled her tight against him.

The softness of her body held firmly against the hard planes of his somehow felt right. She fought to quell the direction of her traitorous thoughts.

Curious at his silence, Lyonesse looked up at him. If the tiny pulse in his cheek was any indication, he was still as angry as she.

''You think I do not care?'' Tightly controlled rage tinged his voice.

Uncertain as to what her own voice would reveal, Lyonesse remained silent and shook her head.

''Did I not swear an oath to protect you and Taniere?''

She took a breath to steady her words before she said, ''Aye, you did and that oath was fulfilled.''

''No. That oath will carry on until I breathe no more.''

''How can you swear an oath of protection and a promise of revenge to the same person?''

''For the love of God, Lyonesse, have you not yet deduced what this *revenge* you fear so much truly entails?''

Faucon ran one hand up her back and gently caressed her tight shoulders. A shiver rippled down her spine. "Do you not see that for every tremor of desire that runs through your body, an answering one builds in mine?"

Lyonesse relaxed against him. She felt his anger leave his body in a rush of air.

"Do you not know that this revenge I so irrationally promised ensnares me in its web as much as it does you?"

"But I... You will not leave and..." She couldn't put her thoughts into words.

"I will not what?" Faucon raked his fingers through her hair, kneading her scalp. "Abandon you? Never." He coaxed her head back with a nudge. "Look at me. Hear me well."

When she stared into his flecked gaze, he softly said, "I will have my revenge on you. I will invade your body, your thoughts, even your very soul. You will never be free of me, Lyonesse." He shook his head before adding, "And I will probably be the one to lose more."

Warmth flooded her, chasing away any remaining doubts and fears that Faucon would bring her harm. In that moment Lyonesse knew she would offer him all.

From the back of her mind came a single thought. Honor. Long ago she'd given a promise to another. Never in her life had she broken a promise. Would she do so now? Could she in all good faith do so simply in the name of passion and desire?

Faucon wiped the frown from her forehead. "I will proceed as slowly as I can, Lyonesse."

She mentally shook her concerns from her mind. "How will you do that?"

He smiled. "Day by day." He brushed his lips against hers. "One kiss at a time."

"Dear Lord, save me."

"'Tis far too late for saving, Lyonesse."

Chapter Thirteen

Guillaume slammed his fist on the food-laden table. "I know not what happened during my absence, Lyonesse, but I will not abide this unbecoming change in you."

Rhys choked on his wine at the man's brazen statement to Lyonesse.

The diners gathered in the hall for the evening meal ceased talking and stared eagerly at the head table. They were as anxious to hear Lyonesse's response as he was.

"I am not the one who has changed."

Rhys had heard that tone before. Her low words were issued from between clenched teeth. He leaned closer, not wanting to miss any of this exchange.

Du Pree bristled visibly. "You have. You are well beyond the age of childhood. 'Tis time you learn to act as befits a wife."

"And who is going to teach me this novelty?"

"As your husband-to-be it is my responsibility, my holy duty to do so."

Rhys knew full well that he'd regret what he was about to do, but he couldn't resist the temptation. He leaned forward. ''Please, why not begin your first lesson now?''

Beneath the table Lyonesse rested her hand on his knee. Her touch was light—he sucked in a quick breath. Her touch *had* been light, until she buried her fingernails through the layers of clothes covering his body and into his leg. When he tried to jerk away from her claws, she hung on. He brought his foot down, gently on top of hers. She let go.

He cleared his throat and repeated his request to a now fuming du Pree. ''What are your holy duties as a husband?''

''Count Faucon, I am certain that anyone else here could explain it much better than I could.''

Rhys leaned forward far enough to pin the man with a pointed glare. ''Maybe so, but since you introduced the topic, it becomes your place to continue.''

He couldn't miss Lyonesse's outraged stare, it burned through him as easily as a red-hot ember. He shrugged. ''I am just making dinner conversation.''

Her look told him louder than words that she didn't believe him. Finally, she turned toward du Pree and prompted, ''Yes, Guillaume, please continue.''

An expression of such total seriousness fell across du Pree's face, Rhys did all he could not to laugh out loud. He rammed a chunk of bread in his mouth before he disgraced himself and angered Lyonesse further. Then he settled in for what would surely be an educational lecture.

"Well, as you know, it is the husband's duty to see to not only the safety, security and welfare of his chosen spouse, but to also see to the salvation of her soul."

Guillaume paused, checking to see if he had their undivided attention. He leaned his forearms on the table and folded his hands as if in prayer. Then he continued. "Part of that salvation is to ensure her God-fearing behavior and righteousness." He shot a quick look of accusation toward Lyonesse.

Rhys was amazed to see the blush rise up and cover her face. Now he leaned forward. "What you mean to say, is that the husband is responsible for his wife's behavior and the discipline required to maintain said behavior."

"Rhys." Lyonesse's warning tone was noted and ignored.

Guillaume lifted his chin a notch. His jaw tightened briefly before he said, "I would not put it quite so vulgarly. But if you insist, then yes, it has always been the husband's responsibility, nay, his religious duty to see that his wife behaves in a manner befitting her station."

Lyonesse's eyebrows rose. "And what manner of

discipline would you employ to ensure your wife's behavior?''

''Nothing too churlish at first.'' Guillaume seemed to consider his ideas for a moment. ''A few days with no food and plenty of hard labor might be enough.''

''And if it was not?'' Lyonesse's voice rose.

''A well-applied rod, no larger than my thumb would be acceptable.''

There was no doubt in Rhys's mind that Guillaume would be the type of man who would willingly ensure discipline all in the name of salvation. How convenient to use the Church's rules to abuse someone smaller and weaker. While he had little liking for the man before, now he had none. And this was the man Lyonesse was supposed to have married? Rhys wondered how much time would have passed before she fed Guillaume his discipline.

Lyonesse shook her head. ''I still do not see how this explains anything. Did anyone stop to think that if a husband and wife loved each other that this discipline you speak of would not be necessary?''

Guillaume looked up and down the length of the table. He lowered his voice. ''Lyonesse, it is blasphemous to speak so. You seek to deny the Church's teachings?''

''Deny? No. I seek only to get an explanation for the ever-changing rules of men.''

''There is nobody else but men who can make rules.''

Lyonesse gasped before looking at Guillaume as if he were mad. ''Nobody else? I will be certain to let Queen Maud know that. I am sure that Empress Matilda needs to be informed, too.''

Guillaume's sigh sounded as if he was well used to dealing with those of lesser mind and intelligence. Though the noise was aimed at Lyonesse, Rhys took offense.

Granted, there were women who wanted and apparently needed a man to tell them what to do, to think for them. And on occasion he'd found it necessary to give direct orders rather than discuss a decision. An occurrence that happened more regularly of late—especially with Lyonesse. But he'd seen firsthand what women could do without a man around to assist them.

While the queen couldn't physically wield a sword, she could lead the troops to the battle. Had she not seen to it that her husband was released from captivity? Had the empress not kept King Stephen jumping for the last few years?

When he and his brothers were younger and his own father was away for months on end, his mother's rule had kept the lands safe and prosperous. Aye, the steward gave most of the orders, but he only repeated the orders he himself had been given from the Lady of Faucon.

Rhys had learned nearly as much at his mother's knee as he had his father's side.

Had not his own capture been led by a woman? Any man who thought that because women were smaller and weaker they did not matter, were simply fools asking for trouble.

Outside of Lyonesse and a few others, it was unlikely that most women would pick up a sword or dagger and run someone through, but it was very likely they could and would give the order for another to do so—and relish the opportunity.

Those not bold enough to pick up and wield a weapon in their own hands, had other methods that worked to their advantage. Was there a woman alive who did not possess wiles worthy of a wild forest cat? The few times he had been simple enough to take a woman's wiles for granted, he had paid dearly. Never again would he be foolish to miscount what a woman could accomplish.

But being a man, Rhys felt it his duty to help Guillaume out all he could. "Now, now, Lyonesse, du Pree is correct. You well know that only men are capable of logical thought." To save himself from the look of pure horror and disbelief that he was certain twisted her face, he looked at a spot above her head. "Even the queen consults with King Stephen before making any decision on her own."

Lyonesse sunk her nails back in his leg. She

needed to read his tone a little better. Did she not recognize sarcasm when she heard it?

Guillaume acted as if he and Rhys were of the same mind. He lifted his goblet. ''Well said, milord.'' After taking a drink of his wine, he began his litany again. ''Yes, and as you know discipline and salvation cannot truly be delivered when one is too attached to the person receiving the experience. So love has no place in a marriage.''

Lyonesse's grip tightened. Rhys reached under the table and grabbed her arm. He pressed his thumb into the soft spot under her wrist. She released her hold. Since he had no intentions of leaving the table with blood running down his leg, he threaded his fingers through hers. When she sought to imbed her nails in his hand, he slid their joined hands toward his groin.

Shock stopped her from attempting to gouge him any further.

After swallowing twice, Lyonesse composed herself and turned her attention back to Guillaume. ''A person cannot live without love.''

''Yes. You begin to see why some men, who cannot live without love, take a mistress.''

Rhys picked up his eating knife and pointed it at Guillaume. ''It may be the perfect solution for some, but what about your wife? That would be unacceptable in my marriage.''

Du Pree laughed at him. The sound made the hairs

on the back of Rhys's neck stand at attention. It ran cold through his veins and settled uneasily in his gut. ''No, I do not see a wife of yours taking a lover.''

By the knave's sly, too smooth tone of voice, there was no doubting the man's inference. Few outside the Faucon lands knew of Alyce's indiscretion. How came du Pree upon that knowledge?

Guillaume leaned forward to peer around Lyonesse. ''What say you, Faucon? How would you discipline a wife who played fast and loose in your bed?''

The man's eyes glittered with a hatred so pure, that it had to have been born from years of practice. Rhys no longer cared to discover from whence it came. The hate was there, as plain as day, and for all to see.

Lyonesse gasped. A twitter of nervous laughter ran the length of the hall.

''Well, Faucon? Would you enforce your husbandly rights as granted by the Church?'' Du Pree sneered and shrugged a shoulder before offering another choice. ''Or would you abandon all human decency and simply kill her? Perhaps you would also deliver her offspring to death's door at the same time.''

Lyonesse gripped Rhys's hand with all of her strength. Not only could she smell his anger, she felt it burn the flesh on her hand. What was wrong with

Guillaume? He had never been one to intentionally goad another into a rage.

When Rhys sought to pull free from her grasp, she forgot his earlier warning and dug her nails into the tightly corded muscles and tendons on top of his hand. She prayed he found control before he crushed her fingers.

Lyonesse frantically searched the hall for her father. After he'd finished eating, he had wandered off. If Faucon took it upon himself to slay Guillaume, she'd be unable to stop him.

With her fingers still entwined in his, Faucon raised his arm above the table. Guillaume's surprised stare darted from Lyonesse's face to where her hand still held on to Rhys's.

She relaxed her grip, then instantly realized that was exactly what Faucon had wanted. Before she could clamp her fingers back around his, he pulled his hand away.

A hushed curse escaped her lips, only to be drowned out by the sound of a sword rasping against a scabbard.

In the time it took her to blink, Rhys stood, swept her from harm's way and pressed the tip of his sword against Guillaume's neck. Lord Ryonne rushed across the now silent hall. "Count Faucon, do not." He motioned to his men. A dozen of them came forward.

Her father would not hesitate to use force against

Rhys. She pushed one of Ryonne's guards out of her way and stood next to Rhys. He said nothing, but the look on his face told her more than words could. Aye, he was angry at Guillaume, but more than anger glimmered in his flecked eyes.

It would take very little for him to ram his sword home. Lyonesse took a steadying breath before laying her hand atop his arm. "Rhys, please."

His attention never wavered from Guillaume's colorless face. "Why? Give me a reason not to remove his miserable tongue from his mouth."

Even though he was taking this a bit too far, she understood his reasoning. She'd take it upon herself to deal with Guillaume, later. First she needed to ensure the fool remained alive long enough.

"You promised King Stephen not to shed Guillaume's blood. Can you remove his tongue without spilling any of his blood on my father's floor?"

The muscles in his arm relaxed beneath her touch. "No, I cannot."

"Then I suppose you might consider sheathing your weapon."

When he lowered the tip of his sword, Ryonne reached out and snatched the weapon from him. First he pointed it at Guillaume. "Take yourself from the hall, but do not leave this keep." He then pointed it at Rhys. "You take yourself outside, and stay there until you cool down."

Lord Ryonne waited until both men left before

motioning at the rest in the hall. "Continue with your meal." When Lyonesse stepped back to the bench, eager to give her quaking legs a rest, he ordered, "Follow me."

She nearly had to run to keep up with his pace as he strode to his chamber. Ryonne waited impatiently at the door, a severe frown creasing his face. She hurried into the room. He slammed the door closed with enough force to knock it from its hinges.

"Have you lost your mind?" His shout bounced off the walls. He tossed Faucon's sword onto a chest. "How could you have let this happen?"

Lyonesse defended herself. "Me? How could I let this happen? I did nothing."

"That was obvious."

"I am not responsible for how the two of them act."

Her father cleared the space between them and stood close enough for her to feel his breath on her face. "Yes, you are."

"How so?"

"Would Faucon be here if not because of you and your foolish pride?"

"Well, no, I suppose not." It was amazing how fast her father could reduce her to a ten-year-old.

"Would du Pree find it necessary to provoke Faucon if not for you?"

"We were only discussing—"

"It matters not what you were discussing. You

could discuss the weather and du Pree would seek a
way to best Faucon."

Again, her father indirectly sought to diminish
Guillaume. Since she herself found Guillaume much
different than the way he used to be, she had to ask,
"What is this change you have had toward
Guillaume?"

Ryonne backed away and walked into the solar.
Lyonesse followed him. "Father, please, I must
know."

"I am not at liberty to say."

"Not at liberty? Only the king could..." She
trailed off. Aye. Only the king could tell her father
to hold his tongue. "My God, Father, what is taking
place? What game are you playing out?"

Suddenly, looking older than his forty-odd years,
Ryonne sat heavily in his chair. "I play no game,
child. I only hold my tongue as ordered."

She dropped to her knees before him. "Then hold
your tongue, but tell me this at least—would you
give your blessings to a marriage between me and
Guillaume?"

He looked away for a moment before running a
hand over her hair. "I will give my blessing to
whichever man you choose."

"Father."

"Lyonesse, please. I can tell you no more."

She rested her forehead on his knee. "Would I be
in danger with the telling?"

"No more danger than you already place yourself in."

She should have known he'd bring the conversation back to the evening meal. "I did not cause that to happen."

"Yes, you did." He waited until she sat up and looked at him. "Child, this is nothing but a choice for you. But for them, it is a challenge. A challenge that neither wants to lose. Each will take every opportunity to belittle the other unless you are wise enough to keep them apart."

Lyonesse laughed softly. "And how do I do that during the meal?"

"I care not how you do it, just see that you do."

"Fine. I will try." Although she had no inkling of how.

"Lyonesse, if Faucon kills du Pree all hell will fall upon Ryonne."

They all worried so much about Faucon's temper. It seemed to her that Guillaume had one of his own. "What if it happens the other way? What if Guillaume kills Faucon?"

Her father was still laughing over that idea when she fled his chamber.

Guillaume paced the confines of the small private chamber he had been allotted. To have been sent to his room like a child was more than he could bear.

This tiny unadorned chamber was no more than a storage closet. This insult would not go unpaid.

How dare Ryonne treat him this way? Did he not realize with whom he dealt?

No. He did not. Someday soon all would know the truth, but not just yet.

In a way, it would be a great relief to enlighten Ryonne. It would be more of a relief to enlighten Ryonne's willful daughter. Maybe then she would show him the respect and obedience he deserved.

He could do nothing until he and Lyonesse were married. The thought twisted his gut. Married to a girl so spoiled that she believed her thoughts mattered. What had Ryonne done to her? It had been his responsibility as her father to see to her upbringing.

Obviously, it would now be up to him as her husband to correct all the mistakes Ryonne had made.

King Stephen was also to blame. It was inconceivable that anyone would give a female a choice in her marriage. He had heard that Stephen was weak and ineffective, but he'd not realized the extent of the king's weakness until now.

Guillaume took a steadying breath. It would work out in the end. He would take it upon himself to correct Stephen's mistakes, too. In truth, Lyonesse had no choice. She would marry him as promised.

He only needed patience for a short while longer. The meal tonight was an error that would not happen again. He would school himself not to goad Faucon further. Just for a few more days. After the wedding night he would be free to be himself and to shape Lyonesse into a proper wife—until he needed her no longer.

Chapter Fourteen

The warm sunshine beating down on the garden did little to lighten Lyonesse's mood. Not even the normally soothing scent from the blooming lavender helped calm her tangled nerves.

King Stephen had given orders for no blood to be shed. Lyonesse thought it a terrible shame. If this lasted much longer, she knew that she would eventually commit a terrible sin by murdering one, or perhaps both, of the men.

The problem lay in deciding which man deserved it more.

Her father had ordered her to keep Rhys and Guillaume apart and she'd tried her best. Creating a lame excuse about wishing to come to know each man better she'd made certain she only shared a meal with one at a time. The rest of the day, she busied herself with chores and ignored both men.

Her plan was simple. She'd have the earlier meal with one and the later meal with another and then switch the order the next day. It wasn't simple. Soon she would need a way to keep track of who she was supposed to be meeting. That, or she'd just quit eating in the hall altogether.

Yesterday, she'd made the mistake of speaking to Faucon while she waited for Guillaume. She'd spent her entire meal explaining why she'd given any of Guillaume's time to Rhys.

Today was just the opposite. The only difference was that while Faucon questioned her about speaking to Guillaume, she'd realized he'd only done so to be a pest. He'd succeeded.

One minute she'd argue with them, the next all was well. It was ridiculous and quickly becoming unbearable.

"They will drive me mad acting like spoiled little children who have yet to decide what they want."

"That is where you are wrong." Rhys hitched his foot up on the end of the bench and leaned forward. "I have always known what I want."

Lyonesse's stomach rolled. How had he snuck up on her? She thought she'd succeeded in training herself to listen and watch for him at every turn. Her skills still needed honing.

She filled her lungs with air and held it a few heartbeats before slowly letting it escape. "Faucon, what do you seek? Are you not joining the other men on a hunt?" She pointed at the wall behind her. "The stables are over there."

He sat down next to her. "No. I decided it would be more entertaining to continue driving you mad."

"It will not take you much longer." Was there anything this man did not overhear? Was there no safe place where she could hide from his ever-present scrutiny?

"What is wrong, Lyonesse?" Faucon leaned forward. "Did you really believe that moments shared over a meal would be enough time spent in my company?" He smiled at her. "How can so few moments be enough for me to win you to wife?" The vision of a bird of prey hovering above its helpless catch flitted across her mind.

"Those few moments provide you plenty of time." Lyonesse returned his perusal and realized her mistake. Did he have to look at her as if he was ready to capture her lips beneath his own? The flutter of countless wings took flight in her stomach. She turned her attention to the stones lining the path. "It matters not. You desire a strumpet to warm your bed, not a wife, Faucon."

"'Tis interesting, the way you are so certain you know what I do or do not want or desire. Is your assumption based on tales, or have you been intimate with enough men to know for certain what a man wants or desires?"

Lyonesse half swallowed her gasp of outrage. Suddenly she knew that neither her mind, nor her emotions were clear enough to be alone with Faucon at this moment. "I...I must go."

Rhys clasped her wrist. "You will stay." His soft words prevented her escape more than his long fingers wrapped gently around her wrist.

"Release me." He shook his head. His eyes sprang to life, nearly twinkling in a way she'd not noticed before. He toyed with her. This was no more than a game and she was the prize. "Please, you do not understand. I cannot be alone with you." All of her earlier determination turned to soft pleading. "Faucon, have mercy. I beg you, let me be."

Rhys looked at her flushed face and shimmering eyes and knew why she wished not to be alone with him. Sometimes it was nigh on impossible to restrain desire, to deny passion. Since he knew the feeling well, he kept his smile to himself. "No, Lyonesse. I cannot let you be."

As if gentling a wild kitten, he stroked her chin. "I will never let you be." He turned her mouth toward his.

Even though it had only been a matter of a few days, it felt like ages since he'd tasted her lips. They'd not been completely alone since the night Guillaume had *miraculously* appeared. Even by the river, her maid had been present. Since then, he'd not seen her except in the crowded hall.

And God help him, as hard as he fought it, he'd missed her.

Rhys slanted his mouth over hers. He'd missed this. The taste of her, the slight hesitation before she succumbed to her own desires with a sigh, the feel of her tongue sweeping across his in an answering caress.

Lyonesse moaned when he threaded his fingers through her hair, tipped her head back and grazed the side of her neck with his lips. Ah, yes, he'd missed feeling her wild pulse beat in unison with his own. He missed her moan, a sound that echoed in his own chest.

With a finesse he possessed only with her, Rhys turned slightly and swept Lyonesse across his lap. She leaned against his chest, drawing one arm around his waist and the other about his neck.

''My maid...''

Her warm, breathless whisper against his ear sent tremors of desire down his spine.

He brushed his mouth back to hers. ''My captain keeps her occupied in the hall.''

Lyonesse tangled her fingers in the hair against his neck. ''How noble of him.''

He stroked her side, deftly loosening the laces of her overgown. Rhys slid his hand beneath the heavier fabric of her gown and brushed his finger across the swell of her breast. The thin linen of her chemise did little to protect her from his touch—or him from the heat of her skin.

His kiss swallowed her gasp. Lyonesse relaxed

against his touch and sought more. Emboldened by her response, he swept his thumb across her breast, pausing to tease and torment her already pebbled nipple.

She leaned into his hand. Blood rushed to his groin. Sweat beaded on his brow. If he didn't stop soon, he'd do something they'd both come to regret.

The king would be present for their wedding ceremony. He would also be present the morning after. He would stand next to Lord Ryonne when the bridal sheets were hung for all to see.

Tongues would wag if no flecks of virgin blood marred those sheets. While blood could be produced at will, Rhys had no wish to humiliate Lyonesse in such a manner.

Desire and passion were new to Lyonesse. He couldn't blame her for something he started. He alone was responsible for controlling this encounter.

Reluctantly, Rhys dragged his mouth from hers. ''Lyonesse.'' He wiped the perspiration from her face and almost drowned in the liquid gaze she turned on him.

Everything about her, from the flush gently tinting her face to her full kiss-swollen lips to the pulse pounding madly against her neck, called him back to her. A call he would answer soon—but not at this moment.

''Lyonesse.'' Gently placing a hand on each side

of her face, he wondered at his own stupidity. "We must stop. Now."

She blinked twice. With each opening of her eyes, he saw passion fade and shame grow.

Lyonesse pushed off his lap and stood facing her herbs and flowers. "I will never understand what you do to me, Faucon."

His ragged laugh seemed to mock him. "I do nothing to you that is not repaid tenfold."

She looked at him over her shoulder. "Then maybe it is best if we are not alone."

"That would be worse." Rhys leaned against a tree planted alongside the bench. "My imagination is much more clever when left to its own devices."

Lyonesse turned to face him. "What will your *imagination* do if I wed Guillaume?"

He seethed at the image of her in Guillaume's arms. His rage grew as a vision of them entwined about each other in bed hammered inside his mind. No. He pushed those thoughts aside, refusing to rise to her senseless baiting. "That is nothing I need worry about."

"You are very certain of yourself." At his silence, she asked, "Why did you come out here? Should you not be with the other men?" She lifted one tawny brow. "Even though my maid is occupied, will not my father come looking for you?"

"No. He swore to keep Guillaume out hunting with the others for the length of the afternoon."

''Is there anything you cannot arrange to your advantage?''

Rhys closed his eyes and settled himself more comfortably along the length of the bench. ''Nothing I can think of.''

He heard the whisper of fabric brush across the stone path as she started to walk past him. Without opening his eyes, he reached out and snagged a handful of her gown. ''Sit down.''

She sat on the ground next to the bench. ''What do you seek, Rhys?''

Shock nearly stopped his heart. Not only had she taken a seat without arguing, she'd used his first name and they didn't even have their hands or lips on each other. Did he dare hope she was softening toward him?

''I only desired to talk before I left on the morrow.''

''Left?''

''Fret not. I will be gone only a day. It will give you and Guillaume a chance for privacy.''

''What are you up to?''

He laughed at the suspicious tone of her voice. ''The men I sent to track the impostor have arrived with news.''

''They found him?''

''Unfortunately, no. But they tracked him to this area and I wish to take a look around myself.''

"At Ryonne?" She gasped. "But my father is out hunting in this area."

Rhys looked down at her. Lyonesse's face had gone pale, her eyes widened. He gently grasped her hand. "He is safe, Lyonesse. Between the men I sent with him and his own, there is little that can bring him harm."

"I thank you." She brought her knees up and rested her chin on top of them.

He released her hand. "I would have thought your first concern would have been for Guillaume, not your father."

"My sire is very dear to me."

"But I thought you loved du Pree so much."

"I will not discuss Guillaume with you. It is unseemly."

"Since you will soon be my wife, I don't find it unseemly."

"You presume much, Faucon."

Ah, that was more normal—they were back to *Faucon*. He looked down at her. "Do you love him?"

Lyonesse closed her eyes for a moment before gazing up at the man lounging so near her. He looked tired. There were dark circles under his eyes. His overlong hair fell across one side of his face.

Without thinking, she reached up and brushed it back. He held her hand to his cheek for a moment before again asking, "Do you love him, Lyonesse?"

His cheek was warm beneath her touch. The slight hint of a beard grazed her hand as she slowly drew it back. ''I am not certain.''

Faucon lifted her chin with the side of his hand. ''Not long ago you sought to kill for the mere memory of him. You were willing to condemn your soul for revenge.''

''I know.'' She tipped her head away from his touch and looked at him. ''What would you do if I had said yes?''

He shrugged. ''You will be my wife regardless of where your heart is involved.''

''You wouldn't care?'' He couldn't possibly mean that.

''No. Why should I?''

''But—''

''But what, Lyonesse? Do you think this love you profess to need has any meaning? Do you think it will make a difference in your marriage? Will love protect Taniere? Will love keep your people safe? Will love put food on your table and clothes on your back? Will love keep the roof over your head?''

His voice was too tight. For someone who controlled himself well, there was far too much anger in his tone. Something was not right. She took in the fierce expression on his face and gazed into his eyes. There it was again. The same thing she'd seen the first day when she'd captured him. Pain. Loss.

Both emotions had been mirrored in his eyes and she'd been certain she'd only imagined it.

She'd been wrong. What could have put such pain in the heart of so strong a warrior?

Lyonesse came up on her knees before him. She laid a palm against his cheek again and stroked her thumb across his lips. ''What do you think love is? Have you never loved anything or anyone in your life? Does not your family love you? Do you not return that feeling?''

''I honor my family. I respect them. I care for them.''

''Is that not love?''

''I am not talking about family. I am speaking of a wasted emotion between a husband and a wife.''

''Are not a husband and a wife family? How can any feelings between them be wasted?'' She frowned at his logic.

When he sought to turn away from her touch, she followed him with her hand and drew him back to face her. ''Rhys, is there anyone you have ever loved?''

Every muscle in his body tightened. When he started to rise, Lyonesse slipped her hand around to the back of his neck and raked her fingers into his hair. ''Rhys, sit back down.''

She wanted to laugh when he did so without arguing. ''If I am to consider becoming your wife, I will not have this between us. What makes you so certain love is a wasted emotion?''

He glared at her. ''There is no considering. You will be my wife.''

He thought to goad her? ''Do not change the subject. Answer me.''

''I do not answer to you.''

It was all she could do to not press her fingernails into his scalp. ''Count Rhys of Faucon, need I remind you that I captured and held the Mighty Falcon in my tower? You no longer frighten me with your fierce looks or nasty tone. So save them for someone much weaker than I.''

For a moment, when the muscles in his face tightened to remind her of stone, she thought she'd gone too far. This must be the look that froze men in their tracks. Lyonesse thanked the Lord that she wasn't a man.

Even so, after all that had passed between the two of them, all the things that he'd said to her, all the times that he kissed her senseless, she knew he'd not harm her. She'd not lied, she was not afraid of him. She held her ground and kept her stare pinned on his.

Finally, after what felt like hours, he relaxed. Then he laughed at her. ''Lyonesse, you can be a wench at times.''

''I have gained much experience at it of late.''

She playfully tugged his hair before standing up. "Walk with me."

They strolled down the garden's narrow path, pausing every now and then to inspect this plant, or that herb. An odd thrill rippled through her every time his arm brushed hers, or her hip grazed his thigh.

Lyonesse could not deny the physical sensations this man had created in her from the first moment she beheld him. Even trussed like a deer ready for slaughter, she'd been awed by his strength and looks. And when she'd tended his wounds, she'd not been able to ignore the heat of his flesh, nor the warmth that had flowed through her fingertips and into her blood.

She could not deny the sinful feelings he aroused in her. But surely it took more than desire or lust to make a marriage satisfying. She knew without a doubt that Faucon was a passionate man. Whether seeking justice or upholding honor, he was passionate in his endeavors. If he cared enough about his quests to fulfill them in such a manner, why could he not have the same degree of passion, or caring for a wife?

Unable to contain her curiosity any longer, Lyonesse asked what she knew to be a dangerous question. "Did you care for your wife and child? Did you honor or respect them?"

She expected him to rage at her, or walk away.

Instead, after a few moments of silence, he turned and placed his hands upon her shoulders.

Pain was clearly etched on every inch of his face. It was evident in the lines grooving his forehead, in the way his brows were drawn together, in the tightness surrounding his mouth and in the flat, unemotional color of his eyes.

She wanted to take back her question. But more than that, she wanted to take away the pain from his heart.

''I did not kill my wife.''

Lyonesse touched his cheek, drawing back her hand when he turned his face away from her touch. ''I have come to believe that much on my own.''

''Nor did I kill her child.''

''*Her* child?''

He hesitated. Lyonesse studied him and saw the pain that wracked him. After filling his chest with air, he answered, ''Aye. The babe who died in her arms was not mine.''

''You cannot know that for a certainty.''

''That was what I thought at first, too. Alyce insisted that she'd always kept my seed from taking and until I gazed upon her child, I did not believe her.''

Lyonesse had seen newborns. They were red, wrinkled and resembled their parents not at all. ''Rhys, 'tis common for a newborn to not look like its parents.''

"Suffice it to say that this child could not have been borne of my loins."

"You believed this child was not yours and you did not kill her?" That amazed Lyonesse. How many other men would have borne that humiliation and shame without bringing some type of horrendous end to the woman's life? No wonder he thought love a wasted emotion. If he had felt anything for his wife, it had more than likely died along with her.

Rhys swallowed the memory of Alyce's death. He tucked it back behind the chains from whence it had escaped. He stepped back from Lyonesse, and from the pain that still chased him.

"How did she die?"

It took a few moments before he was able to get any words past the growing lump in his throat. "She jumped from the tower with the babe in her arms."

"How could she do such a thing? To kill an innocent child as well as herself? Why?"

Rhys turned away. "Enough, Lyonesse. Enough." Countless whys and why-nots chased him nearly every day. The answer was always the same and he could do nothing to change it. Why? Because he'd been foolish enough to care deeply for Alyce— to love her—and she'd hated the very sight of him. He'd given her his heart, his soul and she'd humiliated him and then taken his heart and soul to her grave.

It would never happen again.

He looked into Lyonesse's eyes and saw all the questions running through her mind. But he'd not give her the answers. "Why, Lyonesse? I know not why. Do you think I haven't asked myself that same thing over and over? There are no answers. The only person who could have provided them is dead."

Confusion marred her face. "I do not understand."

"There is nothing to understand." He slid his hand up her neck and pulled her closer. She came into his arms willingly. "It is the past and it is dead. Let it remain that way."

Her heart beat steady against his chest. Her breath warmed his neck. She smelled of fresh air and sunshine. Her nearness, just the very scent of her, chipped steadily away at the chains he'd secured around his heart.

He kissed her forehead and held her slightly away from him. "Lyonesse, I must go. I need to find the impostor. I have not the time to waste here with you."

"I know." She kissed his chin. "However, that is not exactly the way to win my hand."

"If you are looking for pretty words and kind deeds, you need seek them from Guillaume. I have none to offer."

She pulled out of his hold and graced him with an accusing glare. "So be it. Maybe I will. Maybe by the time you return Guillaume will have filled my head with so many pretty words that I'll forget who you are.''

She only teased him, so he humored her. ''If that is your best attempt to make me jealous, you need find another way.''

''I have no need to make you jealous.'' She crossed her arms in front of her and raised one eyebrow. ''Remember, the choice is mine. You cannot force me into a marriage with you.''

Rhys laughed before he pulled her against him. ''I may have no pretty words or kind deeds. But I will protect you, support you, care for your keep, your people and you.''

He passed his lips briefly across hers. ''I will warm you by day and set you afire at night.'' He stroked his thumb along the side of her neck until she trembled beneath his touch.

Rhys lifted her chin and stared down into her now liquid gaze. ''Always, will I keep you safe.''

He lowered his mouth to hers, quickly coaxing an answering response from her lips.

Chapter Fifteen

Lyonesse wiped her hands on the skirt of her gown. After Rhys had left, she'd thought to quell her riotous thoughts by weeding.

It hadn't worked. She still felt stretched as tightly as a readied bowstring. What was wrong with her? Each time Faucon left her senses, her muscles, her very body quivering in anticipation of their next meeting.

She wanted more than just his caresses and stolen kisses. She wanted— *Cease!* If her thoughts kept up in this manner she'd go mad by the end of the day.

The sound of the men returning from the hunt drew her from her self-inflicted torture. She left the garden, hoping for something to divert her wayward mind.

Lyonesse stood in the bailey and wished she'd stayed in the garden. Yes, the men had returned from the hunt. Instead of a boisterous, self-satisfied lot, they reminded her of a group of overtired men returning from a battle lost.

She found Guillaume. He was the only one who appeared to be pleased with his work this day.

''Lyonesse.'' He hailed her from across the bailey. ''Come, see what I have provided for your table.''

She had seen it. And the sight of the boar surprised her. She hunted regularly, but she'd never attempted to kill a boar. That was usually an event, lauded by celebration. Yet the rest of the men unsaddling their horses were too quiet and subdued.

Guillaume approached, seeking to draw her forward. ''Come. See what will grace your table in the days ahead.''

His touch left her cold. She darted away, asking, ''Where is my father?''

He grabbed her arm. ''Do not walk away from me.'' His snarl was menacing. '''Tis time you seek out your husband first, not your father.''

''Husband?'' She turned on him. ''I have no husband. The decision is still mine to make.''

Guillaume laughed at her. But the tone, the look on his face held no humor. ''You will do as your father orders.''

''Perhaps.'' She was not about to argue with him in company of all these men. ''But he has issued no orders concerning you or Faucon.''

''He should not need to.'' Guillaume lowered his voice. ''You swore a vow to me and I know that you will not dishonor yourself, or your father.''

There was the rub. She had sworn a vow. Before God and Ryonne's clergy, she'd promised him her future.

He touched her cheek. ''You have known your place for your whole life, Lyonesse. You will be mine.''

Many times he'd said those very words to her. Until today, this moment, they'd not caused her chest to tighten, or her head to pound. Why now? The words were the same, but the man wasn't, nor were her feelings toward him.

Guillaume lifted her chin with the side of his hand. ''You have nothing to say? Not so very long ago you would have smiled at me and told me how you could not wait for that day to come.''

He told her nothing that she did not already know.

He grasped her chin between his thumb and forefinger. ''What has changed, Lyonesse?''

''Nothing.'' She tried to jerk away from his hold, but he held her fast.

''What have you done?''

Her heart beat faster. She glanced away. ''I have done nothing.''

''Look at me.'' Guillaume stared into her eyes. ''You lie.''

His anger grew unchecked. Rage burned across his face. He raised his hand. ''Why, you—''

''Du Pree.'' Her father rushed forward. ''Touch her and I will kill you.''

Guillaume lowered his hand and released her. A odd look covered his rage. ''Forgive me. I know not what came over me.'' He lifted a shaking hand to his temples. ''It must still be the effects of my ordeal. I can think of no other explanation for this unbidden madness that overtakes me.''

Ryonne frowned, but he said nothing.

How much of Guillaume's explanation was true? While she believed that there were lingering moments when he might be exhausted, or upset from his ordeal, she was not certain it caused the rage that jumped so quickly to his usually mild temper.

She touched his arm, seeking to calm him. ''Let us forget this. Perhaps you would find restoration in a small nap.''

His smile was one-sided. ''I will take your wise advice.'' He reached out and stroked her cheek with one finger. ''I will see you this evening?''

Lyonesse nodded. ''Yes, I will await you at the table.''

She waited until he entered the keep before turning to her father. ''What happened?''

Ryonne dragged a hand down his face before placing it on her shoulder. Lyonesse noticed how it shook. What *had* happened on what was supposed to be a routine hunt?

''It was my fault.''

''What was your fault, Father?''

''He killed one of your men.'' Her father's near whisper shook nearly as much as his hand.

''Who? Which man?''

''One of the boys.''

Lyonesse gasped. She wanted to rant and rave, but she'd not seen her father this upset since her mother's death. After filling her lungs with air, in an attempt to calm her rushing worries, she prompted her sire. ''Please, explain.''

''Guillaume quizzed me about Faucon and when I'd had enough, I told him about the last time Rhys and I had taken down a boar.''

She knew where this part of the story was heading, but she remained silent and let him continue.

''It became mandatory that du Pree best Faucon.'' He paused as if looking for the right words. ''I told him we were not equipped to hunt boar. There were no dogs to confuse and distract the beast. There were no huntsmen to oversee the kill.''

''But he would not listen.''

''No. He was determined to prove that he is better than Faucon in all ways.'' Ryonne took a ragged breath. ''Unfortunately, he found what he sought. His first attempt at killing the animal only enraged it. The crazed beast charged the nearest horse, unseating the stable lad.''

Lyonesse groaned. ''Oh, no, not Simon.''

With a shake of his head, Ryonne confirmed her

fears. "The boar charged and Simon could not rise quick enough. The tusks ripped his throat."

She swallowed hard to hold back the bile threatening to choke her. She'd promised Simon that if he worked hard and learned his job well that one day he would be Taniere's stable master. The man she'd hired for that position had already begun training the boy and said he showed promise.

"I am so sorry, Lyonesse."

She thought for a moment that her father was going to cry along with her. She glanced back at the men still milling about the bailey and bit her lip to keep from sobbing aloud when they lifted Simon's body off the back of a horse.

"Oh, Father." Lyonesse rested her head on his shoulder. "What are we going to do?"

"We are not going to do anything. You, however, need make a decision, and do it quickly."

She shook her head, brushing her cheek against the rough wool of his tunic. "I know not how to choose."

Ryonne pulled her away from his shoulder. His eyes glimmered moist with worry and concern. "Child, as much as I want to, I swore to Stephen I would not sway your mind one way or the other. As the mistress of Taniere, you will be in control of a strategic keep. He wants to see how you choose. He wants to see how wise you are. I cannot break my oath to him."

She hung her head. "If oaths cannot be broken, then my choice is made for me." Her heart broke into a million pieces. She choked back a sob. "I made no oath, no vow, no promise to Faucon."

Her father shook her gently. "Lyonesse, I told you to ignore, to forget anything you knew about either man. That includes any promises, any vows made. You are freed from them."

"But—"

"Nay. There are no buts. The king has already stated that what I say is true. Forget the past. Think, Lyonesse. What will be best for Taniere? What will be best for your children?"

"What about me?"

Ryonne lifted her chin with his forefinger. He silently stared into her eyes. Finally, he smiled. "Think with your heart and you will be fine."

The noise in the crowded hall was deafening. Whispers about Guillaume's deed earlier in the day had grown in volume.

Lyonesse waited for him to join her for the evening meal. How would he take to being called a braggart and a fool for allowing a lad to be killed? How would he react to the opinion that he was dangerous, not only to himself, but to others?

She tapped her fingers on the table. There was no need to wonder, she knew he'd not be happy.

What she'd already thought was going to be a

long night, it now appeared would be even longer. She glanced at Faucon. Along with raising his goblet, he raised one eyebrow.

It would take just a simple twitch of one finger, or a slight nod to bring him to her side. She could not do that.

She did need to make her choice—quickly. This night she wished to dine with Guillaume. She wanted to spend some time with him, talking, without having vows made in the past a consideration.

Now that she knew those promises were null, would she feel differently? Would she find herself wanting to be with him instead of feeling as if she had to do so? She doubted it.

Her father had said to think with her heart. Lyonesse wondered if that were truly the best option.

Regardless of what she wanted, she could not forget Taniere or the responsibilities her husband would assume once they were married.

Who would be the better choice? Faucon, with his vile reputation? She wanted to laugh. The Evil Faucon. The Mighty Falcon. How did he ever get those names? How did he get that reputation?

At times it seemed as if the Faucon she knew and the one talked about in tales were two different men. Perhaps someday she'd discover what lay behind what was nothing more than a cleverly affected mask.

But not everyone knew his guise was nothing

more than rumors. Would it keep others from attacking her keep, or would it draw those who wished to prove their mettle? Something to consider.

Guillaume, who had never taken over the responsibility of tending a keep or the land. He had left all in the hands of his deceased father's steward and paid scant attention to the people or his land. Would he pick up the reins of those tasks at Taniere, or would he think himself above them? And what of this temper he'd returned with? Would it mellow as his memories of his ordeal grew more distant, or would it remain?

Think with her heart. Easier said than done.

The hall suddenly quieted—Guillaume had finally arrived. He sat down heavily on the bench beside her. When he turned to bid her greeting, Lyonesse nearly fainted from the smell of wine on his breath.

It was impossible to hold back her displeasure. ''I see you have been imbibing since we last met.''

Guillaume lifted his already filled goblet. ''Aye. And I fully intend to drink this night away.''

''Why, Guillaume? Why would you do this?''

'''Tis simple. I am trying to forget my days away from you. I am seeking to drink away the pain of putting you through this wasted challenge.'' He held his cup out toward the chamber. ''I am trying to drown the fact that those gathered here are jealous of what I have.'' He looked back at her before tipping his cup toward Faucon. ''And of what I will have.''

Lyonesse sighed. ''You are feeling sorry for yourself.''

''Have I not the right?'' He snatched a wine jug from a serving wench. After refilling his cup, he set it on the table before him. ''I am forced to compete with a man unworthy of you. 'Tis beneath me. 'Tis beneath you to even consider another.''

''Beneath me?''

''Yes.'' He shook his head. ''Beneath you. Far, far beneath you.''

Her disappointment built fire. ''Guillaume, either make sense, or leave.''

''It is unworthy of you to lust so after a man who wants nothing more than Taniere.'' He polished off the contents of his cup and wiped his sleeve across his mouth. ''Especially when you know how much I love and worship you.''

Would he remember this nonsense in the morning?

He leaned close. His breath burned against her neck. ''I can make you lust for me, too.''

Lyonesse leaned away from him. ''What is wrong with you? What has changed you so? You are not the man I remember.''

He stopped her escape with a hand at her back. From the direction where her father and Rhys sat,

Lyonesse heard a bench scrape across the floor. Hopefully one of them was coming to her aid.

''What has changed me?'' Guillaume stroked her neck with his thumb. ''Nothing. 'Tis you who have changed.''

Faucon left the hall. Panic assaulted her. Lyonesse tried to push Guillaume away. ''Stop. Everyone is watching.''

He stared at the nearby diners until they all looked the other way. Then he turned back to Lyonesse. ''See, they care not that we share an intimate moment or two.''

''Guillaume, please.''

He wrapped his hand around the back of her neck. ''Fear not, my love, your father will not permit me to tup you here in the hall.''

Lyonesse fought to control herself. She wanted nothing more than to slap his face. But she would not debase herself in public in that manner. He was right. Her father would not permit him to go too far. But just how far was too far?

Guillaume kissed her cheek. His wet touch did little more than make her stomach churn with disgust. ''You see, Lyonesse, I was to be the one who brought you to the doors of passion. Not another.''

Guilt trickled down her spine. ''There has been no other.''

His hold tightened. ''Do not lie to me. I see the way you look at Faucon. I see your eyes glisten, your lips pout, and your breathing become heavy. I see the desire for him written all over you.''

She'd admit nothing to him. ''You are wrong. You know me better than that.''

''No. I thought I did. But, no. I am not wrong, Lyonesse. Do not seek to start our lives out with lies. Just admit what you feel and I will forgive you.''

''You will forgive me?''

''Yes, and then I will make you forget him.''

She would never forget Faucon. Not as long as she lived. Nor did she require forgiveness from Guillaume for anything.

He trailed his tongue across her jawbone, stopping at her mouth. ''Someone other than I taught you how to kiss like a whore. It had to have been Faucon. Just admit it, Lyonesse. You will feel better for the confession.''

She clenched her jaw. Confession was for the priest, not for some drunken fool. She put her hands against his chest and pushed.

To her complete amazement, he nearly flew away from her. In less than a blink she realized her father had finally had enough.

He pulled Guillaume from the bench. ''What are you doing?''

Guillaume shrugged. ''I was having an intimate moment with my betrothed.''

Ryonne made a face. ''You are in your cups.'' He

pushed Guillaume away from the table. "Go sleep it off."

Guillaume swayed on his feet. Reaching around Ryonne he grabbed the wine pitcher from the table. "Old man, tell me not what to do."

Lyonesse's father drew himself to full height and placed his hand on the pommel of his sword. "Leave my hall. Now."

With a shuffling of benches, Ryonne's men rose as one.

Guillaume nodded at Lyonesse. "I will see you later."

Relief swept through her when he left the hall. Yet another consideration was added to her list. If she chose Guillaume, she'd have to ensure that Taniere had no stores of wine or ale.

Ryonne placed a hand on her shoulder. "You are all right? He did not hurt you?"

"I am fine." She looked up at his worry-creased face. "Do me a favor, though. The next time, be not as long to rescue me."

Lyonesse leaned away from her seat against the wall. After the meal, they'd cleared the floor, placing the benches along the walls for groups of people to hold conversations, or play games of chance.

The warmth of the hall brought fatigue, but before seeking her bed for the night, Lyonesse needed to go over the next day's meals with the cook. She took a lit torch off the wall sconce and headed toward the long hall that connected the kitchens with the keep. It was an extravagance her father had recently built after returning from a mission in France.

The serving girls and the cook enjoyed the shelter it provided, but Lyonesse found it a nuisance. The sound of a slap and a frightened cry reminded her why.

Too often this long, dark hallway was used for other than its intended purpose. She'd lost count of the times she'd bumped into couples embracing along the wall, or tripped over those on the floor who had taken their affections a little further.

Another cry shot through the dark. Lyonesse quickened her steps. That cry was not one of passion. Someone had either become frightened and changed their mind, or did not wish to be in this situation in the first place.

"No. No, please do not."

The echo of a slap reached Lyonesse's ears. Then the sound of tearing fabric made her hurry all the more.

Torchlight illuminated two figures grappling on the floor. Lyonesse rushed forward. "Stop this!"

The man batted at her without looking up. His head was near buried in the nook between the girl's neck and shoulder, and her long, unbound hair half covered him.

Frantic, frightened cries from the girl prompted

Lyonesse to grab the man's tunic at the neck and pull him off his unwilling partner.

He came up in a rage. "Bitch! Leave us be."

Lyonesse stared in shock at Guillaume. He was so drunk with wine and lust he didn't realize who he was shouting at.

The girl scrambled to her knees, grasping at the tattered remnants of her torn gown. Lyonesse motioned the girl to leave. She didn't have to motion twice.

She jerked back to Guillaume. "Who do you think you are? How dare you torment my father's servants in this manner." She swung her free hand at him, gasping when he caught her wrist.

"I know who I am and I will treat a servant in the manner befitting their station." The whites of his eyes were nearly bloody. He smiled in recognition. "Ah, beloved. You have come to take her place. How gracious of you."

Lyonesse backed away. "Keep away from me. Take yourself to bed, Guillaume, as my father ordered and go sleep it off."

"Bah." He swung his hand at empty air. "Your father can command someone else. I'll not listen." He snagged the front of her gown and pulled her toward him. "I have other things to attend to at this moment."

Fear lent strength to her swing. She brought the

torch down on the top of his head. When he released her and fell to the floor, Lyonesse ran.

Millions of stars dotted the night sky. Rhys leaned against the tower wall, staring at the twinkling pinpoints of light.

He should be abed, resting for tomorrow's journey. Too many thoughts had kept him awake.

Far too many decisions to make and things to think about. He was not used to dwelling, or thinking on problems. He was used to seeking solutions and acting upon them.

This inactivity would drive him mad. He laughed softly to himself. Who was he fooling? It was not the inactivity that set his blood frantically racing through his veins making sleep impossible.

Lyonesse invaded his thoughts, coming to him clad only in flowing red-gold hair and a seductive smile.

He envisioned her in his arms. Her firm, silken limbs clung to him, held him close. Red, kiss-swollen lips met his, caress for caress. Her passion-laden voice breathlessly urged him on, beckoned him to end the teasing, to feed the hunger he had created.

Her soft gasps brushed against his ear, sending flashes of fire and ice down his spine. Luminescent emerald eyes glistened with desire. She drew him closer, stroking his back with a velvet touch, raking her nails down his thighs.

He breathed in the scents of lavender, wood smoke and woman. The aromas melded, intoxicating him with growing passion.

Those were the thoughts keeping him awake.

Those and visions of du Pree leaning close to her, kissing her, touching her, sent Rhys outside for air to cool his growing rage.

He had been so certain that he would easily turn Lyonesse's thoughts from Guillaume to himself. Had he been wrong? Did she still care so for the man that she would permit him to drunkenly make a spectacle of himself and her?

What would she do when she discovered that Guillaume was not whom he claimed to be?

Rhys rested his forehead against the cool stone. Melwyn had stumbled upon that revelation by accident and brought the information to Rhys. While everything the men had discovered, and everything he and Melwyn deduced pointed to du Pree, Rhys needed proof before he voiced his concerns to Ryonne and King Stephen.

He would find that proof one way or another. But would it be too late? Would Lyonesse feel honor bound to the man she'd promised to marry long ago?

If he spoke too soon it would appear he was fabricating tales to entice her to choose him. He wanted her to choose of her own free will. He wanted her to come to him willingly, without regrets or feelings of obligation.

He bounced his head against the wall. Hell, right now he just wanted her to come to him.

That wanting made him sick at heart. What had he done? When had she slipped past his barriers? He could think of no one event that had given her entrance. There'd been no great moment of revelation.

It had to have been a combination of many things. Although the desire and passion were welcome and brought great pleasure to his ego, it was more than just desire and passion.

She was brave. Braver than many men he knew. She'd proven that many times over. Each time she'd stood up to him, she'd unwittingly shown her strength.

She was a woman who knew what honor was. He knew barons and earls who did not care for their lands, or their people as she did.

This was not a woman who would use wiles or deceit to gain what she wanted. She used her mind. Lyonesse thought out her tasks and then set her plans into motion. There were commanders who could take a lesson from her.

Little by little these things must have seeped in and built upon each other. Now the problem lay in not letting her know how he felt. The knowledge would give her far too much power over him.

Rhys turned at the sound of the tower door slamming against the wall. He tossed the corner of his mantle over one shoulder, jerked his sword from his scabbard and prepared to defend himself.

''Oh, Rhys!''

He took one look at Lyonesse's ravaged face and let his sword clatter to the wallwalk. There would be no defense against the anguish etched on her features.

She rushed into his open arms, crying, ''Marry me. Tonight. Marry me and take me away from here. Take me home, to Taniere.''

Chapter Sixteen

When he'd wanted her to come to him willingly, this was not what Rhys had in mind. He stroked her hair and held her to his chest, whispering words of comfort. "You are safe now. Hush, Lyonesse. Tell me what has upset you so."

Tremors shook her. He'd seen her in an array of emotions from enraged to passionate, but never had he witnessed the misery that wrapped about her now. More than anger and fear trampled her spirit. As if someone had stolen her hopes and dreams—broken her heart.

Du Pree.

Fury blinded him. It stoked his blood and swept through his veins like a fire gone wild. He clenched his jaw to keep back his curses. He tightened the muscles of his body to keep from going after the knave. Du Pree could wait.

Lyonesse could not.

He led her to an empty guard's room, a small chamber cut into the wall. Here, neither the wind nor prying eyes would find them. The window open-ing faced the bailey and only the light from the near-full moon could bear witness against them.

He released her trembling body long enough to sit down on the floor and pull her onto his lap. She came easily. Too easily. She leaned against his chest without words of protest or even the feeblest of struggles.

Rhys held her close, bathed in the light of the moon, wrapped in the warmth of his mantle and safe in the circle of his arms. He waited until her sobs lessened before again asking, ''Lyonesse, what has happened?''

'''Tis Guillaume.'' Fresh tears welled in her eyes. Tears she snuffled back with a quavering breath be-fore asking, ''What has happened to him? I know not who he has become.'' She buried her face in Rhys's shoulder. ''He was never so cruel, never so vile. I hate him.''

Rhys closed his eyes against the options open to him at this moment. Options that would change his life forever. For better or for worse.

Only God knew how much he wanted this woman. But he'd never be able to live with himself if he used this moment to coerce her.

He stroked her hair, letting the escaped tendrils curl around his fingers, tucking them back into her haphazard braid. ''Lyonesse, you do not hate him.'' He chose his words carefully, not wanting to defend du Pree, but also not wanting to divulge his own hatred for the man. "Surely you realize he was intoxicated? Did he act rashly? I make no excuse for his stupidity, but was he perhaps not in complete control of his actions?"

Lyonesse's muffled response was lost in the folds of his cloak. He caressed the line of her chin before tipping her face away from his shoulder. "Lyonesse?"

The look she turned upon him took his breath away. Aye, she hated du Pree. Her eyes glimmered with a hatred more strong than the one he'd first witnessed the day she'd captured him. What had du Pree done to earn such an emotion from her?

"Aye, he was well under the wine's influence. So much so that he attacked one of my father's maids. When I sought to free the girl, he turned on me." Her voice broke. "He thought to attack the person he seeks to wed."

Rhys's heart catapulted against his chest. The man would die. "Are you injured?" He held her away, looking for signs of harm.

"No." Lyonesse grasped his hands. "I am fine. I hit his head with a torch and ran away."

"Good." He smiled briefly before becoming serious once more. "You are certain you were not harmed?"

She rested her cheek against his shoulder. "I am

certain.'' A shuddering breath escaped her lips. ''Only my heart is injured.''

''See what this love you profess to desire brings? If you did not care for du Pree so much, his actions this night would not have upset you so much.'' Why did the logic he'd employed since Alyce's death suddenly seem wrong to him?

Lyonesse kissed his neck. ''Just because Guillaume is a fool, does not mean I no longer desire love.''

He tried to ignore her mouth against his flesh. But her soft lips and warm breath acted like kindling on a fire.

She ripped the shoulder clasp holding his mantle in place out. The pin fell to the floor. Frantically tearing at his cloak, she swept it aside and ran one hand across his shoulder. ''Rhys, marry me. Take me home.''

''Perhaps I will.'' He'd always known he would, but not just yet.

''Now. Tonight.'' Lyonesse brushed her thumb along his neck, across his ear, finally threading her fingers through his hair. ''Tonight.'' She whispered against his lips before teasing them with the tip of her tongue.

''Why tonight?'' Rhys fought to ignore the blood rushing to his groin.

She turned in his arms, pressing her breasts against his chest. ''I need you tonight.'' She slanted her mouth over his, kissing him with an intensity that would not be denied.

It was all he could do not to take the lead. If she wanted to be the seducer, so be it. But how long would he be able to keep his own desires in check?

Lyonesse broke her persuasive caress. ''Hold me. You need not love me with your heart, but please love me with your body.''

Rhys groaned. ''Lyonesse, why are you doing this?'' He wrapped his arms about her and held her tightly.

''I don't know,'' she admitted in a voice as raspy as his own. ''I need to feel you, to taste you. I need you. Now.''

In a hoarse plea, Rhys whispered, ''Oh, God, help me.'' Before he pulled her to the floor beneath him.

She was certain her heart would burst from its frantic pace inside her chest. She wanted this. She wanted him. Lyonesse wanted to be held by someone who desired her. More than anything else, she wanted him to banish the memory of Guillaume's drunken attack from her mind, and from her heart. She wanted—needed—someone who, even though he'd not admit it, cared for her to hold her, to kiss her and to love her.

Her heart and her mind finally agreed that Rhys was that someone. Though the words would never leave his lips, he cared for her—he had to. She could see it in his eyes, feel in his touch, and taste it on his lips.

''Lyonesse.'' He rose up on his elbows and looked down at her. The golden flecks in his eyes sparkled like the countless stars in the sky. He brushed his fingers across her cheeks. ''Are you certain?''

To her amazement, her hand shook as she reached up to touch his face. But her voice was steady, her heart more than certain. ''Yes.'' She slipped her hand behind his neck and pulled him back down to her. ''Yes. I am certain.''

When he gathered her close in his strong arms, she felt safe. Secure in the knowledge that he would not harm her, would not frighten her. And when he deepened his kiss, she did not hesitate to respond in kind.

He held her tightly and rolled onto his back. She rested atop him. She could feel his heart beat against her own. The hard length of his erection pressed against her stomach. What had been a gentle, but insistent thrumming between her thighs, now flared to a heavy beat.

Lyonesse moved against him, seeking to ease the need.

His lips on hers stilled. He opened his eyes and broke their kiss.

She clutched at his shoulders. ''No. Do not stop.''

She sounded like the whore Guillaume had called her, but she cared not. "Please, Rhys."

"Lyonesse, I cannot. We cannot." He sounded surprised and when she gazed down at him, she saw the confusion etched plainly on his face. He shook his head. "Not like this. Not until you bear my name. Not before our vows are blessed."

"Then marry me tonight." She nearly shouted at him in frustration.

A smile curved his lips. He brushed stray strands of hair from her damp face. "If you can summon the king, awaken your father and find a priest, I will."

She glared at him and snapped, "This is a fine time for the Evil Faucon to start acting like a noble knight." When the shrill tone of her own voice reached her ears, Lyonesse's shame cooled her blood. She apologized. "You did not deserve that. I am sorry." She pushed off him and walked to the window. "I sound like the whore Guillaume accuses me of being."

"Du Pree is an imbecile. You are no whore."

She agreed that Guillaume no longer behaved sanely, but she had to admit, "I have acted as a whore would."

"Do not speak so, Lyonesse. Come back here."

"No." Now that this insatiable need was almost tamed, returning to his side was the last thing she wanted to do. "I cannot."

Lyonesse heard his boots scrape across the floor. She turned to look at him. Rhys sat with his back against the wall, holding out his hand. ''You will come back here and sit down. Of your own free will, or by mine, I care not.''

Nothing in his tone hinted at his mood. No emotion crossed his face. That was her warning. She walked back to his side, took his hand and sat down.

Rhys draped his arm about her shoulders and pulled her closer. ''You will not die from longing.''

''I am not so certain of that.''

He hugged her tight for a moment. ''What will you do about du Pree?''

Lyonesse had no wish to discuss Guillaume. She wasn't certain she could do so without crying again. But when she tried to move away, Rhys hooked a leg over hers, holding her next to him. ''Answer me, Lyonesse. What will you do?''

''I don't know.'' She picked at imaginary dust specks on her gown. ''I will not marry him.'' Her breath nearly choked her. ''Never.''

Rhys covered her fidgeting hands with one of his own. ''He was sotted. Will you not at least talk to him when his mind is clear? Perhaps he can explain.''

Lyonesse's heart froze. She looked at him. ''Do you want me to marry Guillaume?''

Did he want her to marry du Pree? Not in this lifetime or even the next. But Rhys had to be sure she wasn't going to change her mind. "No, Lyonesse, I do not want you to marry du Pree. But you must marry when Stephen returns."

She pulled her hands out from beneath his and touched his cheek. Her fingers were gentle against his skin. "You have told me repeatedly that I would be your wife. Have you changed your mind?"

He pulled her hand to his lips and kissed her fingertips. "And every time I made that claim, you dismissed it as little more than a ploy for revenge."

"The night of our betrothal, I told you I would accept you as my husband."

"Yes, but then du Pree returned. I could not hold you to that vow."

She shook her head adamantly. "I will marry no one else but you."

"Why?" He slipped his hand along her neck. "Why now? To escape du Pree?"

A look of confusion chased across her features. "Is that what you think?"

"What else am I to think?"

Lyonesse worried her bottom lip with her teeth. She frowned at him before looking away.

Rhys felt the pulse along her neck jump to life. Its pace quickened when she gazed back at him. His pulse swelled to match the rhythm hers had set.

"Could you not think that maybe I have come to love you?" Her voice shook with her whispered question.

Nay. He would not be swayed by those words. "How can I believe what I know does not exist?"

She took a deep ragged breath. "What would you believe?"

"The truth."

"I have told you the truth. Shall I instead detail facts that you will accept?"

Rhys nodded. "Please do."

"Fine." She moved as far away from him as his hold would allow—a mere inch or two at best. "I need someone strong to command Taniere. You are strong. I need someone experienced to train and lead my men. You are experienced. I need someone who will treat my people fairly, with honor. You are honorable. I need someone who will give me children." She pointedly studied him, slowly from head to toe. "I am certain you can do that also."

The words made sense. But they sounded so cold. So calculated. So blasted practical. Isn't that what he wanted, though? A marriage based on practical needs.

Instead of voicing his thoughts, he merely stated, "You sound like your father."

"Is that not what you wanted to hear? You refuse to believe caring and love exist anywhere outside of a minstrel's tale, so surely an arrangement that satisfies the needs of both parties must be what you seek."

Her clipped words fueled his temper. Why? She'd

spoken nothing but the truth. And that thought angered him further. "What needs of mine are being met by this arrangement?"

Lyonesse gaped at him. "How would I know? You and my father signed the contract. What needs were met then?"

"A willing woman to warm my bed and give me heirs. Another keep that I do not need."

"Why, you—"

"Enough." Rhys jumped to his feet and stared down at her. "You will marry me."

Lyonesse looked at him as if he'd lost all ability to reason before she, too, stood. "You are being irrational. I know I will marry you."

He pulled her into his embrace and slanted his mouth over hers. There was no tenderness in the kiss, but he didn't care. Yes, he was irrational. He was angry and he knew not why. He wanted more. But he didn't know what. Only one thing *was* clear to him.

He did not want a blasted practical marriage.

Certain he was losing his mind as surely as he'd already lost his soul, he broke the kiss and glared down at her. "Do you still wish to return to Taniere?" She would be safer there. He could leave her with enough men to protect her and Taniere before setting out to discover the truth about du Pree.

"Yes. I do wish to go home." Tears glistened in her eyes. Tears he had put there.

Rhys swallowed his regret. ''Be ready to leave at first light.'' He released her and started for the door.

''Rhys, I do love you.''

He hesitated and denied the longing to turn around and accept what she was so willing to give. The act nearly ripped his heart from his chest. He closed his eyes. An image of Alyce's broken body raced across his mind.

He reached for the door. ''Lyonesse, do not give me pretty phrases that have no worth.''

Lyonesse double-checked her chamber, making sure she'd not left anything she'd need at Taniere behind.

She'd not seen Rhys yet this morning, but Melwyn had collected the chests she'd stacked by the chamber door. They'd already sent the baggage on its way. Helen and her father would see to everything else. He'd promised her maid safe escort back to Taniere.

She'd worried that Rhys would change his mind, but apparently he was still going to escort her to Taniere. Not that she'd truly doubted his word, but she never knew from one heartbeat to the next what he'd say or do.

All night she'd lain awake wondering about his ever-changing moods and came to only two conclusions. One—he did care for her and liked it not.

Two—he cared for her not at all, but would honor his vow to marry her.

"Lyonesse."

She froze at Guillaume's call. She'd known this time would come. But she had hoped not to be alone when it did.

He entered her chamber. "I heard you were leaving."

"Yes." Lyonesse took another look inside the wooden clothes chest, seeking to avoid Guillaume.

He grasped her arm. "Where are you going?"

"Home." She tugged away from him. "To Taniere."

Surprise registered on his face. "Taniere? But the king has not returned. You've not a husband to take along with you."

Oh, Blessed Mary help her. How could she tell him that her husband-to-be *was* taking her home? After last night, Lyonesse had no wish to anger Guillaume while they were alone.

Aye, he had the right to know, but he could hear it from her father. She fished for a way out of explaining anything to him. "I sent word to the king. I have an emergency that needs my attention."

"I thought you had an able steward?"

Lyonesse pulled a gown from the chest and tossed it atop a small pile on her bed. "'Tis my keep. My responsibility."

She walked into the alcove off the side of her

chamber and wondered at her own stupidity when he followed. If he thought to try anything, this would be the perfect place. No one could see them unless they came all the way inside her chamber.

When she changed her direction to leave the alcove, Guillaume blocked her way. "What are you about, Lyonesse?"

"Nothing." Her heart raced with building fear. "Taniere is still mine and there are some things that nobody can decide except me." Perspiration rolled down her back.

He narrowed his eyes and studied her face. She schooled her features to remain impassive.

"You will return to Ryonne?"

"Yes." Next spring perhaps. "As soon as I see to things at Taniere, I will return."

"You are angry about last night."

"Of course I am angry." Lyonesse wanted to rip out her tongue. He'd caught her off guard by abruptly changing the subject. She fumbled for a way to ease the blow of her words. "I am certain you were suffering ill-effects from your ordeal." She kept her hand steady and lightly touched his arm. "You will recover, Guillaume. I know you will."

He pulled her into his embrace. "So you forgive me? You are not seeking to run away from me?"

It was all she could do not to scream. His arms

around her felt like chains, not an embrace. "Of course I forgive you."

"That is good." He lowered his mouth to hers, lacing his fingers through her hair to hold her steady.

She thought her heart would burst from her chest with fear and disgust. She pushed against him. He tightened his hold.

The door to her chamber slammed. Guillaume released her. Lyonesse ran to open the door and looked out in the empty hallway. Who had come into her chamber?

Guillaume crossed to the window. He pulled the shutters closed. "The wind blew through the window opening, that is all." He approached her and tugged on her arm. "Come, Lyonesse. Let me make you my wife in all ways before you leave."

She grasped the door frame and hung on for dear life. He was insane if he thought she'd permit him to foul her so. "Guillaume, I will not do such a thing."

He pried her fingers from the door and pulled her toward the bed. "Be not afraid. This will ensure our marriage."

Rage replaced the pale emotion of fear. "No." She slapped at his hands and hung back. "Do you hear me? No."

"What is happening in here?"

Lyonesse nearly fainted at her father's voice.

Guillaume released her. "I am bidding Lyonesse farewell."

"Then do so and be gone from here."

Guillaume knelt and took her hand in his. "I will await your return." He kissed the top of her hand, sending a shiver of revulsion through her. "Pray, do not be gone too long."

Lyonesse tugged on his hand. "I will return as soon as I am able."

When he leaned forward to give her a kiss, she turned her cheek to his lips. Guillaume bowed briefly, straightened and said, "I will miss you, Lyonesse."

"And I you." When had she learned to lie so easily?

He took his leave without another word.

Her father followed Guillaume to the door and waited until the man went down the steps before coming back into the chamber. "How am I to convince the fool that you wish not to marry him?"

"I care not." Lyonesse rolled her few remaining items into a blanket. "I am not returning here a free woman."

"I know." Ryonne touched her shoulder. "Lyonesse."

She turned to him and threw herself against his chest. "Oh, Father, have I made the right choice?"

He ran a hand down her hair. "You know you have."

"Are you satisfied?"

"How could I not be? Faucon brings his title, wealth and strength to Taniere."

She shook her head against his chest. "No, I meant—"

He cut her off with a soft laugh and held her away from him. "Yes. I am satisfied. You have chosen well. I am certain that your life will be all you ever wished."

"Perhaps." She hoped he was right. "You will explain all to King Stephen?"

"Yes. I fully expect him to order you back here for the marriage ceremony."

"Where else would I be married but in my father's keep?"

He shook his head. "Lyonesse, you may wish to find a clergy to perform the ceremony on your way to Taniere."

"Why would I—" His raised eyebrow and half smile answered her question. Embarrassment heated her face. "Father!"

He shrugged. "I am not so old that I do not remember what it was like to be so close to a comely wench."

She pulled away from him. "Wench? Thank you."

"Milady Lyonesse?"

Lyonesse looked around her father. "Yes, Helen?"

Her maid entered the chamber. "What do you here? I thought you were leaving with Count Faucon."

"I am."

Confusion clouded Helen's face. "But he has already left."

"What?" Lyonesse and her father shouted at the same time.

Lyonesse rushed to the window and threw open the shutters. Helen was correct. Rhys and his men were gone. Peering down the road leading away from Ryonne, she could see the cloud of dust rise from a couple of dozen horses.

She whipped around to her father. "Did he say anything? I don't understand. My things have already been sent ahead to Taniere."

"Nay. He said not a word." Ryonne frowned. "Did you argue with him today?"

"No." She shook her head. "He has no reason..." She turned back to the window opening and stuck her hand out. "Oh, by all the saints."

Her father impatiently asked, "What happened?"

She rushed to her clothes chest and tossed out the gowns lying on top. "Before you came in, Guillaume had captured me in an embrace and was kissing me. I couldn't push him away. But while I was trying, the door to my chamber slammed closed."

"And?"

"Guillaume said the wind had blown it shut." She waved toward the window. "There is no breeze."

"You think it was Rhys."

She pulled her leather armor out of the chest. "I do."

"Daughter, what are you planning?"

"Father, do you not see? He thinks I was in Guillaume's arms willingly. And after what his first wife did to him, he would not abide such a happening." She cursed the man.

"Daughter!"

"Forgive me, but he is a lamebrained lout at times. He knows I do not want Guillaume." She pulled her gown over her head. "He seeks to run away instead of taking a chance."

Her father headed for the door. "I will find an escort."

"No." Lyonesse stopped him. "Find Howard for me. He can ride with me until I catch up to Rhys's men."

"I can escort you to Rhys."

"No." She had something in mind that she did not wish her father to discover. "You need to make certain Guillaume remains here at Ryonne."

Her father narrowed his eyes at her. "You are plotting."

Lyonesse smiled. "Of course I am." She pulled off her shoes and stockings. "It's high time Faucon admits he's wrong."

Chapter Seventeen

From high atop an outcrop, overlooking the path his men followed, Rhys studied his newest *recruit*. Her arrival hadn't been heralded with any words, but his senses, already on alert, had honed in on her presence instantly.

God save him from women and fools. He laughed at himself. There was a useless prayer that would ever go unanswered. It was far too late to save him from Lyonesse and he had already proven himself to be the biggest fool of all time. Hopeless. He deserved whatever fate the heavens had in store for him.

"Milord?" His captain joined him. "What do you think of our new squire?"

"A squire?" How many of his men had fallen for that lie? Her hardened-leather armor did nothing to make her look like a boy. He hoped none of them were that blind. Else all his relentless hours of training had been for naught.

"I guess she thought she looked too old to be a page."

"Did you approach her?"

Melwyn nodded. "Aye. It was all I could do not to give the hoax away."

Rhys considered the possibilities. "Did she realize that you knew?"

"Nay. She was too busy making certain her captain got away without being seen."

"Good."

"What will you do now?"

Rhys saw three choices. Take her back to her father and ride away. Deliver her to Taniere and ride away. Or he could ignore what he'd witnessed in her chamber and prove what a fool he was. "The glen is only a few short hours from here. We will proceed as originally planned."

After a moment of silence, he heard a muffled snicker. "Melwyn, if you are laughing, I will kill you."

"Me?" His captain cleared his throat. "Milord, I would never think to—" His lie trailed off on a strangled cough.

Rhys turned in his saddle. Melwyn looked away. Rhys turned back around and looked down at the line of men. "Am I a fool?"

"Milord, who am I to say? If you asked my wife, she would say all men were."

Rhys flicked the reins he held. "Ryonne will not be there until later this afternoon."

"Do you think he will still come?"

"Yes." Ryonne seemed too anxious to see this through not to arrive as they had planned between them last night. "I gave him no suggestion otherwise."

"Aye, but we left rather abruptly."

Rhys had no wish to be reminded of how, or why they'd departed Ryonne in such haste. He'd discuss that with Lyonesse—later. "Do you think she joins us in this manner without her father's knowledge? I would hazard a guess that Ryonne sent Howard to escort her safely."

Melwyn agreed. "Do you think one day will be enough time to convince her to go along with this plan?"

Rhys turned his horse away from the outcrop. "Convince her?" Had she not been the one to beg for a hasty marriage? Yes, she'd beg for a marriage at night and kiss another man the next morning. "Lyonesse already made her choice." He'd give her the quick ceremony she'd requested. "Had she stayed at Ryonne I would have left her in peace. But she did not."

Melwyn frowned. "But she has no idea that she rode into a wedding party."

Rhys smiled. "You are right." He urged his horse

down the path that led back to his men. "And I do not want her to know."

"She will realize something is afoot when we arrive at the glen."

"Not if she doesn't arrive there until after dark." It was time Lyonesse learned that she was not the only one who could scheme. "By then she'll be too exhausted to even care."

Melwyn's confusion drew creases across his forehead. "'Tis not even noon and it is but a short ride from here."

"And there are many paths that lead in circles."

"But—"

Rhys lifted his hand. "But, nothing. She would rather pass herself off as a squire instead of coming to me as herself. Then let her be a squire. Let this be a test of her manhood."

Lyonesse wiped the dripping sweat from her nose and cursed Faucon. They'd not stopped once this day. She glanced at the men. Some looked as if they'd just returned from a rest. Most appeared as tired as she.

But they probably did not have blisters on their hands from clutching the reins so tightly. They could probably still feel their legs, while hers had gone numb miles back. When or if they ever stopped, she'd not be capable of dismounting without falling flat on her face.

The sun had passed its zenith and began its descent many hours ago. Soon it would be too dark to keep traveling. For that much she was thankful.

Faucon would never drive his men in this manner unless they were headed to battle. The only battle he was riding toward was the one she'd throw at him once they reached Taniere. If they were even headed toward Taniere. She'd lost track of their position hours ago. Perhaps they were chasing the impostor.

Her heart lurched. If they did engage in a battle, Rhys would strangle her when he discovered the truth. Unless she managed to get herself killed in the fighting. She didn't carry a sword. She'd not thought it necessary.

Lyonesse longed to ask someone where they were going, but a real squire would never be bold enough to ask anything.

Nothing along this path seemed familiar to her, but then again she was so tired and sore that she wasn't certain if she'd recognize her own father at this moment. Two nights without sleep had left her exhausted to begin with. To demand her body endure this relentless journey was more than she could bear.

Almost. She would not fall from her horse in front of Faucon and his men. Lyonesse straightened her back. She flexed her arms, forcing the blood to her blistered hands.

Now, if she could just keep her eyes open.

"How fare you, boy?"

Lyonesse shuddered. "Fine, Sir Melwyn." Rhys's captain had asked her that question countless times already. She wondered if he'd discovered her duplicity. No. If he had, he would have gone to Rhys by now.

She hadn't intended to fool anyone. But when she'd come upon Rhys's group of men, she'd not known what else to do. The thought of simply riding up to Rhys and presenting herself hadn't crossed her mind until much later. Sometimes the simplest solutions escaped her.

So for now she was stuck in the guise of squire.

Melwyn tipped his head at her. "We will be making camp shortly. Your assistance will be required with the horses."

"Yes, sir." Maybe one of the beasts would trample her to death. It would be less painful.

She watched Melwyn ride to the front of the line. She noticed that Rhys had finally returned. He'd left the party a while ago and was back with two other men at his side.

When he turned and glanced in her direction, Lyonesse pinned her stare between her horse's ears. She longed to just lean forward and rest her head on the animal's neck.

The two men with him left. A few of Rhys's other men joined the departing party. She sucked in a quick breath. They weren't going to Taniere. They hunted the impostor. That explained why all day long men were coming and going.

Countless questions clouded her already numb mind. Was the man nearby? Were they safe? What if he attacked? She was defenseless. No one knew she wasn't really a squire. Should she hail Rhys? Or tell Melwyn?

Her eyelids closed. It was too much to consider right now. If she could catch a short nap she'd be able to think clearly.

Lyonesse jerked herself upright and forced her eyes to open. Surely it wouldn't be much longer before they stopped.

"How much longer will you ride?"

Rhys looked at his brother Gareth. "Until I say stop."

"'Tis enough, Rhys. She is near asleep now."

"If it bothers you so, why don't you go back to the glen and leave me be?"

Gareth snorted. "Because every time I return there without you and your lady, Darius chews my ears."

Rhys turned around and looked down the short line of men. There were but six in the party now—him, Gareth, Melwyn, two of his men and his new squire.

Lyonesse's head bobbed. Her chin bounced off her chest. Soon. He would call a halt soon.

"You must give her credit."

"For what?" He stared up at his brother.

"She's lasted longer than any of your men."

Rhys countered, "If this was a mission, my men would last as long as need be. Have no fear on that score." Many times they'd ridden for days, taking only short breaks here and there. Most had learned to sleep in the saddle.

"Milord."

Both Rhys and Gareth pulled up on their reins and turned their horses toward Melwyn.

Rhys breathed a sigh of relief. "Finally." His captain had a hand on Lyonesse's shoulder, seeking to hold her upright.

Gareth reached the pair first and caught Lyonesse as she fell out of Melwyn's hold. He settled her across his lap and laughed softly when she looked up at him and whispered, "Rhys, your eyes," before falling asleep against his chest.

Rhys battled the sudden burst of anger that burned his throat. "I will take her."

"Nay. She is fine." Gareth urged his horse toward the camp. "Why don't you go for a nice cold swim?"

"What are you doing?" Rhys caught up with his brother. "This is not your affair."

Without looking at him, Gareth shrugged. "I am saving you from doing anything more stupid this day." He relented, turning a half smile on Rhys.

''Fear not. I will not steal your bride. But before you take her to task for whatever imagined crime she has committed against you, find a way to lose your temper.''

Only a member of his family could get away with this type of high-handed act. ''I never said she committed any crime. 'Tis not like I am going to harm her.''

''Sometimes, Rhys, your mouth does more harm than you know. Go for a swim.''

''One day, *little brother,* you will go too far.''

''I already have.''

Lyonesse snuggled against the warmth beneath her cheek. Something was not quite right, but she was unable to put her finger on it.

She just knew that she was no longer on a saddle. And when the bouncing finally stopped, someone laid her on a bed and pulled a cover over her.

''Sleep well, Lyonesse.''

A smile curved her lips at the sound of her father's voice. She'd never been so tired that she'd imagined things before.

First she'd thought Rhys's eyes turned from gold to green. Then her father's voice. And now strong arms gathered her close and held her safe while she slept.

The sound of men's voices broke into her slumber. Lyonesse sought to escape the sound by burrowing beneath the covers and froze when she backed into a solid form behind her.

Her eyes adjusted to the semidarkness quickly. She surveyed her surroundings. A tent. How did she get here? From the amount of armor and weapons, it had to be a man's tent.

Slowly moving her arm, she reached behind her.

''Good morning.''

Relief gentled the rapid pounding of her heart. ''Rhys.''

He kissed her neck. ''Did you expect someone else?''

''I expected no one.''

''We can discuss that later.'' He moved slightly away from her. ''Can you move?''

Why wouldn't she be able to move? She stretched her legs and gasped at the heat of the fire roaring up them. The pain brought the events of the last day to the fore of her mind.

Lyonesse closed her eyes. ''You knew.''

''From the moment you joined us.'' His breath rushed warm against her ear, sending a shiver down her spine. ''If you do anything so rash again, you will regret the day you were born.''

He caressed her neck with his lips. Lyonesse leaned into his touch. When he slid his hand across her side and down to rest on her stomach, shock chased away his threat. ''Where are my clothes?'' Ignoring the sharp pain her movements caused, she rolled away from him and grabbed the cover from the pallet. "What have you done?"

Rhys came up on his knees and reached for her. "I have done nothing. If you would take but a moment to think, you will realize that I am fully clothed."

She moved too slow, permitting him to catch her wrist. Instead of tugging her back to him, he said, "Lyonesse, I don't want to hurt you. Come here."

"No." She shook her head. He was being kind now. But she knew he was doing nothing more than concealing his anger, waiting to catch her off guard.

He released her and rose. Rhys stuck his head out of the tent and issued soft orders to his men before busying himself about the tent.

"What are you doing?"

"I am gathering our things for a bath."

Lyonesse blinked. "A bath?"

"Yes. You reek of sweat and horse flesh. I doubt if that is what you want our guests to remember about our wedding."

Her heart jumped. She lifted a hand to her temples. "You are making my head ache. What are you talking about?"

"Did you not plead for a quick marriage?"

Lyonesse moved off her knees and sat down on the pallet. "That was two days ago."

"Has something changed since then?"

She fought the urge to laugh hysterically. Had he

lost his mind, or was she dreaming? "Are you not angry with me?"

"Very." He crossed the tent in two strides. "But not as enraged as I was yesterday morning."

Now she wanted to cry in frustration. He *had* seen Guillaume kissing her.

He grasped her chin and tipped her head up to face him. "Do you wish to marry me or du Pree?"

When she tried to pull away from his firm hold, he nearly shouted, "Answer me."

Lyonesse placed her hand over his wrist. "You."

"And do you still wish to do so now? Today?"

"But—"

"Yes or no?"

Oh, yes, he was angry. Yet he'd held her safe and warm through the night. "Yes, I do. Today."

He released her chin and held out his hand. "Then come."

She took his hand and gasped when he pulled her to her feet. There was not an inch of her body that did not scream out with pain. He tugged an oversize loose-fitting gown over her head. It pooled on the floor.

When she turned to fall back onto the pallet, he grabbed the bundle he'd prepared and led her toward a flap in the rear of the tent. "Move, Lyonesse, it will ease the muscles."

"That makes as much sense as anything else does this day."

He laughed. "Trust me."

She rubbed her hip. "Trust you? I keep waiting for you to start yelling." Lyonesse stumbled over the hem of the gown.

Rhys lifted her in his arms. After settling her in his arms, he kissed the end of her nose. "I thought I would save the yelling for after the wedding."

Lyonesse winced. "Why? So no one can stop you from disciplining your wife?"

"Disciplining?" He came to a dead stop. "I am not du Pree. And if you keep bringing him up, you will regret it."

"I am sorry." She rested her cheek against his shoulder. "I spoke out of turn."

"Had I wanted to beat you, I would have done so long ago."

She brushed her fingertips along the side of his too tight neck.

"Stop that."

The look he turned on her did not bode well. So much for waiting until after the wedding before yelling at her. Perhaps it was best they get this out of the way first. "You are angry about what you saw yesterday morning."

"Lyonesse, do not."

She slipped her hand around his neck and raked her fingers through his hair.

"Quit."

She sighed. "Rhys, you do not understand."

"Lyonesse, do not say a word. Just close your mouth."

Each word came out more curt than the last. He wouldn't even look at her as he carried her through the woods. This could not go on. He had to realize this time, he was wrong.

If she clung to him, there was no possible way for him to ignore her. "I was not kissing Guillaume."

Rhys stopped again. He swallowed hard. "If you say one more word, I will leave you right here." He took a deep breath. "Even if I have to keep you chained in a tower, you will not get the chance to again play me false. Do you understand?"

This was outrageous. She opened her mouth, but before she could say anything in her defense, he repeated, "Not one word."

Lyonesse wanted to scream in rage. She wanted to beat on his back. Chained in a tower indeed. Who did he think he was? He would never understand what he witnessed if she could not speak. With a huff of expelled breath, she laid her head back on his shoulder. Surely he didn't mean for her to remain silent forever.

Finally, Rhys walked out of the forest and into a clearing. Lyonesse looked around and marveled at the wondrous sight before her. A gurgling stream cascaded over and around rocks to empty into a small pool. Through the clear water, multicolored pebbles appeared to shimmer.

The grassy bank provided cover for the deer and rabbits pausing to drink from the pool. Upon spying her and Rhys, the animals took refuge behind the misplaced boulders dotting the clearing.

The air was crisp, and only the sounds of nature broke the silence. The splashing of the stream as it fed the pool, the birds singing from the trees and the gentle rustling of leaves in the light breeze.

Rhys dropped the bundle he carried and stepped closer to the water's edge. ''Can you swim?''

''No.''

He took another step closer. ''That is too bad.''

Lyonesse's stomach tightened. ''You wouldn't.''

He released her and pulled her arms from around his neck. ''I would.''

She tried to cling to him. ''It will be cold.''

He pried her fingers from his tunic. ''I will warm you.''

She filled her lungs with air and released it in a rush. ''Pardon me?''

Rhys pushed her into the water. ''You heard me.'' He began stripping off his clothes.

The chill of the water forgotten, Lyonesse stared at him, speechless.

Naked, he waded toward her. ''My, my, for someone who was so anxious to talk, you suddenly seem bereft of words.''

Even if her life had depended on it, she wouldn't have been able to get words past the thickness closing her throat.

The muscles in his long legs bunched with each step he took toward her. Lifting her gaze, she swallowed past the lump. There could be no denying that he was more than ready for the wedding night. She quickly shifted her gaze to the flat planes of his stomach and up the ripple of muscles encasing his ribs.

Rhys snapped his fingers and waved his hand in front of his face. ''Up here, Lyonesse.''

Spellbound, she followed his voice and stared up at him.

He stopped before her and pulled her from the water. ''Take this off.'' He pulled the gown over her head.

''No. I have nothing to wear.'' She slapped at his hands.

He ignored her attempts to make him stop and nodded toward the bank. ''Fear not. We both have dry clothes.''

She grabbed his hands. ''What is going on?''

After unbraiding her hair, he spun her around and pressed down on her shoulders. ''Sit. We are taking a bath and then we will be married.''

She scooted around on the pebbly bottom of the pond, making a more comfortable seat. The clear water, while not as cold as she'd first thought, lapped against the undersides of her breasts and hid nothing. ''How?''

He'd gone to fetch some things from the shore and was heading back to her, with a pitcher and soap in hand. Lyonesse quickly turned her head forward, seeking to hide the telltale blush heating her face.

''How?'' He sat behind her and ran soapy hands over her back. ''We'll finish our bath, dress and join the others for the ceremony.''

''Where?''

''Here.''

''Rhys!''

He easily slid his hands around her body and pulled her back against his chest. His touch took her breath away. When she shuddered against him, he asked, ''Do you think you are the only one who can plot and plan?''

She crossed her arms over her naked breasts. Rhys chuckled and ran his hands down the length of her arms. His fingers brushed the tops of her breasts. She gasped and tried to ignore the fire he built. ''No, but I do not understand how you arranged this.''

''Me?'' He scooped up a pitcher full of water and began rinsing the soap off her back and arms. ''Not I.''

Now she was truly baffled. ''Then who?''

''Your father.'' He moved to her side. ''Lean forward.''

''My father?'' Water poured over her head.

"Yes, he suggested this location." Rhys raked soapy hands through her tangled hair. "He said you were conceived here."

This was the glen that her mother had so often spoken about. When she tried to lift her head to get a better view, Rhys pushed it back down. "Let me finish here."

"But that glen is not far from Ryonne. It cannot be the same one."

"Oh, it is."

She sputtered when he dumped another pitcher of water over her head. Before she could drag her clinging hair away from her face, Rhys began washing her leg.

"Stop that." She tried to pull away, but he hung on to her ankle. "Rhys, please."

He flashed her a wicked smile. "Please, what?"

Lyonesse narrowed her eyes. "You are enjoying this far too much, milord."

He ignored her struggles and trailed his fingertips up her shin, over her knee and across the top of her thigh.

Quickly finding a way to stop him, Lyonesse crossed her other leg over the one he held. "I said, stop."

Rhys stared at her locked legs and then at her face. His eyes glimmered bright. He stole her heart with another smile. She tightened her legs.

"I only thought to give you a bath." He repositioned himself in front of her. "But, if you would rather play." Still hanging on to her, he pulled her locked ankles atop his shoulder and held her there with one hand.

Lyonesse leaned back, seeking enough purchase to scoot away from him. When he laughed, she stopped. By the tone of his laugh, she'd made a mistake in his favor.

Rhys slid his free hand down the backside of her legs. Slowly stroking and kneading the sensitive flesh, he instinctively followed the course of the fire.

With the side of his hand he traced and retraced the crease where her crossed legs met. Her muscles turned useless. She couldn't have escaped had she wanted to.

He lowered her legs from his shoulder. Easily coaxing them apart, he wrapped them around his waist and drew her forward.

Lyonesse came willingly. Pressing her breasts against his chest, threading her fingers through his hair, she whispered his name.

He swallowed her whisper with a kiss, pulling her closer still. His desire burned hot and hard between them.

Too soon he broke their kiss and slid her away. The air rushing between them chilled her heated flesh and she sought the warmth of his body.

Rhys held her shoulders. "Not yet." His words

sounded as breathless as she felt. "Not until after the ceremony."

Lyonesse groaned in frustration and rested her forehead against his chest. "Then perhaps we need to hurry."

His response was lost in Melwyn's shout from the edge of the forest. "King Stephen is here."

Chapter Eighteen

King Stephen pinned them with a glare when they returned to camp. Lyonesse released Rhys's hand and after quickly greeting the king properly, rushed to her father's side.

"What took you so long?" Stephen near snarled.

Rhys bowed, then shrugged. The king's attitude changed with the wind and Rhys had long ago learned to ignore snarls of impatience. "I did not realize you were arriving this soon."

"Yes, well, that is true enough." Stephen's mood lightened. "I understand a wedding is to take place this day?"

"By your grace, yes it will."

"Don't seek to placate me, Faucon. You would have gone ahead without my grace."

Instead of agreeing, Rhys took the safest course of action and remained silent.

Stephen paced. Rhys held back a groan. The king paced when he was thinking. The last thing Rhys wanted today was for Stephen to think up a way to keep him from Lyonesse.

"Sire? Did you not give Lyonesse permission to marry either me or du Pree?"

"Yes. Upon my return to Ryonne." Stephen swept the clearing with a wave of his arm. "This is not Ryonne."

"But we are not far from Ryonne's lands and Baldwin, Lord Ryonne, is present."

"And you think that close enough to my orders to suffice?"

Rhys knew full well how thin any excuse he made would sound. Before he could think of words to sufficiently soothe the king, an elbow hit him squarely in the side.

"My lord. Sire. Forgive my brother his foolishness." Gareth took a step toward the king. He leaned his head down, as if he were telling a great secret. "You see, Rhys knows so little of love that it has taken him quite off guard."

Stephen glanced around Gareth and asked, "Is this true?"

Speechless at his brother's audacity, Rhys could only nod.

"See?" Gareth shook his head and placed a hand over his chest. "Now, experienced men, such as you and I, can deal rationally with these bouts of emotion." He swung his arm around and pointed at Rhys. "But those less experienced, like Rhys, become...'' He paused and made a great show of choosing the proper word. ''Well, they become near brainless.''

Stephen nodded. ''Yes, I can see how that might be so.''

To Rhys's horror, Gareth dropped to one knee. ''I pray you milord, sire, forgive my brother his moment of insanity.''

King Stephen tugged at his beard with his thumb and forefinger. He motioned Gareth up from the ground and looked from one brother to the next. He settled his focus on Rhys. ''Why must you always be so serious? Why can you not be more like Gareth here? We find him quite amusing.''

Rhys glared at his brother. ''Oh, I find him quite amusing, too.'' Visions of Gareth's slow torture danced in his head.

Stephen laughed and then approached Rhys, slapping him on the shoulder. ''So, you wish to become tied to a wife?''

If the queen had heard the phrasing of that question, Stephen would eat cold venison for a month. ''Aye, sire. I do.''

''Good.'' The king urged Rhys toward Lord Ryonne. ''Du Pree is in custody?''

Rhys dug his heels into the soft ground, bringing their short walk to an instant halt. Lyonesse gasped and stepped forward. Lord Ryonne coughed and shook his head.

"Milord?" Rhys looked from Stephen to Ryonne. "What is this about du Pree?"

"Ah." King Stephen studied the branches of the surrounding trees before gesturing toward his tent. "By the looks of things I can see we need to speak."

He ushered Rhys, Lyonesse and Ryonne into the tent and waited for all to take a seat on the scattering of small benches before asking, "Rhys, did you find the murderer?"

"No, but I am fairly certain of his identity."

"How so?"

Rhys spared a glance at Lyonesse. She would not like what she was about to hear. "My men tracked and back-tracked the impostor for days. All the signs of his coming and going led to and from Ryonne."

"Nay."

While he felt sympathy for the disbelief he heard in her voice, he ignored Lyonesse and continued. "Obviously, it could not be Ryonne himself, so it had to be someone inside. Someone who could come and go at will and someone who could order men to do his bidding."

"But Guillaume was not at Ryonne when the impostor first appeared." Lyonesse's attempt to defend her former betrothed fell on deaf ears. She leaned toward Rhys. "It had to be Sir John. He was capable."

"'Tis what I thought at first, too." He explained to a confused King Stephen and Ryonne. "John was angry that Lyonesse did not kill me outright when she captured me. Howard had to order the man from Taniere to keep him from harming Lyonesse.''

''Yes.'' Lyonesse continued the explanation. ''And that's who attacked Taniere.''

''No.'' Rhys shook his head.

''But Guillaume had not yet returned from his ordeal.''

Ryonne cleared his throat. ''There was no ordeal, Lyonesse. It was a subterfuge to hide his true mission.''

''You knew this all along?'' Rhys stared at Ryonne. ''Yet you said nothing?''

Stephen interrupted. ''It was your task to find du Pree.''

There was a piece of information someone might have shared with him before this. Rhys crossed his arms against his chest. ''Perhaps someone could start at the beginning.''

King Stephen sighed. ''Guillaume du Pree is a spy for my beloved cousin, Empress Matilda. We have suspected him for some time, but we had no proof.''

''Had no proof?'' Rhys asked the obvious. ''And you do now?''

''No. We were counting on you to provide it.''

''Me?'' What began as an annoyance grew to anger. ''And someone simply forgot to inform me of this mission?'' Rhys leaned forward. ''May I speak freely?''

Stephen sat back in his chair. ''I am elated that you request permission this time.''

Rhys took that as an affirmative. ''When I was accused of murdering du Pree, you gave me one month to either find the true murderer, or face a trial by sword. A trial that would jeopardize everything my family holds dear. Yet you knew the entire time that du Pree was not dead?''

''You understand that quite well. You had been implicated for some reason that I could not fathom. I wanted you to discover that reason without letting on that you knew the truth. The simplest way to do so was to not tell you.''

Lyonesse leaned forward and glared at her father. ''And you knew, too? You let me believe the body brought to Ryonne was Guillaume's when it was not?''

''Yes.'' Ryonne looked at Stephen before explaining. ''For the same reason as was with Rhys. The body had been delivered to you intentionally and we wanted to discover why.''

''Did you?'' Rhys had heard as much as he wanted to hear.

The king and Ryonne answered in unison. ''No.''

Rhys stood and held his hand out to Lyonesse. Without hesitation she rose and clasped her hand in his. ''Sire, Lord Ryonne, before either of you deign to further play with our lives, I am going to attend my marriage ceremony.''

Lyonesse squeezed his hand. "'Tis about time."

"Count Faucon." Stephen's voice rose.

"No." Rhys held up his free hand. "I humbly apologize for what could be construed as an act of treason, but I came here this day to wed Lyonesse and do so before you send me off on another wild chase. Unless you intend to slay me where I now stand, I am going to get married."

"But du Pree—"

Rhys stopped Ryonne's words with a look. "Can wait until tomorrow." He headed toward the flap of the tent. "You can attend your daughter's wedding or not. It is up to you."

His heart drummed loudly in his ears as he stepped through the flap, taking Lyonesse along with him. He half expected King Stephen to order the royal guards to cut him down. He paused about five steps away from the tent and turned around.

Stephen and Ryonne stood outside the tent. No one made a sound. Not even the birds were foolish enough to break the heavy silence.

Finally, Stephen nodded. "Let us table this discussion until tomorrow. For now, we have a wedding to attend."

Lyonesse studied her husband from across the clearing. *Husband.* Still an odd word in her thoughts.

The ceremony had been brief. Nothing more than an exchange of vows, promises for today and the future. It had meant much to hear Faucon give his promise so solemnly. Normally, when he discussed matters of the heart, sarcasm rolled off his tongue. But his vows had held not a trace of anything but sincerity.

''Milady Faucon.''

Lyonesse looked up at the man standing beside her. Darius, the quiet brother. While all three Faucon brothers looked nearly alike, each had something that set him apart. Gareth, the minstrel at heart, was the size of a mountain, yet his silver-streaked hair gave him the appearance of a wolf. Darius, the wanderer, reminded her of a panther—dark and sleek. And Rhys, the protector, the falcon with eyes of gold.

She patted the spot next to her on the log. ''Please, join me.''

Darius declined. ''Nay, I wished only to bid you a happy future.''

She noted the bundle slung over his shoulder. ''You are leaving so soon?''

''I have been gone from Faucon for many weeks.'' He smiled. ''Looking for my missing brother. Now that I know all is well, I need to return home.''

Here was a man who held unspoken secrets in the depths of his soul. Secrets Lyonesse had no wish to reveal. ''You care for the keep in Rhys's absence?'' As a younger son, what had Darius to call his own?

"Yes, milady. Falconsgate is near my own property, so it poses no difficulty."

Interesting. A younger son with property of his own. Lyonesse's musing were forgotten as Rhys caught her gaze and held it while he steadily approached.

A ripple of anticipation quickened her breath. Firelight reflected in his eyes. Golden specks flared to life, creating twin beacons of light. The Devil Faucon stalked her, and she eagerly awaited her capture.

"Milord Darius," Lyonesse's words fell thickly from her lips, "have a safe journey home." His answering laugh evaporated in the night.

"Lyonesse." Faucon stood before her, a promise etched clearly on his features. A silent promise that swelled in her heart and warmed her blood.

When he held out his hand, she threaded her fingers through his, willingly prepared to follow wherever he led.

This woman he'd taken to wife had little reason to trust him so completely. Yet the unwavering gaze resting so easily upon him spoke of complete and utter trust.

Desire seeped into his veins. The steadily growing warmth surprised him. This was not the wild storm of lust, but something stronger. Buried deep inside his memory, a longing awoke, catching him unaware.

Unprepared for the emotions welling within his chest, Rhys closed his eyes against the tide of feelings. But he could not shut out Alyce's final words. Words that haunted him still. *No woman will ever love you. All will use you and cast you aside.*

"Rhys?"

The soft, questioning voice pulled him from his torment. Lyonesse stroked his cheek.

He stared down into her liquid gaze and knew it was already too late. He was lost. Bound to this woman. Securely held by threads more powerful than any chains.

Yet the knowledge did not fill him with dread. The past be damned. He would worry about tomorrow when the day arrived.

He drew Lyonesse to his side and escorted her to the glen. Off the footpath, away from the pond, he led her to a circular formation of boulders that formed a roofless chamber.

Here, in this open chamber of paganlike magic, he would kiss the last traces of Guillaume from her memory. He would weave his own silken threads, securely binding her desires, her needs, to him. Here, in this place of whispered dreams, they could soar on the wings of desire.

He guided her around rock walls taller than himself and drew Lyonesse into the circle. The glow of a full moon bathed the chamber in muted light.

She gasped. He smiled, pleased that this oddly formed chamber met with her approval. Slowly, silently, Lyonesse walked the perimeter of the circle. A myriad of expressions played across her face. The flitting emotions echoed his own.

A breeze rustled across the grass and echoed between the stones. In a hushed, chanting voice the wind whispered promises to him.

After completing the circle, Lyonesse placed a hand on his arm. ''My mother had often spoken about this place of magic. I am glad you found it—was it difficult?''

Rhys tossed his mantle to the ground before turning to take her in his arms. ''Nay. Once your father provided the directions, I more or less stumbled upon it in my search for a private place in which to seduce my wife.''

''You have gone to much work for this seduction.''

''I hope my labors were not in vain. I have expectations of much success.''

''You speak nonsense.'' Lyonesse leaned forward, seeking to hide her embarrassment in the folds of his tunic.

Her embarrassment bothered him not a whit. But he did not want her hiding like a shy, frightened child.

"Oh, nay, Lyonesse, I will ravish you from head to toe, leaving not a speck of your flesh untouched. I will worship you with my hands and my lips." After taking a deep breath, he continued, "Before this night is over, you will beg me to never leave your bed." He lowered his voice. "I promise you will cry out with a passion never before known by any woman." He sought to swallow his mirth.

She pulled away from his embrace. Her laughter weakened the blows she rained on his chest. "You are an arrogant fool."

He gently grasped her chin, brushing his thumb over her lower lip. "That is better." He urged her closer and stroked her cheek. She willingly came back into his arms. "Do not hide from me, Lyonesse. I have not the inclination to seduce an unwilling maiden."

Her breath warmed his neck. "You know that I am far from unwilling. But I find myself suddenly uncertain. I know not what you expect."

He lightly rubbed the soft skin beneath her ear. "Only that you feel. That is all I expect." Rhys tipped her chin up and lowered his lips to hers. "Do not think, nor worry. Simply follow your feelings."

Her mouth was warm and responsive. Threading his fingers through her tumbled locks, Rhys deepened their kiss.

The warmth of desire flamed. His heart pounded recklessly within his ribs. He held her tighter and felt the steady rhythm of her heartbeat against his chest.

He wanted to caress her, to feel her skin against his. He wanted to see her body bathed in the light of the moon.

Rhys lifted her in his arms and carried her to his cloak. She moaned softly when he broke their kiss and laid her on the makeshift bed. He stretched out beside her and unlocked the clasp of her mantle.

''Rhys, look.''

He followed her wide-eyed gaze and saw the cause of her surprise. He, too, marveled at the spectacle above them.

The sky twinkled and glimmered with countless stars. Heaven had designed nature's ceiling to their secret nest.

She pointed at a streaking star. ''Quick, make a wish.''

He propped himself up on his elbow and gazed down at her flushed face. ''The heavens have already filled my desires. Place your wish upon the star.''

She shook her head, reaching up to touch his face, whispered, ''I wish only to be loved by the Devil Faucon.''

His heart ceased to beat, then slammed against the inside of his chest, knocking the breath from him. He closed his eyes. ''Lyonesse, I promise you that I will always care deeply for you. Ever will I protect you and see that all your desires are fulfilled." He looked down at her. "But this love does not exist in my soul. I have none to give."

Uncertainty crossed her face, marring the pale smoothness with fine creases. She bit her bottom lip for a moment before stating, "You have promised me forever. That will be long enough for me to teach you how to love."

"Ah, minx, married less than one day and you plot and plan the future."

Lyonesse relaxed beneath him, stroking his cheek. "Let it begin now, Rhys. Let our future start now."

His control slipped a notch at her request. His growing need pressed him to hurry. But a small portion of his senses reminded him they had all night. They had the rest of their lives for satisfying lust. But this night would come only once.

Rhys untied the laces on her gown. "I want to feel your silken skin beneath my touch." Tipping her head back with a gentle nudge, he whispered, "I want to taste every inch of you."

She gasped softly as he rained light, teasing kisses along her throat.

In one fluid motion, Rhys leaned away, pulled both the gown and chemise over her head and slid them easily from her body.

A tremor of pleasure coursed through him. She was beautiful. His gaze feasted on perfection from her slender neck, across rounded breasts and down to her narrowing waist.

Her skin was so pale beneath his dark hand. No fur had ever felt as soft. No silk could match the smooth suppleness of her flesh.

Lightly, as if handling a fledgling bird, Rhys brushed his palm across her breasts. Her soft moan of pleasure brought a groan to his lips.

The flame of desire raged within him. "You are more beautiful than I imagined."

Her throaty laugh tripped across his ears. "'Tis not as if you have not seen me before."

"But never as my wife." *Wife.* The word echoed through his heart, into his soul.

Lyonesse rested her hand against his chest. "And you? Are you more beautiful as my husband?" Her voice was as breathless as his own.

It took no further prompting for him to shed his clothing.

"Ah, yes." Lyonesse ran her nails lightly down his chest. "You are more beautiful."

He gathered her into his arms. "Aye, this battle-weary body is indeed lovely."

Any retort she would have made to his sarcasm was lost beneath his lips. Their breath mingled. Tongues entwined. Fingertips traced and memorized curves and peaks, scars and muscles.

Rhys could feel the heavy pounding of her heart

beneath his touch. The steady beat matched his own. She moved against him, seeking closer contact.

Like a willing pupil, Lyonesse followed his lead with little coaching. Her touch mimicked his own. Stroking his back, gently grazing a nipple. She petted and explored until he thought he could stand no more.

This sweet, torturous embrace chipped away at his will. It would take more than kisses and caresses to cool the inferno growing between them.

The need to satisfy the wild urges rocked him. He wanted to toss control aside and satiate this driving lust.

Yet he wanted the passion to last forever. To revel in each moment. To savor every touch, every kiss. And he wanted her to share the passionate response fully—completely.

Drawing hard on the reins of his control, Rhys gathered her tightly in his arms. Lyonesse settled against the length of him, soft silken flesh yielded against battle-hewn muscle.

He ran a hand down her back and up her side, cupping a breast. "You are so soft."

Her nipple swelled beneath his thumb. The response urged him on. Kneading the sensitive pearl with his fingers, he groaned when she pressed harder against him.

Her lips were hot against his neck. Her teeth

lightly grazed his flesh, sending shudders of desire down his spine.

Nestled against the soft juncture of her thighs, the hard proof of his need strained between them. His body demanded he release the reins of control.

Rhys kissed her damp brow. Rolling her onto her back, he skimmed his lips down her neck. The salty taste of her skin inflamed his senses further.

Lyonesse arched her back and gasped when he took a nipple into his mouth. She smelled faintly of roses and woman. But the delicate taste and the perfumed scent were not enough to quench his appetite.

He moved back to her mouth, her ragged breath mingling with his own. "Lyonesse, I want you." He brushed his lips across hers. "I need you."

She threaded her fingers in his hair and pulled him closer. "I am afire, Rhys."

Lyonesse's whisper, thick with desire, took his breath away. She returned his near-brutal kiss with a full measure of her own desire. The heated caress left little doubt that she needed and wanted him, too.

He glided his palm down her quivering belly. Finding and parting silken curls, he dipped into her hidden cleft.

She pressed against his hand, moaning softly. She was hot. So hot.

Rhys steeled his will against the urgency driving him wild. Slowly he stroked and circled her swollen bud. Her nails raked his back.

She tore away from their ravaging kiss, breathlessly crying his name. She strained against his teasing hand, parting her legs. Her breaths came in short, quick gasps as she pulsed beneath his touch.

He could wait no longer.

Rhys positioned himself over her. Before reclaiming her mouth with his own, he groaned, ''I do not want to hurt you.''

As he slowly, gently sought entrance into her body, Lyonesse entwined her legs around his hips and surged up against him. He slipped easily through her barrier and felt her tighten around him.

Slowly at first, they soon found the rhythm that lent them wings. Spiraling higher and higher into the heavens, they reached the zenith with a cry on their lips.

In that instant, Rhys knew he'd been correct. In this place of paganlike magic they had indeed woven silken threads. Strong yet gentle chains that would hold them together forever.

Sated from a night of lovemaking, Rhys slept curled protectively around Lyonesse. Until something, the snap of a twig or an unfamiliar shuffling, awoke him.

''Lyon—''

Before he could complete his one-word warning, a heavy object hit him on the back of the head, sending him into a sightless, soundless sleep.

Chapter Nineteen

Bright morning sunshine blinded Rhys. His head throbbed without mercy, his stomach churned, threatening to choke him on bile.

A bead of sweat trickled slowly down the side of his face. Yet the morning air was cool. He grimaced and lifted a hand to the irritation. When he brought his hand away, blood covered his fingertips.

"Lyonesse?" He rolled over. His breath strangled him. The spot beside him was empty and cold.

He tried jumping to his feet and fell flat on his face. His ankles were tied together by a torn length of Lyonesse's chemise.

Dear Lord, what had happened? He sat up, rubbing the back of his head and finding a lump. A jagged memory of last night jolted him into awareness.

They had fallen asleep in each other's arms. He vaguely remembered sensing footsteps before a solid object had crashed down on him, sending him back into the darkness of sleep.

Only one person would do such a treacherous thing. Du Pree. No one else had cause to attack him, or to take Lyonesse.

Rhys ripped apart the fabric confining him and jumped to his feet. He glanced for his clothes, only to find them missing. He cared not. He'd walk naked through the flames of hell to find her.

Rhys covered the distance quickly. Entering the camp he shouted a cry to arms, ''Faucon! To me!'' before striding directly into his tent. Without waiting for a squire, he tossed on the first garments he found and shrugged his chain mail over his head and down his body before strapping on his sword.

His men came running, pulling on boots, clothes, armor and weapons as they rushed to obey his cry.

Not seeing his brother's tent, he flagged down Melwyn. ''Where is Gareth?'' He could use his brother's sword arm.

Melwyn grunted, nodding toward the king's abode. ''After you left last night, he was sent on a mission.''

''By all the Saints, does Stephen never quit? What kind of mission was so important that Gareth leave immediately?''

''I know not.''

Rhys cursed. There was nothing he could do to call Gareth back. He had not the time to wait for his brother's return. He issued orders to ready the men to ride and went to find Ryonne.

The flap to King Stephen's tent whipped open. Stephen stared at the flurry of activity before asking, "What is the meaning of this, Faucon?"

Rhys paused briefly on his way to awaken Ryonne. "My wife is missing. She was taken from me by force during the night."

The king spotted the blood still on Rhys's face and gasped. "Good Lord, man, you are injured. Who did this?"

Rhys brushed his concern away. "'Tis nothing. It will heal. I need find my wife." The words caught in his throat.

"What do you mean by find her? Why is she not with you?" Ryonne ran up behind Rhys. The accusation rang clear in the man's tone. "I gave her into your care less than a day ago and you have let her come to harm already?"

Anger at Stephen and Ryonne twisted in his gut. It was deceitful enough that they played games with his and Lyonesse's life. But to be questioned by them was beyond his endurance.

At this moment, Rhys didn't care if both of these men branded him a traitor and had him drawn and quartered. They could do whatever they wanted to— after he found Lyonesse.

"Harm?" Rhys spun around. "*I* let her come to harm?" He motioned his men to mount their horses, all the while pinning Ryonne with a hard stare.

"Who left du Pree running free even though he was a suspected spy and traitor?"

Rhys swung around to ask Stephen, "Who used us, without our knowledge, to bait this suspected traitor?"

He swallowed hard, seeking to tame the tremor building in his throat. "I hold both of you responsible for her welfare."

Melwyn led Rhys's horse across the campsite. Rhys took the reins and mounted. Before leaving the camp, he looked down at Stephen and Ryonne. "Since you both so enjoy intrigue, see if you can scheme my wife's safe return."

Lyonesse lifted a hand to her throbbing head. Never had she hurt so. When she tried to open her eyes, the light blinded her. If she didn't know better, she'd think that an entire herd of horses had trampled her.

She tried to sit up, but her legs would not move more than a hair's breadth. Lyonesse tugged at her leg, only to find it securely tied to a bed frame. *Bed frame?*

Carefully peering out between her barely slitted eyelids, she gazed about. Obviously, this wasn't the stone circle. Nor was it Faucon's tent. She rose up on her elbows. This was—a tower cell at Taniere. How did she come to be here?

She couldn't remember. There'd been a struggle

and she'd been hit over the head. She recalled awakening in the back of a hay wagon, only to have someone force a vile concoction down her throat, sending her back into a dreamless sleep. Lyonesse fought to calm her breathing and her racing heart. Something was dreadfully wrong.

There should be comfort in the fact that she was at Taniere. How? Who would do such a thing on her wedding night?

Lyonesse sucked in a great breath of air at the thought running through her mind. *No.* He would not. Guillaume would never attempt such a foolish act.

The door to the cell slammed open, bouncing against the wall. She closed her eyes, not wanting to see who was entering, yet needing to know.

''Cover yourself.''

She swallowed her groan. He would. He did. Lyonesse opened her eyes and looked at Guillaume. ''What is this about?''

He stepped toward the bed. ''It is about you covering your nakedness.'' He tossed a gown at her. ''The sight sickens me, but I found nothing at your camp with which to clothe you.''

''*You* found nothing?'' While pulling the gown over her head, she asked, ''How did I get here? Where is Rhys?''

Guillaume sat on the edge of the bed. Lyonesse

scooted as far away as her cloth leg shackle would allow.

"Since we have known each other for so long, I suppose there is no harm in telling you."

He looked like a man torn, hopeless and defeated, yet she could not understand either emotion.

He patted her leg. "Had you done as you were supposed to, none of this would be happening now. Sir John would still be alive. Faucon would be with his maker in hell." He gave her a look of apology. "And you, my dear, would be in the king's dungeon, but I would plead prettily for your life. Which would be unsuccessful, but for my efforts, I would gain Taniere."

Lyonesse could make no sense of his ramblings. It would serve her well to play dumb. She'd not let on that she knew about him being a suspected traitor. She swallowed her confusion and asked, "Guillaume, what plans did I not follow? I do not understand what you are speaking about." She tried to appear concerned. "Are you not feeling well? Are the effects from your ordeal bothering you?"

"What plans?" His voice rose. "The plans to kill Faucon." He pulled a knife from his belt and fingered the edge. "You were not to hold him for ransom. You were to kill him."

"That is what John said," Lyonesse whispered. Fear grew in her belly at the implications of Guillaume's words.

"That oaf only repeated what I told him."

The fear spread from the clenching in her gut, to tremors running down her legs. She needed to keep him talking. Surely Faucon, King Stephen, or her father would eventually look for her here. "How would killing Faucon make everything right?"

"Since he was on the king's mission to find my murderer, you would have been interfering. It would have been an easy thing to plant the seeds of treason in the ears at court."

Lyonesse shook her head. "I do not understand. How could you plant any seeds when you were not there?"

His laughter filled the room. "What do you think the clergyman from du Pree was for? Did he not do a fine job of delivering the news of my death? Did he not do a better job of dropping hints for Faucon to follow to Taniere?" He waved a hand in the air. "Rumors of treason would be easier than either of those things."

Lord, have mercy. Lyonesse could not believe what she heard. "Your clergyman? How will he answer to the Church? How will he answer to God?"

Guillaume shrugged. "He is already answering to God."

"You..." She drew in a steadying breath. "You killed him?"

The blade flashed in front of her eyes. His smile was inches from her. "Yes. Just as I will kill you."

This was the man she'd been promised to. This was the man she'd known her entire life. Somewhere inside him there had to be a thread of honor and dignity left. "Guillaume, what did I do to deserve this?"

He sat back down at the end of the bed. "'Tis not what you did or did not do. 'Tis simply who you are not."

"And that is?"

"You are not Alyce."

Alyce? Who in the name of God was Alyce? Lyonesse's heart jumped to her throat—Rhys's dead wife? What did Guillaume have to do with...oh, no. It couldn't be possible. But it made such sick sense, that she had the dreadful feeling it was true.

Foolishly, she had to ask, "Were you Alyce's lover?"

"Lover?" Guillaume stood and paced across the floor in the small room. "Lover?" He shook his head. "Nay. I was her love, her very heart. I was her soul and she mine."

Lyonesse closed her eyes. Her heart bled for Rhys. He would be crushed when he learned this news. "You have planned this entire event. From having Rhys accused of your murder, to implicating me." She stared at Guillaume. "How long have you planned and plotted mine and Rhys's demise?"

He returned her stare. "Since the day Alyce was killed."

"No." Lyonesse shook her head. "No, Guillaume. She was not killed. She took her own life and her son's."

He rushed forward and slapped the mattress alongside of her. "Lies! She did not kill herself nor Faucon's child."

"It is not a lie."

Guillaume raised his hands as if to steady himself. "No. You will not force me to act too soon." He backed away from the bed. "You will stay in this tower until Faucon arrives."

He reached for the door and smiled at her before saying, "And then he will learn what hell truly is."

Lyonesse gasped. "What are you planning?"

"Faucon will feel the same pain and loss I did upon learning of Alyce's murder. But his punishment will be greater. He will watch helplessly as I throw you from the tower."

Melwyn looked about the village. "Are you certain he is here?"

"Yes. Do you not think he left enough clues along the way? He wants me to find him. Can you not spot his men hiding amongst the others?" Rhys nodded to a man standing alongside the blacksmith's hut. "That one there."

He pulled his horse to a prancing stop before the hut. He pointed at the man and asked, "You there, where is your master?"

The man pounded his fist on the side of the hut until the blacksmith and his wife appeared.

Rhys eyed the couple. They kept away from the other man and would not meet Rhys's gaze. He turned his attention on the man. Not only did he meet Rhys's gaze, he lifted one eyebrow as if flaunting his arrogance before his betters.

Did du Pree not know how to train his men? They'd never make good spies. He pointed at the man and yelled, ''Seize him.''

Faucon's men had not even taken the man into custody before he started blathering. ''Milord, milord. Do not kill me. I will do anything. I will tell you anything you wish to know.''

Rhys suspected as much. Fortunately for him, du Pree hired mercenaries as deceitful as himself. He looked down at the groveling fool. ''Kill you? Why would I kill you?''

His smooth, even voice had the desired effect, because the now pale man blathered more. ''My master is at the keep and awaits your arrival before killing your lady.''

The reputation that preceded him truly was useful at times. Rhys jerked his head toward the blacksmith's hut and ordered his men. ''Hold the fool in there. Tie him to anything that will not move.'' He looked at the smithy. ''I do not imagine that the good blacksmith will permit my prisoner to be freed.''

The blacksmith opened his mouth and gave Rhys a nearly toothless grin. "Nay, sir, I be glad to hold him for you."

"When I return, I will make it worth your while."

The smithy's wife stepped forward. "Milord, God be with you and the lady."

He nodded his thanks before motioning his men back the way they had come. Rhys gathered the men at a small clearing. He sent a few to keep an eye out for King Stephen and Ryonne. They could not be permitted to approach Taniere Keep.

A few more were sent back into the village with orders to round up anymore of du Pree's men they could find.

He beckoned Melwyn forward. "I need someone to question the prisoner."

"Milord, I would be delighted to perform the task."

Rhys looked at his captain's face and realized the man would be too delighted. "No, Melwyn. Not you. The last three prisoners you questioned died before I got any answers. I need someone with a lighter hand."

Melwyn's expression flattened out to near despair. Rhys laughed. "Perhaps I will let you question du Pree."

His captain's smile returned. "Aye, sir, thank you."

"I am glad it takes so little to keep you happy."

When his sarcasm went ignored, he continued, "After you see to that, we need to go over the entrances to Taniere. I am sure you were privy to more of them than I was."

Rhys waited for Melwyn to complete his first order. While he did, he tried not to think about Lyonesse. Just knowing she was in du Pree's hands made him sick at heart. If he thought about the things that could happen, he would lose his mind.

That was something neither he, nor Lyonesse could afford.

He gritted his teeth. Later. He would think of all the horrid things later. He and Lyonesse could discuss them at length after she was free. For now, he could think only of how to get her out of du Pree's clutches.

Melwyn returned quickly. "Milord, if the stream is down it will prove our best chance for entering Taniere."

"The stream?"

"Aye. If it is low enough, you can follow it a short way beneath the keep to the garden's well."

"This is not the time for you to speak nonsense, Melwyn. I need your help, not some wild scheme involving a stream."

"'Tis not so wild a scheme, Faucon. Your man is right." Lord Ryonne stepped out of the shadows. "My father diverted a section of the stream so that it flowed beneath the ground, under the wall and into the well.''

Rhys frowned. ''I have never heard of such a thing.''

''Neither had I until he explained that in the olden days, the Romans used underground streams to feed their pools. Some were natural, and some man-made. My father, ever on the lookout for something new, tried it here at Taniere. He thought to build a pool of sorts in my mother's garden.''

''And it worked?''

''Not exactly. The old workings are still there and since it has not rained, you should be able to follow it to the well.''

''Praying I don't drown, how do I get out of the well?'' Rhys was willing to try anything, but he'd not go on a fool's mission with no hope for success.

''There are toeholds up the side of the well. They will be quite slick, but they are there.''

Rhys studied the man. ''You have seen these toeholds? You have used this method to gain entrance to the keep?''

''No. I have had no reason to do so. But Howard always complained that the well should be filled in because the possibility of a surprise attack existed.''

He couldn't just walk through the gate—not even in disguise. Du Pree would have every person entering the gates inspected. Nor could he permit his men to approach the walls. Those methods would only ensure Lyonesse's death. ''Get me the prisoner's clothes.'' It would be his only chance.

Lyonesse stared out the arrow slit at the darkening sky. Her head throbbed, her body ached and her heart broke. Hour by hour little pieces of it crumbled into shattered bits.

Her life, her dreams had consisted of nothing but lies. Her *beloved* Guillaume. Had the thought of it all not hurt so badly she would laugh. What a joke. A sick, sad jest.

All their plans, all their talks of the future had been nothing but one lie after another.

Guillaume had filled her head with fanciful ideas of what the future would hold for them. Love. Children. They'd live a long and happy life at Taniere. He'd take care of her and their children. She'd want for nothing.

And all the time he'd loved another.

The irony and devastation of his betrayal washed over her, leaving her shivering and cold. She'd vowed revenge for his death. She'd plotted with Sir John to kill Faucon for murdering Guillaume. And in the end she would die at Guillaume's hand.

And in the end, Faucon had her heart. Lyonesse's chest constricted with pain. Even though Rhys swore he had no love in his soul, she knew he was wrong. She'd seen it there last night. In the moonlight it had glistened from his eyes as brightly as the stars in the sky.

She'd felt it in his touch. And she'd fallen asleep knowing it would not take a lifetime to teach him to love.

Nothing she did, not holding her breath, biting her lower lip or covering her mouth with her hand could stop the cry from escaping. Hot tears streaked down her face.

''Crying will not save you from your fate.''

Lyonesse jumped. Lost in pain and grief, she'd not heard Guillaume enter the chamber. She wiped at the tears. ''How can you do this? How can you kill me?''

He shrugged. ''Killing becomes easy after a while.''

''My God, you talk as if you have killed dozens of men.''

Guillaume shrugged. ''The first one is the hardest.''

Lyonesse wanted to vomit. How could he discuss this so rationally? ''I am surprised that you even remember the first death you have caused.''

''It is not hard to remember, especially when the man was my friend and near brother.''

The look he turned on her boded nothing but evil. She shrank away from him, away from the words he had just uttered. ''No. Not Leonard. Not my brother.''

"I was truly sorry for his death. But he recognized me in the skirmish and I could not permit him to tell anyone that I fought for Empress Matilda."

"It was you who tossed Leonard's shield at my gates."

"Yes. Had I known that Sir John had already been turned out, I never would have approached. He was to have opened the gates and permitted my entry to *rescue* Faucon."

Lyonesse gasped in horror. "What had you planned? Were you going to kill him and then blame me?"

"Do not play dense, Lyonesse. Of course I would have laid the blame at your feet."

His admission brought another cry from her lips. "How could you?"

"'Tis easy." He cut through the cloth chain about her ankle. "After the first few times, it becomes rather like hunting. Except four-legged prey gives more sport."

She kicked out at him. "You are a monster." Lyonesse rolled off the other side of the bed. "Stay away from me."

Guillaume smiled as he approached. "You can fight me as you wish, Lyonesse, but it will do you no good." He drew his sword. "You will still die this night."

Lyonesse stared at the weapon. A quick death now by his blade would save Rhys the pain of watching her fall to her death. She took a step forward.

He swung his blade aside. ''Oh, no. I can see what you think to do.'' He grasped her wrist before she could back away. ''I've no wish to spare Faucon one heartbeat of your death.''

''Please, do not do this.'' Lyonesse despised the weakness in her voice. She hated the tremor and the tears that fell freely. ''Guillaume, please, for the love of God, do not.''

He dragged her toward the door and up the stairs to the tower wall walk. ''The love of God?'' His laugh sent shivers of fear down her spine. ''There is no God, Lyonesse. Have you not yet learned that?''

''No. You are wrong, Guillaume.'' Surely there was a God. Else she had no hope.

Rhys stood at the bottom of the pitch-black well shivering. Whether from cold or rage, he could not tell. While the underground stream had not been water-filled, the fine layer of dank mud coating the bottom had been frigid. But he'd not let a minor annoyance like stench or muck thwart Lyonesse's rescue.

He felt along the sides of the well seeking the toeholds with his fingertips. He could not find them, but the shaft was narrow enough to shimmy up. He pressed his back tightly against one side of the well and planted his feet against the other. Armed with a determination to succeed, he stretched out his arms; placing his palms flat against the sides, he pushed up.

Halfway up the shaft he stopped to catch his breath and give his straining muscles a brief rest. Rhys looked up and saw nothing but utter darkness. Neither stars nor the moon broke the night sky. It was as stark and empty as his heart had been only a few short weeks ago.

Little light or joy had filled his heart until a small grieving lioness had sought to capture the Mighty Falcon. She'd succeeded in capturing more than just his body. She'd caught and gentled his soul.

Rhys swallowed hard against the tightness building in his throat. Only last night he'd promised to care for her, at the same time vowing that he'd never have any love to give.

A bitter curse left his mouth. What a blind, stupid fool. It should not have taken du Pree's deceit to make him realize the depth of his feelings for Lyonesse.

Pain clenched his gut. Fear's icy fingers clutched his heart. He would not fail. With a mighty shove, Rhys began his final ascent up the shaft. He would hold Lyonesse in his arms this very night and she would know just how much he loved her.

He found the top of the well and hauled himself over the edge, surprising a trysting couple on a nearby bench. Startled, the man shoved his paramour behind him. ''Who goes there?''

Rhys pulled his sword from its scabbard. His eyes quickly adjusted to the torchlight in the garden. Only one man and one woman seemed to occupy this private space. He'd not come this far to be stopped by a pair of lovebirds. ''Stand aside.''

The man stepped forward, whispering, ''Lord Faucon?''

''Aye.'' He placed the tip of his sword against the man's chest. ''And you are?''

''One of Taniere's guards, milord.''

It was all Rhys could do not to run his weapon through flesh and bone. ''Guard? Why are you not protecting your lady?''

The man had the decency to look shamefaced. ''When Lord du Pree arrived with the lady, his men disarmed us and forced us from the keep and the walls.''

''Why did you not send for help?''

''None are permitted to leave.''

An added boon he'd not expected. He'd assumed du Pree would have killed Taniere's men. ''How many of you are there?''

The man shrugged. ''Perhaps a handful. No more than ten. The few who put up a fight were killed on the spot.''

''It will be enough.'' He stepped back and looked

down the well before asking, "Will your woman find those loyal to Taniere and send them to me?"

She stood and answered for herself. "Gladly, milord."

"Go, find the men quickly and return here."

He glanced from the man to the well and stated, "You have a mission to complete." He would send this man to Melwyn with further orders for securing Lyonesse's keep.

After giving Taniere's men their instructions and sending the one off for Melwyn, Rhys headed toward the keep. Hidden by the cover of darkness, he crossed the bailey. Nobody knew where du Pree held Lyonesse, but Rhys had a gut feeling and he'd learned long ago to trust his battle instinct.

With Taniere's men keeping du Pree's busy, Rhys entered the keep. He kept close to the wall, out of the torchlight and away from the men gathered in the hall. Sword at the ready, he headed for the stairs that led to the tallest tower.

If what du Pree's mercenary said was true, the man had long ago stolen something that once belonged to him. He would not get the chance again. If any harm befell Lyonesse, Guillaume du Pree would beg for death.

Chapter Twenty

Guillaume pushed her out onto the walkway, shouting, "Faucon! I know you are hiding in the night. I have something of yours. Come, see what hell is."

Lyonesse gasped at his insanity. Rhys was not out there hiding. For whatever reason, he had not been able to rescue her and even if he was close, she doubted if he would succeed before she died. Her heart ached with a near unbearable pain.

The night wind blew across her flesh, chilling her to the bone. Clouds obscured the moon and the stars. The inky blackness of the night caressed her in its icy embrace.

Guillaume poked her in the back with the point of his sword. "Get over there." He pushed her toward the crenellated wall. "On the wall, Lyonesse."

Step by painful step, he forced her toward the wall, bringing her closer to her fate.

She would die—soon. As much as she wanted to fall to her knees and beg, Lyonesse refused to die like a coward. She turned and stared at Guillaume.

"This night will haunt you for the rest of your miserable life."

He laughed. "It will have good company. Many nights already haunt me and I live with them."

Lyonesse looked over the edge of the wall. The ground seemed leagues away. Would the pain of hitting the hard rocks below be as great as that in her chest?

Would it hurt as much as knowing she would never again see Rhys? Would it be as painful as knowing she would never again feel his lips on hers, never again lie in his arms?

"I do wish things could have been different, Lyonesse." Guillaume prodded her with the sword. "But your fate awaits."

"Aye, du Pree, her fate does await." Rhys stepped out from the shadow of the door, his sword held before him. "But not at your hands."

Lyonesse nearly fainted.

Guillaume swung around, pulling her in front of him like a shield. "How?"

"How?" Rhys laughed. "'Tis my keep. Should I not know every nook and cranny?"

Guillaume edged toward the door. "Taniere is not yours."

Rhys quickly searched Lyonesse for signs of physical injury and thankfully saw none. But he knew she had to be frightened by the threat of death—a happening he'd not permit. Lyonesse was his wife, his love, his very soul and he'd be damned if anyone was taking that from him.

He moved between them and the door. "You will not escape me this time, du Pree. Release her."

Guillaume shook his head. "Nay, Faucon. I take from you what you took from me."

"Alyce?" Du Pree's man had talked more freely under threat of torture than Rhys had imagined he would. And oddly enough, the knowledge gleaned did not tear at his heart. Lyonesse's love protected him from the pain garnered in the past. "She was always yours for the taking."

"You think your lies will change my mind?"

"Lies?" Rhys shrugged. "She cursed me before leaping from the tower."

"Alyce never would have jumped to her death. You lie, Faucon. You lie to save your own love and it will not work. At least you have the chance to say farewell—a chance that was stolen from me by your senseless destruction."

"I do not lie, du Pree. Regardless of what wagging tongues have said, Alyce jumped to her death. She leaped to the wall with your son in her arms, cursed me for all time before jumping into the air. I could do nothing to stop her."

"My son? How do you know it was my child?"

"She had more than one lover?" Rhys kept his gaze fixed on du Pree, waiting for the man let his guard down.

"Nay. She had no other lover."

"Tell me, du Pree, is there a mark on your shoulder blade?"

Rhys did not have to wait for Guillaume's answer. Lyonesse's gasp told him all he needed to know. He'd been correct all along. The babe had not been a Faucon. It had been marked by its father and that man stood before him.

When du Pree did not respond, Rhys asked, "Would it not have been easier for the two of you to simply admit what was occurring instead of betraying the vows Alyce had taken?"

"And if we had?" Du Pree's voice shook.

Rhys knew his chance was close at hand. "I would have let her go." He didn't know if that was true or not, nor did he care. But he hoped the answer would give du Pree pause.

"No." Guillaume's sword wavered.

Rhys leaped forward. He held the tip of his sword against du Pree's neck and tore Lyonesse from the man's grasp, shoving her behind his back.

Guillaume swung his weapon halfheartedly. His eyes were wide and unfocused. His face and lips pale. "All has been for naught." The words were a mere ragged whisper in the night.

Easily dodging du Pree's sword, Rhys prodded the man toward the door. As much as he wanted to kill this man for even thinking to harm Lyonesse, he could not risk the chance of this coming between them. Let King Stephen deal with the traitor.

Du Pree stopped and raised his weapon, holding it in both hands. "I will not become a prisoner. I wish to die instead."

Rhys knocked the weapon from Guillaume's grip. "However much you deserve death, I will not kill you."

Defeat washed over du Pree's face, a look Rhys had seen on other men's faces countless times. Before he could reach out and grab hold of Guillaume, the man rushed to the wall. Leaping up on the thick stone, he turned and glanced at Lyonesse for one heartbeat before disappearing into the night.

Lyonesse slipped to the floor with a cry on her lips. Shock held Rhys momentarily in place.

"No!"

Lyonesse bolted awake from her nightmare with a scream of terror. Wildly glancing about the room, she found herself in her chamber at Taniere.

Strong arms encircled her, pulling her back down into safety. "Lyonesse, it is over." Rhys gathered her into his embrace, wrapping her in warmth and security.

The fog cleared. Guillaume had captured her and dashed all her memories to shards of broken glass.

He had threatened to toss her from the tower and instead had leaped to his own death.

She took a deep shuddering breath. She could live with the knowledge that all her dreams had been a lie. She could live with Guillaume's deceit and death. Once this day was past, she could live with whatever the future held.

Rhys had come for her and that was all that mattered.

She clung to him, her tears soaking his tunic. ''Rhys.'' She sought to bury herself in his chest. ''Rhys, love me.''

He raked his fingers through her hair and brought his mouth down on hers. His demanding caress warmed her, brought life to her heart, banishing the fear and the pain.

He broke their kiss and pulled her face against his damp chest. His heart beat furious against her cheek. She could feel his chest tighten and relax as he fought for words.

''Lyonesse, I...'' His embrace tightened. ''Lyonesse, can you ever forgive the fool you married?''

''Forgive you?'' She stroked his cheek. ''For what?''

He pulled away, leaving just enough room for the chilled early morning breeze to rush between them. His steady gaze shimmered gold in the torchlight. ''I promised to protect you and failed miserably.''

''No. That was not your fault. Nobody could have

foreseen what happened, Rhys. Guillaume, he—''
She choked back the tremor shaking her words.
''Through their own selfish reasons, Guillaume had
lost his true love and I think, his soul and sanity.
You could not have prevented him from seeking
vengeance.''

''Perhaps. Perhaps not. It is something we will
never know.'' He stroked her face, tracing her jaw-
line, across her cheek and over her lips. ''But I made
another promise. One to always care for you.''

''Aye.'' She leaned across the tiny distance between them and playfully kissed his chin. ''And I
promised to spend forever teaching you how to
love.''

He laughed softly. ''Your task is complete. I will
ever be grateful that the Lioness of Taniere captured
the Mighty Falcon.'' Rhys placed a soft kiss on her
lips. ''You broke the chains that bound my heart and
wrapped silken threads of your own around my soul.
I am your willing prisoner.''

Rhys slid a hand to each side of her face. ''You,
my love, are the very breath I take. You are my soul,
my heart. I desire nothing more than to love you for
the rest of our days.''

She saw the truth of his words shimmer in his
gold-flecked eyes and felt it in his touch. Her heart
soared. The past was buried. Only the future lay be-

fore them. Lyonesse wrapped her arms about his neck and blinked back her tears. "And you, my Devil Faucon, are my life."

*   *   *   *   *

HISTORICAL ROMANCE™

LARGE PRINT

A LADY OF RARE QUALITY
Anne Ashley

They have never seen Viscount Greythorpe listen so intently when a lady speaks. To have caught the eye of this esteemed gentleman, Miss Annis Milbank must be a lady of rare quality indeed. Innocent to the world, the question of who the beautiful Annis will marry has never been foremost in her mind… However, Viscount Greythorpe is confident she will soon be his…

THE NORMAN'S BRIDE
Terri Brisbin

Recalling nothing of her own identity, Isabel was sure her rescuer, Royce, had once been a knight, for he expressed a chivalry that his simple way of life could not hide. William Royce de Severin could not quell his desire for this intriguing woman. Unbroken in spirit, she made him hunger for the impossible – a life free of dark secrets, with Isabel by his side.

TALK OF THE TON
Mary Nichols

Her name was on everyone's lips. They were agog to find out what Miss Elizabeth Harley had been doing down at the docks. And in such shocking apparel! Elizabeth had not meant to sully her good name. All she had craved was a chance to travel. Andrew Melhurst had come to her rescue when she needed him most, but should she consider marrying him to save her reputation?

MILLS & BOON®

Live the emotion

HIST0307 LP

HISTORICAL ROMANCE™

LARGE PRINT

AN IMPROPER COMPANION
Anne Herries

Daniel, Earl of Cavendish, finds the frivolity of the *ton* dull
after serving in the Peninsula War. Boredom disappears
when he is drawn into the mystery surrounding the
abduction of gently bred girls. His investigation endangers
his mother's companion, Miss Elizabeth Travers. Tainted
by scandal, her cool response commands Daniel's respect –
while her beauty demands so much more…

THE VISCOUNT
Lyn Stone

The young man who appears late at night at Viscount
Duquesne's door is not all he seems. Dressed as a boy to
escape the hellhole in which she has been imprisoned, Lady
Lily Bradshaw must throw herself on the mercy of a
ruthless rake. Viscount Duquesne soon finds himself
captivated by this bold lady – and he can't resist her
audacious request for a helping hand…in marriage!

THE VAGABOND DUCHESS
Claire Thornton

He had promised to return – but Jack Bow was dead.
And Temperance Challinor's life was changed for ever.
She must protect her unborn child – by pretending to
be Jack's widow. A foolproof plan. Until she arrives at
Jack's home…and the counterfeit widow of a vagabond
becomes the real wife of a very much alive *duke*!

MILLS & BOON®

Live the emotion

HIST0407 LP